ONE BOAT SERVICE

Dragon Island Adventures
Book One

J MILO

For Vickie

TABLE OF CONTENTS

PROLOGUE

*T*HE SHARP PAIN IN HER *shoulders woke her. Half-light of the moonglow illuminated the space. The trees outside swayed from a light gust casting eerie shadows across the unpainted walls and hardwood floor. Something large rustled in the corner and she heard a light tapping at the filth shrouded window above her head. The wind rustled the brush and off in the distance she heard a boat's whistle, "What the??? Where the hell am I?" she croaked through her parched throat and chapped lips. Her whole body ached, and her head was spinning, "Must have been drugged." Craning her neck, she looked at the window and spied a small bird hopping along the outer sill stopping occasionally to peck at the space between the glass and the frame. She tried sitting up but the pain and nausea forced her back down where she fell asleep again.*

Sometime later, was it ten minutes or two hours, she wondered as she lay there? She tried to clear the cobwebs from her mind and assess her situation. Her hands were tied with zip-ties and there was a chain pulled tight around her left ankle and secured with a small padlock. Her eyes traced the chain to an eyebolt anchored to the wooden floor. She pulled on the chain but there was no give. Struggling to sit, another wave of nausea threatened to send her back into the darkness. Pausing for a few deep breaths she was finally able to reach a sitting position. Her movement startled the creature in the corner, and it skittered to a hole in the wall where it disappeared, its long tail trailing behind.

She searched the dark room and spotted two shapes lying on the floor across from her. Her eyes drifted toward the door when one of the shapes made a slight movement and a low groan pierced the silence. She croaked out a squeaky cry, "Oh my God, someone's here. Hello, can you hear me?" The shape let out another groan and began softly crying.

Suddenly the shape rolled over and a dark face stared at her. Her lips pulled back and white teeth reflected the dim light, "Welcome to paradise, honey. I'm Cillia. What's your name? How'd you get here?"

The girl wimpered "My name's Maya. What is this? What's going on?" and started sobbing.

Cillia sat up with a groan, scooted toward Maya and whispered, "Don't know the answers to any of those questions. The last thing I remember before waking up here I was walking down the street in Tacoma after work when someone grabbed me, jamming a cloth over my mouth. Tried to fight and I think I scratched the son of a bitch before I went out like a light. Next thing I know, I'm tied up here with my little honky bunkmate over there."

The other shape rolled over and sat up. The moonlight illuminated a dirt-streaked pale face and blond hair, "I'm Judy. My story's like Cillia's. I was grabbed off the street in Salem and woke up here. Been here about three nights, I think. Not sure where we are, but we're in deep doo-doo! We have to get out of here! I've been working on it and I almost have one hand free." She jerked her arm and gave out a grunt and held up her arm, "Yes, I did it! It's bleed-

ing like hell but now maybe I can work on the chain." She pulled herself to the eyebolt, holding her chain and began working it back and forth, "I think it might be coming loose! Help me find something to pry with."

The three women felt around in the dark. Cobwebs brushed their faces as they slid around the floor. Cillia let out a little scream when something she touched bit her, "Oh man that's sick! I may get rabies or something!"

Maya shouted from the other side of the room, "Wait, I think I found something! It feels like an iron bar." She slid toward Judy and handed her a short piece of rebar, "Try this. Hurry!"

Cillia hissed, "Quiet, someone's coming." Nearby the percussive whop-whop of a helicopter pierced the air and the door swung open. A large shadow cast by the moon fell across the dusty floor and a voice broke the quiet, "Okay ladies, time for a little trip."

CHAPTER 1

I STOOD AT THE END OF the bar and watched across the smoke-filled room as a group of my fellow agents horsed around at the pool table. Others were hovering around a table of bar flies, chatting them up and hoping to get lucky. The lady agents hovered around the jukebox where indecipherable music and the boom of a beat pounded out of the speakers. Everyone was in a boisterous mood, everyone that is except yours truly, the honoree at this retirement party, "*Damnit*', I thought '*I'm not ready to be put out to pasture. I'm going to miss these guys.*"

Jessie sauntered over, her hips swaying to the beat. Jessie stood six one and was the toughest agent in the room. She was also my direct supervisor at the Albuquerque NCIS office. Her dark face smiled; deep amber eyes boring into mine, "Hey little baby, how about one last dance with your old boss?"

Jessie was the fellow agent I would miss the most. Fifteen years my senior she was the other retiree being honored tonight. She had been my big sister since Sister Kathleen found me abandoned and sobbing on the convent steps so many years ago. Sister Kathleen and Jessie were the family that stepped in for long forgotten parents who tried to drown their demons in a bottle. Life in a convent for a ten-year-old boy would have probably turned me into a priest, but Jessie made sure that I experienced normal boy stuff. Sister Kathleen took care of my soul and Jessie turned me into a man.

The two of them ushered me through elementary and high school and into college where Jessie convinced me to join the ROTC program. During summer breaks, Jessie developed and then finely honed skills in me that colleges never offered and most students didn't even know existed. Following my graduation and completion of Marine Corps OCS, she arranged for my assignment to her NCIS unit as a shavetail lieutenant. Six years later I transitioned to a civilian role as a lead investigator.

And here we were ten years after that; Jessie had earned a full retirement and I had earned a medical retirement with a bum leg. That leg had been injured at the same time the bad guys took out my partner, Gibby, after a bust gone bad. Gibby was the only other person that I considered a member of my family and I still blamed myself for her death.

I grinned and stood up, "You know Big Sis, I never was much of a dancer. Something you and Sister Kathleen neglected during my youth. I should probably write a blog about the abuse you two inflicted upon me during my formative years. But if you're willing to put your feet at risk, let's give it a go."

I took her arm and guided her to the small parquet square that served as a dance floor. We danced in silence for a while and she looked into my eyes her mouth turned down into a pout, "What are a couple of worn-out misfits going to do without our badges?"

I couldn't help myself, so with my best faux-Mexican accent, I held her at arms-length and growled, "We don't need no stinking badges!" Jessie let out a full belly laugh and punched my arm. She still had a hell of a punch and I was pretty sure I'd never use that arm again. She pulled me into a full hug whispering, "Zeke, my little baby" and just rested her head on my chest for the rest of the dance, both of us giggling.

After the song ended, I migrated back to the bar, grabbed my beer, stepped out the back door and into the alley to clear some of the smoke from my eyes. Leaning against a brick wall, I pulled a joint from a small plastic case and lit it. The tension in my shoulders slowly eased while I watched a rat scurry from one trash bin to another.

Standing there, lost in thought, I was startled when Jessie spoke from behind, "You know, I could bust you for possession of a Schedule 1 substance." She walked to my front, took the joint and sucked in a lungful, "But, then again, I'm retired" She leaned back against the wall and smiled, "Seriously, I'm setting up a consulting agency here in Albuquerque. I've hired on a couple of other retired agents who will work part-time as cases arise. I've already lined up a consulting gig with the FBI. I want you to join me as my partner."

I took her hand in mine and stared into those sparkling amber orbs, "Thank you Big Sis, but I'm not sure that's where I should be at this time. Besides, you don't need a gimpy has-been weighing down your enterprise. She faced me with a scowl and began to protest, but I put a finger to her lips and continued, "You and Sister K own a part of my heart and I will never be far from you, but it's time for me to spread my wings and see if I can fly on my own. I'm really happy you have this great opportunity. Maybe, if there's a case that fits, I might do some gig work for you, but I need to see what else is out there."

I put my arm around her shoulders, and she leaned her head against me. We stayed like that, sipping our beers and taking hits off the joint for a long time.

It was pushing eleven when I worked the room saying my goodbyes and then hopped into an Uber for the short ride to my apartment. As soon as I slid the key into the lock I heard skittering nails scratching the floor on the other side. Lobo jumped up and spun around with a bark as I opened the door. She sat and held out her paw to me and I reached down to shake it and ruffle the fur on her head. To be honest, Lobo was the final member of my small family. I'd responded to a want-ad announcing free puppies at a ranch on the west side of town. As soon as I'd seen her soft brown eyes looking up at me, I'd been hooked. She's a border collie with other breeds mixed in. The rancher thought that a coyote might be in the mix. She's two and a half and whatever her genetic makeup, Lobo was the smartest dog I've ever met. And her loyalty to me was unquestioned. She accompanied Gibby and me on many operations and had put her fifty pounds on the line for each of us several times. She and I would always mourn the loss of Gibby.

After Lobo and I shared greetings with lots of licks and a dog biscuit, I pulled the mail off the floor and sorted through it. Among the bills and fliers was an official looking letter from an attorney's office in Seattle. *Great, just what I need, someone's probably suing me! Well, you can't get blood out of a turnip.*

I started to throw the offensive envelope in the trash before my curiosity got the better of me. I slit the seam with a pen knife, skipped the heading, and started to read.

Dear Mr. Jones,

Our office represents the estate of Mr. Robert Auburn Sullivan, deceased. Our investigation leads us to believe that you are his only surviving relative. It is imperative that you contact us at your earliest convenience to discuss his estate. Please call 206-699-7865 between the hours of 9AM and 4PM PDT.

Sincerely,

Jacob Epstein, Esq.

I chuckled to myself and threw the letter on the coffee table, "Lobo, my girl, I believe they've got the wrong person. Those two reprobates that brought me into this world didn't have any relatives that I'm aware of. Let's go out for your walk before we turn in."

Lobo sat up, put both of her paws on my leg and licked my hand.

———•———

The next morning Lobo and I jumped into Karla, my 1968 Karmann-Ghia and headed across town. Lobo sat in the passenger seat, her tongue hanging out, the wind across the convertible's windscreen ruffling her fur. When she tired of the scenery she hopped into the backseat, curled up and began snoring. We were headed to the 50-meter pool at West Mesa Aquatic center where I had a six-thirty reservation to punish my body doing speed work. I used to alternate running days with swimming, but my busted knee wouldn't allow me to run distance anymore. Now I hit the pool four days a week and mixed it up with karate one or two times a week.

Pulling into a parking space, I reached to the floor and retrieved Lobo's collapsible water bowl, filled it from an old plastic milk jug and set it on the ground where she could hydrate if she woke up. Lobo spent my workout sessions curled up in the back seat of Karla. She's not one to work up a sweat unless she's chasing squirrels.

•————————•

My eyes were red and my arms and shoulders were burning as I limped over and climbed into Karla. Lobo jumped into the passenger seat, looked at me, and then pointed her nose straight ahead. She knew we were headed to her favorite part of the workout, breakfast at Jalisco's in Barelas.

As I drove into the parking lot, the enticing aroma of masa and spices made my mouth water. Lobo hopped over the car door and scrambled into the small café before I could turn off the ignition and climb out. *I gotta teach that dog patience and manners someday!*

"Buenos Dias Senor Zeke, welcome!" I was enveloped across my abdomen in arms attached to a pretty Hispanic woman as soon as I stepped into the dimly lit café, "Senor Lobo is already at your table." Sonia smiled a full tooth grin that turned into a question and tightened her arms around me, "We haven't seen you for a while. We missed you and Lobo."

Sonia and her husband Miguel were the proprietors of possibly the best Mexican restaurant in Albuquerque. They were busy this morning just like every day. The locals kept the secret of this culinary gem to themselves to keep out the tourists, but business was always brisk. I took Sonia's shoulders in my hands and pulled her back and kissed both cheeks, "Bella Sonia, I missed you too. Is that mean bandido of a husband around or can we sneak into the back and make mad passionate love?"

Sonia giggled and slapped me on my arm. A loud voice bellowed out from the kitchen, "I heard that. You have insulted mi esposa. Therefore, I must exact revenge and inflict punishment on you. Maybe I'll turn you and that miserable mongrel into Carne Asada!" A short rotund man with a drooping mustache charged out the door and grabbed my hand in a vice-like grip that made me wince, "Zeke, How are you, my friend?" He stepped back and looked me over top to bottom, his eyes pausing at my knee.

While Sonia had immigrated from Mexico as a child, Miguel was fifth-generation American. Born in East Los Angeles, a wise judge had given a seventeen-year-old gang banger a choice - five years in prison or an enlistment in the Marine Corps. Fortunately for the Marines he chose the latter. The regimen and pride of the Corps had worked wonders on him. He turned out to be a natural and earned a bronze star and purple heart in Afghanistan. He met and fell in love with Sonia and the two of them opened their little restaurant after his enlistment ended. Miguel couldn't boil water when the two met, but Sonia and her sisters patiently turned him into a Michelin three-star chef.

Extracting my hand from his vice-like grip, I massaged my fingers and said, "I'm doing well. The knee is coming along. How are those bambinos?" Miguel and Sonia had a stable of five young ones ranging from three to twelve. They were the most polite and helpful kids I'd ever run across.

"They are all well and eating us out of house and home. They're constantly hungry and I can tell by the way Lobo is drooling that you two are also in need of nourishment. Please sit down, and we'll get your specials started."

My special is Huevos Ranchero with a twist. Miguel topped the eggs with Chile Verde and slices of avocado, rice and refried beans on the side. Just the power breakfast I needed after a hard workout. Lobo's meal consisted of sauteed strips of beef mixed with rice. We both loved our meals at Jalisco's, but I would need to add a couple of notches to my belt if we ate there more than once every couple of weeks.

With our tummies happy, we said our goodbyes with bunches of hugs, waddled out to Karla, hopped in, and headed home.

·———————·

The letter from the attorney was still sitting on the coffee table taunting me. I grabbed it, scanned it, and crumpled it into a ball ready to throw it in the trash when I stopped. Something was tickling the back of my mind, a vague memory, a conversation between my mother and my father where she mentioned a brother who wouldn't have anything to do with her. *Well, the guy couldn't have been half bad. It can't hurt to talk to the attorney and, worst case, tell him that he needed to keep looking.*

I glanced at my watch and did some calculations. It was nearing nine here in New Mexico making it well within the attorney's office hours. I hesitated for a minute and then pulled my cell phone out of my pocket and dialed. After navigating through the office receptionist and then his personal secretary Mr. Epstein answered. He spent thirty minutes patiently describing the situation and letting me know there was no doubt that I had an uncle and that I was, indeed, his only heir.

Mr. Epstein had been my uncle's attorney and good friend for many years. My uncle, Robert (Robbie) Auburn Sullivan, was twelve years older than my mother and, because of the age difference, never very close to her. According to Epstein, she was terribly wild and left home at sixteen. She and my father would show up at their parents every few years to wreak havoc and sponge money. After my grandparents passed away, she did the same with Uncle Robbie. The last time he'd seen them, they were hauling a young child along. Robbie was concerned about the child's welfare and tried to convince them to leave the baby, that would be me, with him, but they wouldn't have it. They needed the welfare money that a child would bring to keep them flush with booze.

Robbie had been a Seattle policeman and following a career that spanned from beat cop to Detective III, opened a bookshop in Oyster Cove on Whatley Island near Seattle. Because of his police background he dabbled in private investigations for Epstein's clients on the island and an occasional wayward spouse or runaway for the locals.

Robbie had passed away, unexpectedly, six months ago from an aortic aneurysm brought on by a two pack-a-day habit. His will had been very specific in excluding my mother and father from any proceeds. Along with some charities, I was the sole beneficiary of the bookstore and a tidy, not so little, savings account. His will did stipulate that I continue to employ Silas McKenna as the bookstore's clerk. Silas had helped Robbie open the store many years ago and was a dear friend. Robbie wanted to ensure Silas was cared for. We ended the call with my promise to let him know how I wanted to handle the estate within a week.

After hanging up I sat on a chair on the small patio staring at the Albuquerque skyline for a long time. Lobo looked up at me with one of her crazy grins and climbed upon my lap. I scratched behind her ears, "Well, well, well! What do you think of that Lobo? We have an uncle!" Somehow that, and the fact that he'd cared about me, brought a smile to my face, "What the hell am I going to do with a bookstore? It's time to get some advice from Big Sis and Sister K." Lobo woofed and gave me a slobbery kiss as I picked up the phone and told Siri to call Jessie.

———•———

After a lot of thought and much heartfelt discussion, I let Sister K and Jessie know that I wanted to try my hand at being a proprietor. Sister Kathleen had vetted the situation on Whatley Island as only she could. She called the archdiocese of Seattle and got numbers for all the churches in the area. After speaking with the priests and staff at the parishes, these conversations resulted in a tentative approval of my move, but only after she received assurances from me that I would not ever miss Sunday Mass and I would call her twice a week. Her voice broke when she softly uttered, "Ezekiel Jones, you are going to be even farther away. I will miss you terribly! But it may be God's way to help you get over that terrible business with Gibby. At least you won't be cavorting with criminals. Please be safe and call from the road every night and as soon as you get there."

She paused, let out a long sigh and then continued, "Oh, by the way, take down this number for Father O'Rourke. He's the parish priest at Mary, Mother of Mercy in Oyster Bay. He's expecting your call and will be reporting back to me." Sometimes, I thought I was raised by a couple of drill instructors.

Jessie was a tougher sell. She had been my big sister and mentor since that first day at the convent. We had been joined at the hip, so to say, and she wasn't letting go without a serious discussion, "What the hell, Zeke? You're just going to move thousands of miles from me?" She sputtered "And, to run a bookstore? C'mon, get real. What do you know about selling books? And on a friggin' island!" Tears began to form and she blinked hard to dispel them.

I sat down next to her and pulled her to me. She struggled, but then leaned into me, "Big Sis, you are my best and dearest friend. I don't know how my life would have turned out if it weren't for you and Sister K. If you're adamant, I won't go, but I really think this move is what I need. I will only be a couple of hours by plane and there is no distance that can diminish our bond and my love for you. Please understand."

She buried her head into my chest and I felt a slight nod, "Ezekiel Jones, if you don't call me every day from this damn bookstore, I swear I'll drive up there, rip your arm off and beat you over the head with the bloody stump." I knew she was serious, and it filled me with warmth that these two women had so much love for this orphan.

Lobo crawled onto the couch and then onto our laps. She whined and licked the tears leaking down Jessie's beautiful black face until she finally let out a sigh and put her arms around both of us. *Who knew Lobo was a therapy dog among her many skills?*

CHAPTER 2

I T WAS TWO DAYS BEFORE I was to leave, and I had just returned from a rather exhausting session at the small martial arts academy located in a strip mall a few blocks from my apartment. The sensei was teaching me new techniques to compensate for my bum knee and had thrown me about like a rag doll. As I prepared to leave for the walk home with Lobo, he pulled me aside to lecture me on the importance of focusing my mind.

When I got back to the apartment, I grabbed a bottle of water from the fridge and plopped myself down on the patio chair. Thoughts of the move swirled in my head. I started going over the to-do list in my mind when my cell phone rang. It was a Denver area code, and I almost blocked it thinking it was spam, but some sixth sense pushed me to answering.

"Zeke this is Sissy."

Now there was a shock from the past. Sissy and I had been a thing ten years ago until she had disappeared from my life. At the time, I thought we might even become permanent, but she couldn't adjust to my irregular hours and the potential dangers of my chosen profession. We'd turned to bickering and an impassible distance grew between us. I had hopes that we could patch things up until I came home to an empty apartment and a note. She had taken a promotion at her firm's San Francisco office. It had hurt at the time. Still, it didn't take me long to realize we weren't meant to be.

I guess I got lost in my thoughts until she spoke again, "Zeke, are you there? It's important that I see you. I'm in the hospital and dying with stage IV pancreatic cancer. Can you come to Denver?"

Talk about a sucker punch! My heart came to my throat and tears exploded from my eyes. I pressed her for more information, but she started crying, insisting that she see me in person and wouldn't expand on her reasons. I'm a softy for tears and despite the pain of our breakup, she still held a piece of my heart. I told her that I would be there in two days on my way to Washington. We finished the conversation with small talk and I hung up. Lobo sensed my pain, made a high-pitched whine and licked my fingers. My voice shook as I reached down to pet her, "Well, Lobo isn't that a kick in the ass? Feel like meeting an old lover?" She jumped up, faced toward the Ghia and looked back at me expectantly. I let out a sound between a sob and a chuckle, "Yep, we're going on another adventure, but you need to cool your jets for a couple of days. How about a nice long walk to clear our minds?"

———•———

We were on the road at five-thirty, Lobo's head hanging out the side window, the wind turning her ears into wings. The drive to Denver took almost seven hours. We began climbing shortly after we left Albuquerque, passing through high-mesa country dotted with pinon trees across red earth stopping to top off the tank and grab a cup of coffee in Trinidad. And, of course, Lobo left a calling card behind the gas station. The traffic in Colorado Springs slowed us down a bit and we pulled into the Hospice facility parking lot on the north side of Denver at 12:30.

The Hospice was discretely situated amongst a serene landscape framed by a grove of aspen trees. Gravel paths and tables populated the expansive lawn. Lobo and I made our way to the large doors that opened to a sunny lobby. The lady at the desk gave me Sissy's room number and confirmed that dogs were welcome as love providers to the patients.

As I turned to walk down the hall towards Sissy's room I noticed a young girl sitting in one of the cushioned chairs. Her eyes were red among a face splashed with freckles and she looked miserable. Something about the girl tickled my brain, but I couldn't put my finger on what it was. As I walked past, she looked up with hope in her eyes and then wiped her nose on her sleeve and stared at Lobo and me. *Poor thing! This must be hard on the children of the patients.*

Sissy's room was soft-lit and I hardly recognized her. She was emaciated and pale. There were tubes running into her nostril and an IV wound its way to the vein of her left arm. A bandana covered her head. She looked up with tired eyes and smiled when we entered, "Hello Zeke." She reached out a hand on a toothpick size arm. Her voice was so light I had to strain to hear, "Thank you for coming."

I took her hand, leaned over and brushed her sallow cheek with a kiss, "Hello Sissy." I sat on the edge of the bed and tears started pooling in my eyes.

She reached up and brushed the tears off my cheek, "Please don't cry. It's okay. I've made my peace with God and I accept that this is his plan for me." She grinned the lopsided Sissy grin that I remembered, "Even though it pretty much sucks." Glancing down, she spied Lobo, "And who is this lovely girl?" I told her about Lobo, and she put her paws on the bed's rails and lifted her head toward Sissy, "You're such a good dog. Jump up here and give me a kiss." Lobo looked at me, I nodded, and she sprung immediately to the bed and laid her head on Sissy's chest. Stroking Lobo's head Sissy fixed her gaze on me, "I owe you an apology and an explanation.

I'm so sorry for the way I left. Our relationship wasn't working and we both knew it. I knew another heart-to-heart discussion wasn't going to cure it, so I took the coward's way out. The promotion in San Francisco was a great opportunity, both professional and personal. I hope you will forgive me."

I stroked her hand and whispered, "It's alright. There's nothing to forgive. I've had a lot of time to think about it and you hit the nail on the head. We were eventually going to destroy each other. Your leaving was a blessing in disguise. A nice, quick end where we could heal without always getting the scab continually ripped off."

Sissy buried her head into Lobo's fur, shuddered and let out a whimper, "Oh Zeke, you are so levelheaded and understanding, I've always loved you for it. There's a reason I asked to see you rather than putting my apology in a letter." Picking up my hand she stroked my fingers, "I didn't realize I was pregnant until a month after I moved to San Francisco…"

My head shot up and turned toward the lobby and that mysteriously familiar young girl. I turned back to Sissy my mind spinning, "Ours? How?" More rhetorical than questioning. That young girl out there was undeniably a product of our love making.

"I thought about reaching out to you but didn't want her to be the reason we stayed together. It would have destroyed both of us in the long run. And abortion was never an option! That young person growing inside me was a living being and a wonderful product of our time together. She's been the center of my universe ever since they laid her on my chest in the delivery room."

I started to speak until she put her finger to my lips, "Please let me finish. That little girl out there is completely innocent of my deception. Her name is Maxine, or Max, and she is everything a parent would want." She held her hand up, "She's scarily smart and pure enjoyment to be around. She reminds me so much of you."

"She's aware of my condition and she's come to grips with it quite maturely for a nine-year-old. I've always been open with her about us, so she knows a lot about you. She's anxious to meet you and has been on pins and needles since I told her you were visiting."

Burying her head in Lobo's fur she continued, "Zeke, she has no one beside the two of us. My parents passed away a while back and there are no siblings or others in my family. She raised her head and stared into my eyes with tears streaming down her cheeks, "I know it's all new to you and it's asking a lot, but please take care of her, Zeke. Give her all the love you have in that huge heart of yours. Please promise me!"

Her words came out as a groan. I pulled her to me and kissed the top of her head, "There is nothing I'd rather do. But, isn't it up to her? I mean I'm a stranger!"

She wrapped her arms around my neck and kissed me softly, "Max knows everything about you because I shared every detail I could while she was growing. She knows

I'm leaving and she is anxious to start a life with you. Please?"

I buried my head in her shoulder, my eyes leaking buckets, "I promise that I'll give her the best life possible."

Sissy sat up, emptied her nose into a tissue and smiled, "Why don't you go introduce yourself to your daughter and give me a chance to fix my face. Whenever the two of you are ready, come back in and we'll chat."

She watched me through red-rimmed eyes as I walked over and knelt in front of her. Blond curly hair framed her face and freckles dotted a pug nose. Her blue eyes were opened wide, and her gaze bore into me, "Hello Maxine, my name is Zeke and I'm your father. I didn't know that I was missing you until today, but if you let me, I promise to make up for lost time."

She put her hand against my face and stared deeply into my eyes for a moment, "You're just like I imagined. I'm glad you're here. But, please, can I call you Dad." She wrapped her thin arms around my neck and gave me the best hug I've ever had. We talked for a long time. She told me about her life, her school and asked me about Lobo. After an hour, we went back to join Sissy and Lobo.

Sissy died three days later. Scores of people attended the funeral and let me know what a special person Sissy had been. I called Jessie and Sister K and had long discussions with both. Sister K made sure I went to confession while Jessie was completely thrilled at becoming an aunt. They flew up for the funeral and doted on Max to the complete exclusion of Lobo and me. The four of us, and Lobo of course, sat around after the wake eating cold catered food. Sister K and Jessie competed with each other, telling embarrassing Zeke anecdotes and fully absorbing Max into our little family. I sat in a cushioned chair sipping a beer and looked on as they shared girl stories and giggled. Lobo would alternate between them and throw in a lick here and there. A warm feeling filled my soul as I watched the three women that were woven into my heart.

CHAPTER 3

S ISSY HAD BEEN METICULOUS IN crossing the t's and dotting the i's with the mounds of bureaucracy required for me to have custody of Max. Even so, it took a struggle to wind our way through the few remaining documents and a DNA test. I certainly didn't need the test to prove Max was mine and even if the test had proved otherwise, I would never abandon her. She was now part of Zeke's Clan!

Sister K and Jessie made good use of the time by schooling me on the needs of girls and young women. Some of it was a little embarrassing to the three of us, but we plowed through. Jessie had fully embraced her role as doting aunt and insisted on taking Max shopping for a new wardrobe. I could hear the two of them giggling and whispering when they returned, bags overflowing with enough apparel to clothe the entire Denver homeless population. Max ran up to me and twirled around in a bright yellow dress adorned with bright flowers and pink Converse All-Stars, "Look what I bought, Dad! Isn't this beautiful?" She pulled me up and we swung around in a circle, laughter percolating from her pretty mouth.

I pulled her to me for a hug and then held her at arm's length, "I believe you're the belle of the ball, sweetie" She shrieked with joy when I picked her up swinging her around and around, her new high-tops floating behind.

Two weeks after the funeral, we were finally ready to head out. The sun had been up for an hour when Sister K gave me a hug, "My dear Zeke, I'm going to miss you so much. I know that you'll take care of this precious young lady, but I'm going to worry just the same."

"That's what makes you special, Sister. You worry about everyone. But you don't just worry, you back up your worries with prayers and actions. Something within me always knows when you're praying for me. And just like that first day you took me in, your prayers carry me through. As soon as we're settled, I'll arrange for you to fly up. I'll miss you bunches until then."

Sister K wiped a tear from her eye and went to have one last hug with Max. And there was Jessie standing in front of me looking miserable. She grabbed me with both arms and buried her head into my shoulder, "Damn, this is hard! You're leaving a big hole in my life. I don't know what I'm going to do without having to keep your sorry ass out of trouble. Please, Zeke, don't let me lose you."

I pulled her to me and stared into those beautiful amber orbs, "Big Sis, it'll take a lot more than a few miles to come between us. I can't go too long without my Jessie fix. So, I expect to see you up there next month. No excuses. In the meantime, we can all FaceTime every night." I shuddered and then squeezed her, "You're right, this is hard, and I'm scared out of my wits. I don't want to separate from the two of you! And what do I know about being a father? Maybe this is a mistake!"

Jessie pulled back from me and 'bonked' me on the head, "Ezekiel Jones, that is not how we raised you! This is going to be hard for all of us, but you need this and that little nine-year-old needs you! You'll be a great dad. So, buck up!"

One last hug and Max, Lobo and I piled into Karla, tooted the horn, threw kisses into the air and pulled away.

———•———

We wanted to take our time to give us a chance to become more familiar with each other, so we headed north toward Cheyenne. Max was petting Lobo and I joined her and said, "There's a package on the seat back there that I'm pretty sure is for you. Why don't you get it and open it. Lobo would appreciate having the extra space."

Max ripped at the brown paper covering and gave me a sideways glance at the Ariat label. Her look turned to puzzlement when she pulled out a glittery pink pair of cowboy boots, "These are pretty, but I'm not really a cowgirl." Her eyebrows bunched together in confusion, "What's this all about?" I just smiled.

Two hours later we drove down a wide thoroughfare and under a huge banner announcing 'Cheyenne Frontier Days' and parked just in time to see hundreds of cattle being herded by mounted cowboys and cowgirls down the middle of the avenue. Max bounced in her seat, clapped her hands and let out a shriek, "Oh wow! Help me get my boots on Dad!" Pulling on her boots, she bounded down the street, her dress bouncing up and down in pursuit of the cattle entering the pens in the park. Lobo wanted to herd the cattle so I slipped a leash around her neck and we jogged to keep up.

We spent the remainder of the day wandering through the Old Frontier Town exhibits and watching women and men demonstrate their skills at the rodeo. While we were watching the women barrel race, Max slipped her hand into mine and looked up with a grin, "Maybe I might want to be a cowgirl after all. Do you think I could get a horse?"

"That's a pretty big responsibility. Just like everything, a lot of work goes into caring for a horse before you can ride and then even more work after that. How do you feel about shoveling horse poop?"

Max made a face and then the grin returned, "How about I start with some riding lessons?" *Very practical girl.*

After watching the wild horse race, we wandered over and chowed down on barbequed brisket, beans, and corn on the cob at the chuckwagons followed by double scoops of ice cream. Later, after a stomach lurching few rides at the midway, my knee was screaming and Max's head was drooping. I picked her up, laid her in the front seat while Lobo jumped into the back, and we drove to our hotel. Max was softly snoring when we arrived. I gently lifted her little body, carried her to the room and tucked her in. Lobo crawled onto the bed, curled up next to her and went to sleep. I sat across the room watching Max's little chest rise and fall softly, in amazement. *I am truly blessed.*

After feasting on cowboy flapjacks the next morning, we were back on the road. The sun was warm and the sky peppered with little puffs of clouds. Lobo sat in the back, tongue hanging out in the wind. A fully rested Max began a non-stop dialog, bouncing from excited chatter about the scenery to pointed questions for me, "Dad, what are your parents like? I mean, they're my grandparents, right? Did you tell them about me? I know Jessie's my aunt, but do you have any other brothers and sisters?"

Thinking about Jessie brought a smile to my face, "I'll always tell you the truth so I'm not going to sugar-coat it. It happened a long time ago, but my parents abandoned me when I was about your age. Sister Kathleen and Jessie pretty much adopted me and they were my only family until you came along. I found out about an uncle I didn't know I had just a few weeks before I found out about you. There are no other relatives that I'm aware of."

I must have looked sad because Max jumped up in her seat and wrapped her thin arms around my neck, "Oh Daddy, it must be serendipity that we found each other. Two almost-orphans coming together when we need each other most."

'Serendipity?' Where did a nine-year-old come up with that?

I tousled her hair, "You got it, sweetie! I don't know where I'd be if I hadn't found you."

She turned in her seat and looked at me seriously, "Technically, we found you dad." And, then she let out a huge belly laugh, reached up and tousled my hair. We zipped down the road laughing while Lobo howled.

It was a long, but thoroughly delightful day of driving and chatting under azure skies before we pulled into the hotel parking lot in Great Falls. After checking in we took Lobo for a long walk along the banks of the Missouri River. Max's eyes were drooping when room service arrived with burgers and shakes for each of us and a hamburger patty for Lobo. After her shower, she lasted for fifteen minutes watching cartoons before nodding off, snoring gently. I pulled the covers up to her chin and tucked her in. She pulled one hand from the covers and stroked my face, mumbling, "Good night, Daddy," before slipping into a deep slumber.

After enjoying the hotel's free breakfast the next morning, we were off again. Lobo was sleeping in the back, but Max was fully rested and began peppering me with more questions, "Were you really an NCIS agent? That sounds soooo exciting! NCIS is one of the few TV shows Mom and I would watch together. She said it reminded her of you." A sad look clouded her pretty face and I reached over and pulled her close to me.

"Being an NCIS agent isn't really like you see in those shows. Most of the work is boring. A lot of paperwork and unexciting white-collar crime."

Max was animated and the questions poured out before I could respond to them, "But Mom said it was dangerous and that she was always worried about you! Did you catch a lot of crooks? How many did you shoot? Did you have a partner? I think agent Torres is cute! Kasie's really smart. I think I might want to be a forensic scientist like her. What's the scariest case you were on?"

When she paused to take a breath, I edged in a few responses "Your Mom was right to worry, but the danger level was usually pretty low. While I caught my share of crooks, I only pulled my gun a handful of times. My last case was probably the scariest in my career. It was a drug bust that went wrong. I did have a partner and she was killed during that raid."

She must have sensed my melancholy because she grabbed my hand in both of hers and gazed directly into my eyes, "I'm sorry. I can tell that you miss her. What was her name?" Her eyes shaped into a question, "Were you good friends…or were you more? Like lovers?"

I took my hand from hers and looked straight ahead, willing the tears from my eyes, "No nothing like that. Her name was Gibby and she was just the closest friend I had. We bonded from the start and always had each other's back. Only this time I couldn't protect her." I rubbed my knee, "I took one in my knee and couldn't follow her and the team into the melee. And, yes I miss her! I should have been there and she would have been okay!" A tear fought its way through my squinted eyes and trickled down my cheek.

Lobo whined and Max reached across wrapping her thin arms around my torso, "Oh Daddy I'm sorry I made you sad. I'm here now and I'll watch your back, I promise."

A laugh or sob, I'm not sure which, gurgled out of my throat, "Thank you. That means a lot. You don't know how happy I am to have you as my partner. We're going to make a great team."

We drove in silence through the Blackfeet Indian Reservation for a while. Lobo sat up and licked my face before retiring to the backseat.

The sun was approaching the horizon as we sped past fields of golden wheat and muted green alfalfa fields. The back road highway was quiet with very little traffic. Max sat up with a devilish gleam in her eye, "Mom said I was too young to drive. Will you teach me? I watched her all the time and I know I can do it."

I chuckled as I worked up a response. Clearing my throat, I looked into her clear blue eyes, "You know, I wasn't much older than you when I learned to drive the old farm truck around the convent property. Sister Kathleen and the other nuns grew vegetables, fruit and lavender for sale at the local farmers' market and she would let me load the truck and drive it to the gate. But she made me promise not to drive off the property until I got my license." I winked, "Seems like if I could do it, so can you. But there's one stickler. I'm a driving purist and I believe that anyone who learns to drive must learn in a car with stick shift." Her confused look brought a snicker from me. I grabbed the gear shift sticking up from the floorboards, shifted down into third and let her feel the deceleration, "Did you feel that? I just changed the gears that control how fast we're going. Your mom's car would change gears automatically, so she didn't have to worry about moving this lever all the time. Kind of like an early version of artificial intelligence."

Her eyes lit up and her words rapidly spilled out, "I get it! Some cars even do more, just like Teslas. They drive themselves! You just sit back and tell the car where you want to go and it takes you there while you play video games or sleep or whatever."

"That's right. I suppose self-driving cars are the future but give me a four-on-the-floor anytime. For me riding in a Tesla wouldn't be much better than riding a bus. I mean where's the fun? And . . . I'm not sure I would trust the driver." I pulled to the shoulder of the road and said, "Get on my lap and we'll have our first driving lesson."

While she climbed onto my lap, Lobo took her place in the passenger seat and off we went, Maxine squealing and hooting while Lobo barked. I let her steer for a while, with only a little weaving, until the traffic got heavier. She slid over onto her seat, grinned up at me and yelped, "That was a blast! Can I practice with the gear shift next time?"

Thoughts of shredded gears flashed through my mind, but I didn't hesitate for a moment, "That sounds like fun. Maybe after we get settled."

A crimson sun was slipping behind the mountains as we pulled into the hotel in Couer d'Alene for the night. Lobo jumped out and baptized a bush near the circular driveway and we gathered our bags. The valet jumped into the driver's seat and then looked at us with a confused expression. He turned beet red and stuttered, "Oops, sorry sir, but I'm not familiar with a stick shift. I think you might have to park yourself."

I took the keys from him and smiled, "That's okay. Why don't you take care of the bags. My daughter and I will park the car." Max and I started giggling as soon as he disappeared into the lobby.

———•———

We were becoming anxious about getting to our new home and we were up with the sun. The hotel's buffet breakfast seemed to sate Max's bottomless stomach, at least for a while. I sipped my coffee and slipped Lobo slices of bacon while she devoured a bowl of cereal, two pancakes, an omelet, hash browns and a huge cinnamon roll. She smiled slyly as she finished a fruit plate piled high with strawberries and cantaloupe, wiped the milk mustache from her lip and wrapped another cinnamon roll in a napkin, "This is just in case we can't find a restaurant for lunch."

I filled a to-go cup with java and paid the bill while Max visited the restroom. Clutching her precious cinnamon, bun she raced Lobo to the car shouting, "I call shotgun!" to Lobo who was just happy to be with her as he hopped into the backseat.

In the name of expediency, we agreed to skip the backroads and jumped on the interstate. A while later we sailed past a sprawling Spokane and turned west into the arid environment of eastern Washington. A checkerboard of vast fields of pale-yellow wheat and purple tinted green alfalfa streamed by on both sides of the highway.

Two hours later we made a pit stop at Moses Lake. We walked Lobo around and watched hundreds of migratory birds clustered around the water. Their calls and shrieks created a pleasant cacophony drowning out some of the highway noise. Max grabbed a soft drink at the convenience store to help wash down the gut bomb that was slowly bleeding melted icing into the napkin.

The majestic snowcapped peak of Mount Rainier loomed in the distance as we began to climb up from the valley and the air became less dry. Pine forests replaced irrigated fields. Max squealed and jumped up and down at the sight of a doe and its fawn, causing Lobo to pop up from his slumber with a bark. Pockets of snow appeared in shady areas as we climbed. I used the curves and elevation changes to demonstrate how manually shifting gears helped me control Karla.

We summited at Snoqualmie Pass where gashes in the mountainside stripped of trees were reminders of the ski lifts in the area. Waterfalls graced us with bursts of rainbow-sparkled mist. Max's stomach was growling and I could tell Lobo needed to visit a tree so we pulled in at a roadside restaurant for lunch. I nibbled on my tuna sandwich while Max slipped pieces of her grilled cheese sandwich to Lobo in between French fries. She took a long pull on the straw of her chocolate milkshake and grimaced, cried out and grabbed her head. She startled me and I started to reach for her when she cried out, "Ow! Ow! Ow! Head freeze!" Ice cream dribbled down her chin and she giggled, "This milkshake is delicious."

Max visited the restroom while I paid the check and picked out a giant jawbreaker that she had been eying. Outside the air was fresh and scented with pine. Lobo spotted a squirrel chittering on the side of a tree and gave chase before giving up and loping back. We wandered around the area for a while to stretch our legs and then we were back on the road again. After a few miles I pointed ahead, "We're getting close. There are two routes to the island. We can come in from the north across a bridge or we can take a ferry from the south. What do you think?"

Max laughed out loud, "Oh my gosh, a fairy? Does the fairy magically transport us?" and then punched me in the arm, "Just kidding Dad. I know what a ferry is. I've been reading up about Whatley Island. I think I would like to take the ferry. They say that sometimes you can see whales. Orcas even!" Her face lit up. "It takes less than half hour to cross. As soon as we get some cellular, the ferry has a web page with departure times. And I'll bring up 'Maps' for the best route."

My little navigator!

Halfway down the mountain we pulled to the side of the road. A light rain had begun so we pulled the rag top up and latched it to the top of the windscreen. The steam from our breaths fogged the windows until we opened the wind wings and the temperature and humidity stabilized.

Half hour later the road straightened, the ground leveled out and we left the forest behind to cruise past Seattle's outlying communities. Max was fiddling with her phone and looked up, "Looks like we will have an hour wait. There are normally two ferries, but they only have enough crew for one boat service."

We drove through the small town of Mukilteo, past a school on the right and pulled behind a queue of vehicles idling in the right lane half-way down the hill. A short time later the car ahead began inching ahead for a few blocks and came to another stop. We were idling next to a roadside café so I gave Max a twenty and she and Lobo ran in for snacks and a coffee for me. We chatted and listened to an oldies radio station while Max devoured a bag of chips and bottle of lemonade. Lobo sat in the back and worked on some beef jerky.

An hour later we pulled up to a kiosk and bought tickets for the crossing. The attendant doted on Lobo and slipped him a doggie bone as we pulled away and filed into lane two. The big ferry tooted it's horn, bounced between pilings and into the dock. The ferry dropped its ramp and disgorged its contents; motorcycles roared up the ramp followed by a myriad of trucks and cars of all sizes. Then it was our turn. A crew person waved our lane forward. We drove into the belly of the boat and up a ramp. A crew member guided us up close to the vehicle in front where I set the parking brake and turned off the engine.

As soon as we parked on the middle deck, Max was up and headed for the stairway to the observation deck. Her voice trailed behind her, "Isn't this cool Dad? I'll see you up there." I shouted at her to be careful, but the noise of the big diesel engines drowned me out and she disappeared. Lobo was a little anxious from the loud noises and strange surroundings, so I ruffled her coat and patted her head to calm her. I slipped a leash around her neck and we headed up the stairwell.

Lobo pulled from side to side as she investigated the deliciously new mysterious odors. I pulled her along and just as we stepped onto the outside observation deck the clouds split and the sun blessed us with its warmth. The water glistened with thousands of sparkling gems of light. Max was twirling around and singing an unintelligible ditty when we reached her. Falling into my arms she let out a belly laugh and tittered, "Isn't this wonderful? I've never seen so much water! I just love it."

She shrieked and ran to the railing, bouncing up and down. She pointed over the railing at a churned-up area of the sound, "Look! I think I saw a whale!" Just then an Orca breached and fell onto its backside, "Oh my gosh! That's so beautiful! I can't wait to tell . . . ." Her words trailed off and her face fell.

I pulled her to me and held her tight while she sobbed, "It's okay sweetie. Let it all out. I miss her too. But I know your Mom is watching you and smiling down from heaven." Lobo whined and raised her paw to Max's leg. We both got down to the dog's level and Max wrapped her arms around Lobo's neck and squeaked, "I love you, Lobo! You always cheer me up. You're my best friend." Lobo reciprocated with a slobbery lick and we both laughed.

Lobo's going to be busy. She's my best friend, too!

We spent the remainder of the crossing hugging Lobo, looking out across the waters of Puget Sound and watching sea birds; some floating lazily in the gentle swells and others drifting on the thermals waiting for a wayward fish to appear near the surface. As we approached the island, we spotted a seal balancing on an exposed rock covered in barnacles and arching its back toward the sun.

CHAPTER 4

T HE FERRY'S HORN BLEW A mournful sound, and
we scrambled back to the car as the boat bumped
against the dock pilings and settled itself against the loading ramp. The big diesel engines growled as they kept the
nose of the boat pressed against the shore. The air was
heavy with the briny, musky odor of low tide. Fishermen
crowded the pier, their poles angled against the railing in
the hope of a strike. Seagulls floated overhead looking for
the chance to steal a catch or someone's sandwich. To the
left, I spotted beach houses crowding the shore and more
stately homes on the hill above among the trees.

We followed the line of cars and exited the boat at the
opposite end than we had boarded. The ramp was steep
and we scooted up and onto Whatley Island, driving past
the lines of cars waiting to sail in the opposite direction.
The road bent up steeply and around a curve where we
were faced with a hodge-podge of clapboard buildings
laid out with no discernable logic or pattern. Along each
side of the road were light industry businesses next to
retail outlets and restaurants. A few real estate offices and
churches were sprinkled in the mix.

Heading north, the structures became few and far between, replaced by dense foliage lining both sides of the
road. Jam-packed growths of ferns and blackberry bushes

competed for space, interrupted only occasionally by non-native kudzu. Thick stands of pine and fir towered above in regal pose. Occasionally, an orphan eucalyptus tree stood proudly in contrast with its adobe-red bark sloughing off its twisted, naked trunks.

Max became animated by the apparently prolific deer population. We passed both lone does and those accompanied by a couple of fawns with their spotted torsos. Coming around a corner we had to stop behind a line of traffic waiting for a young four-point buck to amble across the road. Max was working her phone and read to me, "The deer population is dense on Whatley because there are no natural predators on the island." Her face darkened as she continued, "Because the island is naturally isolated not only from predators, but also from other herds, the deer here are horribly inbred and genetic weaknesses manifest themselves. While most are reasonably healthy, there is a much higher incidence of genetic disorders. That's sad."

I thought for a minute, "It's very sad. I'm not a biologist or nature scientist, but I wonder why they don't just capture some deer from the mainland and introduce them to the herd. The new blood would soon propagate the island. Probably too simplistic."

Max sat up and grinned at me, "That's a great idea, Dad! Maybe we can talk to someone to get it done."

"Well sweetie, we're going to be busy setting up our new digs. Let's get settled first. I think we'll have plenty to keep us busy for a while." I reached over and squeezed her hand and was rewarded with a bright smile and then peppered with questions sprinkled with excited discourse.

"I can't wait to get there. I'm really excited. What do you think Oyster Cove is like? Will there be other kids there? I can't wait to make some new friends! Do you really own a bookstore? That's just the best thing in the world! I love to read!"

She stopped to take a breath and I wedged into the conversation and told her what little I knew about the store, "Yes, but I don't own a bookstore, we do. We're a team, right? I just learned about the store at the same time I learned about you. I didn't even know I had an uncle. From what I can find out, he was a real character who also did private investigations on the side."

"That's so cool! I think we should be private investigators, too! We could be like the Hardy boys or Nancy Drew." She drew a breath and got a devilish grin on her face, "'Maxine and Associates, Private Eyes!' I like the sound of that."

I was taking a drink and almost blew coffee out of my nose with my laughter, "Hey, wait a minute, how come you get top billing? Maybe it should be 'Ezekiel and Maxine, Investigators!'"

Max turned toward the rear seat and cackled, "We're forgetting about the brains of the family. I've got it! It has to be 'Lobo, Max and That-Other-Guy, PI's!'" Lobo jumped up and barked.

We kept busy thinking up silly detective agency names while we cruised past small towns and verdant farms nestled among stands of pine and fir. A cooler sat at the edge of the driveway leading to one farm. A sign scribbled in uneven black letters on the backside of a cardboard box proclaimed, *Eggs for Sale, $4/Dozen.* A cash box rested upon the top of the cooler. Another farm advertised, *Fresh Cut Flowers, $5/bouquet.*

•————•

The air was pleasantly warm and a light breeze ruffled our hair as we approached a stoplight. A large white sign directed us to the right and 'Historic Oyster Cove'. The street carried us past a small regional hospital on our right and professional buildings on our left. We passed a weathered Catholic Church dominating the top of the hill and I beeped the horn to say hi to Jesus before the car dipped down presenting us with a gorgeous view of the quaint town nestled along the edge of a small, sheltered bay. The panoramic scene was right out of a Norman Rockwell painting. Max gasped, "Oh my gosh! Is this our new home? It's absolutely beautiful! I'm going to love it here!" She rubbed Lobo's head and the dog lifted her nose in the air for a sniff.

We followed the street as it curved left, threading us between clapboard buildings on a narrow lane. The buildings on the right were clinging to the side of the hill and dangling above the water's edge. Halfway down the street I was the first to spot the sign, 'Dragon Island Fine Books' was printed in large letters. Below, in smaller script, announced 'Discreet Inquiries' above a plate glass window crammed with book displays. I pointed to it and Max laughed, "That's a pretty good name. But I like some of ours better, especially 'Lobo's Detecting and Sleuthing, We dig up the Dirt!' Let's check it out."

I pulled nose-first into a diagonal parking spot on the left and Max and Lobo immediately hopped out. She came around and grabbed my hand pulling me across the street, "Don't you just love it? Look at all the books! Hurry!"

A small bell tinkled when we opened the door and the enticing, musty 'bibliosmia' of the tomes within delighted my senses. A distinguished looking fellow with a pencil-thin moustache, thinning silvery hair and a muted green cardigan stood behind the counter attending to a middle-aged woman purchasing a stack of paperbacks. He turned our way and a hint of recognition lit up his bright blue eyes, "Welcome. I'll be with you shortly. Please have a look around."

The front of the store was populated with a half-dozen tables, each displaying the latest releases of a different genre; Poetry, Drama, Fiction, Action and Adventure, Young Adult and Mystery. A small table to the side held a dozen books under a 'Local Authors' sign. We wandered through the neat stacks with shelves of hardcover and paperbacks. A large picture window looking out over the water dominated the back of the store. Small tables were neatly arranged with comfortable chairs allowing customers to relax and peruse their literary interests. A pitcher of iced tea and one of iced water sat next to small plastic cups on a sideboard. *That's a good idea. I might add carafes of White and Red Wine, though.* I chuckled, *Maybe a cigar humidor!*

One of the tables off to the side was populated by a pretty teenage girl and a boy about Max's age. They both had books open, their heads down and were writing in spiral notebooks. Max led Lobo over and began chatting with them, making new friends as only innocents can.

I chose a chair on the other side to give them space and looked out at the boats lining up at a T-shaped pier to the left. The boaters would jump out and haul a long hose over to fuel up. A café at the end of the pier was doing a brisk business, all the outside tables were crowded with customers and a young waiter took orders and another rushed to fill glasses and bring heaping plates to tables. The water ahead was calm and some pelicans floated calmly in the swells while cormorants sat on the pier's pilings and spread their wings to dry them. A blue heron stood frozen above its intended prey in the shallows while small birds dove for insects around her.

I heard the shopkeeper's heels on the wooden floor as he approached, and I stood and reached out my hand. His grip was strong, his hand was warm and his fingers long and slender. He held himself proudly erect and smiled warmly. His voice had a slight undertone of an accent I couldn't place.

"You must be Master Ezekiel. Allow me to introduce myself. My name is Silas McKenna, and I am, or I should say I was the assistant store manager." He bowed slightly "We have been waiting for your arrival. I trust you had a safe and uneventful trip. You must be knackered. Is there anything I can get you, water, tea, coffee . . . perhaps a wee drop?"

"I'm good for now." I waved at the chair across the table, "Please sit down. You needn't be so formal. Please call me Zeke. Tell me about yourself. I detect a bit of an accent. How did you end up running a bookstore on a somewhat isolated island?"

His knees creaked and popped as he settled himself into the chair, "Old habits are difficult to break and I'm probably too old to try, so if you don't mind, I'll continue to be formal. It's too deeply ingrained. I worked as a man-servant for twenty years before your uncle rescued me and gave me this wonderful position in paradise." Even though he smiled, I sensed a sadness that he couldn't camouflage. "Now, I suppose you'll be making changes. I've packed up all my things and will happily spend time getting you up to speed about the ins and outs of the shop."

"You're correct, I will be making changes." I pointed across the room at Max, "You see that little girl over there. She's the new Assistant Manager." Silas' face fell and I hurried on, "But, that presents me with a problem. I don't know the first thing about running a business much less a bookstore. I was hoping you would stay on as the manager." His face went from crestfallen to buoyant in an instant. I pulled a sheaf of papers from my jacket pocket and spread them before me, "You see, my uncle Robbie included a letter with his will. He explained that the two of you were long-time lovers. He wanted to include you in the disposition of his assets, but you refused. You felt his belongings should go to his only living relative. He asked me to keep you on and wanted to make sure you were cared for as you grew older."

His eyes had misted and there was a slight tremor in his hand. I continued, "Now, here's the deal, Silas. I was abandoned as a child. Two wonderful women raised me and never asked for anything in return except love. And now I have that sweet young daughter over there. They are my family just like you were Uncle Robbie's family. And since my family now includes an uncle I never knew, you have become a member of Zeke's Clan."

He smiled and began to reply until I held up my hand. I slid the papers across the table and he picked them up and held them at arms-length, squinting. I handed him my dime store readers and he nodded and began reading. I continued, "That first set is the legal documentation making you one-third owner of 'Dragon Island Fine Books and Discreet Inquiries.'" He started to protest, and I interrupted giving him my best stern-faced NCIS agent look, "It's what Uncle Robbie would have wanted."

His hands were trembling while he scanned the document. I continued, "The other papers in that stack describe the health insurance program we are instituting for all

Dragon Island Fine Books employees including you. There is also a description of the 401K plan that we've set up. The store will match any contributions by you up to six percent. I recommend you use the raise you're getting with your new position to contribute."

Silas stood and faced the window and after a few moments silently whispered, "Robbie was my soulmate. His death left a hole in my heart that I thought would never heal. I felt so alone these last months and my future was murky with unknowns." He turned and looked at me, a broad smile belying the tears that trickled down his cheeks, "Your kindness, Master Ezekiel, has helped close that hole. And I'm not speaking of these generous gifts, I'm talking about your embracing me as a member of your family! What did you call it, Zeke's Clan? That rather resonates doesn't it." He grabbed my shoulder and squeezed, "You have my eternal gratitude."

I stood up and pulled him to me for an awkward hug, "Now about that wee drop, Uncle Silas?"

●———————●

We toasted each other with weighted crystal glasses of amber liquid and fell into a comfortable banter, talking about the island, the town and the bookstore. I finally convinced him to, at least, shorten my name to Master Zeke. As our conversation trailed off, I nodded toward Max and her new friends, "Who are those children?"

A broad smile spread across his face, "Robbie was an extremely kind person. Charlene, or Charlie and Mike belong to a young widow. She works days and can't afford a full-time babysitter so he would let them stay here while she was working. We helped her homeschool them.

They're very well-mannered and quietly do their homework or read." His face fell and he became uneasy, "If it's a problem, I can ask her to make other arrangements."

I watched the three of them chatting and giggling for a few moments, "No, not at all. Do you think we could get Maxine into Silas' homeschool program?"

Silas poured another dollop of whiskey into each of our glasses, lifted his to me and barked, "I believe you're in luck Master Zeke, we happen to have one opening." We silently sipped our drinks staring out at the expanse of Puget Sound while our friendship solidified in the bonhomie atmosphere. *Family, good books and good whiskey! Doesn't get much better than this. Maybe a cigar?*

Max caught me looking over and pulled her new friends over to us, a smile lighting up her face, "Hey Dad, I already made some friends. This is Charlie and Mike."

They both impressed me with their manners. The girl shyly squeaked, "Very nice to meet you Mr. Jones. My real name is Charlene but everyone calls me Charlie. Max told us about you."

The boy stood straight and held out his hand and gripped my hand firmly and with a bright voice chirped, "Hello, sir. Nice to meet you." He became animated, couldn't contain himself and sputtered, "Is it true you were an NCIS agent? That's so cool! Do you have a gun? I want to be just like Gibbs."

Charlie put her hand on his shoulder and spoke silently, "Mikey, why don't you let Mr. Jones relax. I'm sure he'll tell you all about being an agent later."

I chuckled, "That's okay Mike. We'll have a lot of time to tell stories. Maxine, please say hi to your Uncle Silas." They both looked startled, "He and Uncle Robbie were together and now we have a new member of our family."

Max walked over to Silas and put her hands up to his face and smiled, "It's a pleasure to meet you Uncle Silas. I'm sorry about Uncle Robbie, but I'm glad that you're with us now." She wrapped her arms around his neck and gave him one of her famous hugs.

Silas blinked and his voice broke, "I'm delighted to make your acquaintance young lady. And thank you for allowing me into your life."

We chatted with the kids for a while and then Max lit up and exclaimed with a grin, "Charlie says there's an ice cream store down the street. Can we go get some? Please!"

I looked at Silas and he spoke up, "It's only a block away, the traffic crawls on this street and there are adults everywhere. There's not much danger. Mike and Charlie go there often.

I pulled some bills from my wallet and handed them to Max, "I'll take a double scoop, one pistachio and one vanilla on a cake cone." Silas declined and the children scampered out in a flurry of giggles.

After they left, I pointed at the ceiling and asked Silas, "Do you live in the apartment above?" His face took on a whimsical look, "No, the apartment was Robbie's and has been vacant since he bought the place. He never spent any time there. We shared quarters in my cottage a few blocks away." He gave me a knowing look, "If you're planning on living there you might want to consider upgrading the appliances and certainly all the décor. I believe it was last done in the seventies. Ghastly! Come, I'll show you."

I followed him up an outside stairway to the apartment door. A musty odor enveloped us as the door swung open to a large open space living area. There were two bedrooms, one in a loft above a nice sized kitchen. A large picture window treated us to a gorgeous view of the bay. The green rug and yellow appliances were a blast from the past. I pulled up a corner of the rug and found wide plank ash flooring that seemed to be in excellent shape, "This wood is very nice. It's too bad they covered it up. We're booked into a bed and breakfast for now. You don't happen to know a good handyman that could fix this place up quickly?"

Silas nodded with a smile, "Normally, things on Whatley move at a snail's pace. It's called 'island time'. But, when I heard you would be moving here, I thought you might want to fix this place up so I took the liberty to contact a friend who does remodels. She's already laid out a plan for the space and preordered the appliances. She can have it ready in a few weeks. Would you care to peruse her plans?"

"I'm afraid that I'm 'décor challenged' and wouldn't have a clue. I'm sure that whatever she comes up with will be more than suitable. Please tell her to proceed."

We went back downstairs just as the kids arrived with ice-creamed faces. Max handed me a cone with green and ivory stickiness seeping down the side. The four of us sat on a bench outside licking our frozen delights while Silas returned to the shop to attend to a customer. I sat back and relaxed and took in the weathered ambiance of the town. The clapboard buildings housed an assortment of businesses. Those that I could see from my perch included a lavender shop *How could anyone sell enough lavender to make a living???*, a yarn shop *Ditto*, a couple of souvenir stores, a Spa and Salon and a diner.

The kids were amicably chattering away, my tummy was happy, and I dozed relaxing from the long drive. My eyes shot open when Mike shouted, "There's mom" and he and Charlie ran up the street. I watched them run into the arms of a striking woman in her mid-thirties. Her copper-colored hair surrounded a softly sculpted face. Her blue eyes laughed with the children as they hugged before they looked up at me. Our eyes locked and my heart skipped.

I stood as she walked up to me and her velvety voice practically purred, "Hello, Mr. Jones. I'm Anne Murphy." She reached out to shake my hand with long delicate fingers, "I see you already met my two urchins. I hope they haven't driven you crazy." She bent to look around me at Max who'd suddenly become uncharacteristically shy, "Who's this pretty girl?"

"Please just call me Zeke." I gently nudged Max to the front, took her shoulders and turned her toward the pretty lady, "This young lady is my daughter, Maxine." Max smiled shyly and said hello.

Anne knelt down to Max's level looking deeply into her eyes, "Hello, Maxine. You're very pretty." She reached out and took Max's hand in hers, "I'll bet you take after your mother. Is she with you?"

Max immediately warmed to this nice woman, and then whispered, "My Mom died. It's just me and my Dad. I have two aunts, Jessie and Sister K. I just found out about my uncle Silas." She giggled and reached down, "And Lobo's my best friend."

Anne stood, a cryptic smile flashed across her face, "Well Zeke, did Silas explain our situation? Now that you're here I can make other arrangements." The pretty lips of her mouth turned down softly and she tried to hide it, but I sensed worry mixed with sadness.

There was no way I was going to disrupt those kids' lives even if their mother wasn't beautiful, "I won't hear of it. Your kids are great. Besides, I was hoping that Max could join their home schooling. I could help with some of the lessons if you'd show me the ropes." *Geez, Zeke, do you think you could be more obvious? Get a grip!*

"Well, that's a huge relief. I'm not sure what we would have done without the help Robbie and Silas, and now you, have given us." Her face lit up and she chuckled, "How are you with math? I'm afraid it's not my strong suit and Silas is as lost as I am." She gazed at me with those green eyes, the question seemed to amuse her.

"As luck would have it, my math skills are decent. I think we can handle up to Trig and a little calculus." I looked over at the children as they played with Lobo on a small patch of lawn, "It looks like Max and Mike will be studying the same things, but Charlie is probably Algebra Two or Trig. If you'll give me the lesson guides, I'll study them and try to dredge my memory."

"Thank you, Zeke, that's so kind." She turned and called, "Come on kids, let's get home." She smiled, reached out her hand and gripped my hand, "Goodbye for now. I'll see you tomorrow when I drop them off." She put her arms around her children's shoulders, and they walked across the street and up the hill. When they reached the crest, she turned, grinned and waved before disappearing.

Maxine looked up at me with a devilish grin, "She's really pretty. I think that maybe you're smitten." *Smitten? Where does this kid come up with these words? She's a walking Merriam-Webster!*

I reached down and picked her up swinging her around while she shrieked and Lobo jumped up barking. I growled, "You're the only one I'm smitten with! You, Jessie and Sister K are more than enough women for me."

Max was still giggling when I put her on my shoulders, walked down the street and into the bookstore.

CHAPTER 5

I WOKE AT FIVE THE NEXT morning and traipsed down to the shore. I pulled on a wet suit and waded into the cold waters of Puget Sound. It had been a long time since I'd done any open water swimming, so I limited my first outing to twenty minutes looping around the pier and then returning. Small dogfish lazing along the rocky bottom skittered away as my shadow reached them. Two sea otters splashed ahead of me, diving and frolicking in the calm waters of the cove. I reached shore, sat on a rock and began to peel off the wetsuit when a young female deputy walked down the slope of the beach to me. She had a pretty face crowned with straight black hair, her high cheek bones hinting at Native American genes. The name tag pinned above her left breast read 'PCSD Deputy T. White Feather'. Her uniform had been tailored to accentuate a sinuous figure. *Man, this place is chock full of beautiful women!*

She removed her obligatory mirrored Foster Grants exposing light blue eyes and long eyelashes. She smiled as she watched me struggle with the wetsuit, "Sorry, sir, but swimming near the pier is restricted. There are just too many boats. It's a dangerous situation. May I have your name, sir?" She appraised me critically, not giving any indication of whether she liked what she saw, "Don't suppose you have any identification?"

I pulled a towel from my bag and reached back in searching for my wallet. I pulled it out and opened it to remove my driver's license but before I closed it, she spotted my NCIS identification card. She glanced at me, "You an agent?"

I started toweling off, smiled and pointed at the scars stitched across my knee, "Was. Medical Retirement. You going to arrest me?" I grinned, "I sure could use a cup of coffee. Any good places around here?"

She got a wicked look in her eyes, "I could put the cuffs on, but you're in luck and I'm in a good mood so I'll let you off with a warning this time. Follow me. I was just headed for a cup myself."

I slipped into my flip-flops, pulled a T-shirt over my head, grabbed the bag and scurried after her, "My treat, unless it would be considered a bribe? I didn't catch your first name Deputy White Feather." *Looks just as nice from the back as the front!*

She ignored my question while we walked up to Beach Street, turned left and stopped at a bakery located at the end of a row of buildings. She turned to me at the doorway and smirked, "I don't think a five-dollar cappuccino will break the threshold for reporting, but then again there's a donut calling my name. You know how we cops are about our donuts."

I cracked up, "Since I'm a recently retired, highly trained law enforcement specialist let's call this a professional exchange addressing the efficacy of donuts versus that cinnamon roll that has my name on it."

I let her order her drink and pastry and then ordered a black coffee, the roll and half dozen assorted pastries to-go. She raised her eyebrows into an unspoken question, "Sweet tooth? You'll need to swim a lot farther after all those."

A small table by the window opened up as I paid so we scurried over and sat down. I took a sip of my coffee, then explained, "You're right, I can't afford any extra calories. These are for my daughter and her new friends. This should get them through a morning of home schooling." Her eyes darkened at the mention of a daughter, and she sat back putting a new space between us. I chuckled and continued, "Maxine's mother passed away recently, and we moved here to start a new life. Any chance I'll learn your first name?"

"Sure, my name's Theresa or Terry." Her shoulders visibly relaxed and her eyes took on a sorrowful look, "I'm so sorry for your loss. That must have been devastating for both of you."

I explained the situation between Max's mother and me and then went on to tell her about my long-lost uncle and the bookstore. She knew the bookstore and frequented it. We fell into an easy banter, and she told me about herself. Her mother was a member of the Snohomish tribe and she'd been raised on the reservation. Her father was white and hadn't been seen since she was a year old. She'd studied Criminal Law at Washington State and joined the Puget County Sheriff's Department two years ago as soon as she graduated.

She became animated when she explained her reason for entering law enforcement; her sister had disappeared when she was young. She explained that the disappearance of young Native Americans was a widespread problem and she hoped to make a difference. She leaned forward with an intent look, "The disappearance of Native

American kids goes largely unnoticed, but more and more Anglos, Hispanics and Orientals are missing lately! Because of that, the problem is getting more attention, but most cases are written off as disgruntled teens running away from home." She leaned forward, her eyes intense, "Human trafficking is a big problem across the country, but it's especially bad here because of our proximity to the Canadian border and the extensive waterways."

We talked for a few more minutes until she glanced at her watch, "It's been nice talking to you Zeke, but breaktime's over. I've got to go bust bad guys. I'll stop by the bookstore. I want to meet your daughter." She stood, shook my hand, looked around and leaned forward to whisper in my ear, "A word of caution, steer clear of the sheriff. Since I'm the token minority female, I'm not privy to his inner circle, but there's something not right in that office."

Every male in the café, and some females, watched her walk away. *Very interesting…if I were ten years younger, I'd be hanging around the sheriff's station.*

———•———

I showered, dressed and opened my bedroom door to a beaming, chocolate-covered face, "These are delicious, dad!" She sat in an easy chair in her pajamas and a blanket wrapped around her shoulders. Lobo lay beside her with crumbs speckling her snout and a guilty look.

"Hey Munchkin, if I didn't know that you're a bottomless pit I'd be worried about you ruining your appetite. Why don't you brush your teeth and get dressed, the breakfast spread downstairs looks pretty tasty."

Our bellies were happily full of the continental break-fast when we walked to the shop and greeted Silas as we traipsed into the store. Max ran over to one of the shelves, pulled out a copy of 'Anne of Green Gables' and plopped down at one of the tables in the back. Lobo curled up at her feet while Silas began to show me the ropes for running a bookstore. A short while later, Anne, Charlie and Mike arrived. The two children ran over to join Max and Lobo bringing happy chitter to the quiet environment.

Silas handed Anne a cup of tea and the two of them explained the routine they had set up for the kids. Anne began, "Since it's summer vacation, we lighten the studies and fill in with enough activities to keep Charlie and Mike and now Max busy. In addition to some classes, they must read at least one book a week and write a report on it. Most kids would balk at that, but I'm blessed with two bookworms. Do you think Max will be okay with that?"

I pointed to Max as she held up her book and excitedly jabbered to her friends describing what she'd read, "I don't think she'll have any problem with that. She's already a walking encyclopedia. But I'm sure you don't keep active kids like those inside all the time. Do they participate in sports? How about other friends?"

"Mikey plays little league baseball and youth soccer. He has lots of friends from the teams as well as in our neighborhood." She scrunched up her face, her voice dropping an octave, "Charlie was playing softball, but she's getting to the age where athletic activities are taking a backseat to hanging out and meeting boys. Her friends are okay, they're just entering the terrible teens and all the changes women go through at her age. Anyway, after the kids have finished their assignments it's usually lunch time." She handed me a paper sack stocked with sandwiches, fruit and cookies, "After lunch they have free time. They need to let Silas know where they'll be and check in every hour. Mike usually heads to the ballfield and Charlie and her friends hang out around the ice cream shop. Four o'clock is the witching hour when they must return. I get off at five and join them."

"Sounds like a pretty good system. Max and I will need to figure out extracurricular activities for her. I'm going to cruise around the island this afternoon to orient myself. Would it be okay to take Charlie and Mike with us on a field trip if they want to go?"

Her smile was warm, and her voice took on a lilt, "That sounds like fun. I'm sure they would love to go with you." She glanced at the large clock above the desk, "I've got to run. My shift starts in ten minutes. Mikey, Charlie come give me a kiss." Needless to say, I was terribly jealous of Mike and Charlene.

<hr>

Silas spent the next hour giving me the rundown on best sellers, classics, isbns, genres, spines and inventory turnover. My head was spinning, and my eyes crossed, "Silas, I'm absolutely certain that you are capable of running the store, but I'm afraid I won't be much help. I'm just not built that way. Let's leave you running the day-to-day operations and keep me in the background? I can take care of the books and help where I can. I know you and Robbie worked as a team and it wouldn't be fair to load all responsibilities on you. What do you think about hiring an assistant?"

Silas picked up a nearby book and softly stroked its cover, "Master Zeke, I think you are selling yourself short.

You would do fine here, but if it's not in your blood it won't be enjoyable for you. I'm concerned about the extra expense of another employee, however."

I put my hand on his shoulder and smiled, "I've looked at the financials and it really won't be a problem. The store earns more than enough to cover another salary and still provide us owners with a little profit at the end of the year. And, since I won't be taking a salary there's even more in the coffers. My retirement stipend is more than adequate for Max's and my needs. But you're now a part owner and have much more knowledge about the operation, so I'll be okay with whatever you decide."

"Thank you for your confidence in me. Since you so eloquently explained the situation to me, I believe my old bones could use a little help around here." A sly grin spread across his face, "I'll try not to be a hard taskmaster."

We carried on a light conversation for a few minutes until Silas went to help a customer. I pulled my phone from my pocket and dialed the rectory at Mary, Mother of Mercy. The secretary told me that Father O'Rourke could see me in twenty minutes. I told Silas where I was headed, kissed Max on her head before Lobo and I jumped into Karla and headed up the hill.

Father O'Rourke was somewhere in his fifties, medium build with unruly carrot top-hair, a warm smile and vicious grip. Massaging my hand while I sat in the chair he offered, I introduced myself and asked if he remembered that Sister Kathleen had called him about me. His eyes crinkled and he let out a huge belly laugh, "How could I forget? She's quite the pistol! Very protective of you. She told me about your relationship and gave me clear instructions on 'caring for her boy'. His grin widened, "Of course, I'm not going to do that. You seem like a responsible young man and I'm not a babysitter. Besides, she had many years to set you on the right path. She and I had a good laugh about that. But I believe she's making plans to join the retirement convent down the road."

"She's an amazing woman and if you think I'm okay you can thank her. She and her friend Jessie did every-thing right with me and any flaws are my responsibility not theirs. She mentioned her move up here when I spoke with her last night and, honestly, I can't wait for her to get here. I miss her and Jessie already."

We chatted for a while. Sissy had been a Lutheran, so I arranged for the necessary steps to bring Max fully into the Catholic faith including First Communion, Reconciliation and eventually Confirmation. Before I got up to leave, he showered me with fliers for adult bible studies and men's prayer groups. I promised him I would review those and see if anything clicked.

●────────────●

By the time I'd returned to the shop, the kids had finished reading. Silas had ordered a BLT for Max at the café down the street and the three of them were digging into their lunch. Silas was nursing a Cobb salad while he enjoyed the children's happy talk. He pushed a Turkey sandwich toward me as I sat down. The kids chattered about the books they were reading while we savored our lunch.

They finally ran out of steam and were concentrating on their meals when I asked, "I'm going to drive around to familiarize myself with the island. You guys want to join me? I could use your help, so I don't get lost."

Max giggled and poked me in the stomach, "Ha, Ha! Don't be a Troglodyte, Dad, how can you get lost when you have a navigation app on your phone?" *Troglodyte, hmmm?*

City girl didn't understand the lack of cell coverage in some areas. But I wasn't ready to correct her figuring she'll get the idea when we're out in the sticks, "Okay sweetie, you caught me, I just want your company. What do you say? Might be a milkshake waiting for us when we get back." I stood up and headed for the door, Lobo running ahead.

Excitement flashed in her eyes when Max jumped up looking at her friends, "Let's go guys. It sounds like a blast, especially the milkshake part." *Amazing what a little bribery will get you. I better dial back on the rewards.*

Charlie and Mike jumped up and all three chased after me. Charlie shouted 'shotgun' and they climbed into the Ghia, Charlie in the passenger seat, the other two squeezed into the small jumper seat, Lobo in the middle.

———•———

I put Karla's ragtop down so we could enjoy the gorgeous seventy-degree day. The sun was shining in the southwest and whispery clouds scudded over the sound. Mount Baker dominated the horizon, part of its snow-covered peak blanketed by clouds. We drove around the town so I could get a feel for the neighborhoods. Pretty cottages dominated green lawns. Deer were everywhere and I had to stop more than once to allow a doe and her fawn to cross in front of us. Charlie and Mike were used to the docile beasts, but Max squealed with delight every time one appeared.

The beach side of the town consisted of restaurants and toney shops catering to the tourists. Driving up the hill and away from the beach we passed a library, Masonic Temple and another church scattered among Victorian houses converted to B&Bs. The main street crossed the highway at the town's one stoplight. Beyond, lay clapboard buildings housing various businesses, a grocery store and three schools for elementary, middle, and high school students. The kids pointed out different points of interest. Then we were in open country populated by small farms and ranches.

Country roads meandered aimlessly through stands of pine and fir, so we just followed our nose, stopping to pick blackberries from the huge stickered plants spreading along the roadside. After we had our fill and Lobo had chased a couple of rabbits, we jumped back into Karla to continue the tour, eventually ending up on the seaside of the island. An old fort and lighthouse stood on a hill overlooking a terminal for the ferry to the Olympic Peninsula. We parked and got out to wander around the grounds and bulwarks. We watched people fishing from the rocks of the breakwater before heading back to the car.

We followed the shoreline past a large brackish pond on the left and beach cottages on the right. Hundreds of seabirds crowded the shoreline, shrieking and taking to the air when disturbed. Coming to a Y in the road I turned in the general direction of Oyster Cove. We drove up a hill and around a bend. Cresting the hill, we were blessed with the sight of a beautiful equestrian facility. A twenty-foot iron gate spread across the driveway. 'Oyster Cove Thoroughbreds' was spelled out in fancy iron lettering across the arch at the top. The place must have been at least a couple of hundred acres of pastures leading all the way to the ocean, fenced and cross-fenced. The barn and outbuildings were brilliant white with red roofs. A paved driveway, bordered on both sides with red and yellow rose bushes, led through the pastures to a sprawling ranch house. Horses grazed on the lush grass, and one looked up, whinnied and began running alongside the road, matching my speed. The kids laughed and waved while Lobo barked a greeting.

A line of pines stretched along the tree line providing a buffer between the ranch and the next property, another horse facility but of a smaller and more modest nature, maybe about five acres. It was fenced and cross-fenced as well, but with barbed wire and a hot wire running across the top strands. The pastures were neat and well-tended, but the grass was sparse. Several horses populated the paddocks and pastures. Two horses stood by the fence near the road; one was off-white and the other a deep chestnut, but the startling thing about them was their condition. They appeared to be emaciated, ribs and hip bones stuck out and their walk was weary. The white one had obviously been injured and walked with a painful limp.

Charlie saw them first, let out a whimper and began to cry, "That's so sad. Why are they like that? Doesn't anyone care for them?" Mike and Max became visibly upset while I pulled over. We jumped out and approached the fence. As soon as we did the big white one nickered and approached while the chestnut held back. Charlie ran to the fence and the horse immediately came to her and nuzzled her with her big head. She picked a clump of dandelions and fed them to her. Tears were streaming down her face, "She's so sweet. Can't we do something?" She stroked the big horse's head and slowly the chestnut sidled over and nudged her arm to get a piece of the action.

I was hot under the collar. I could never stomach animal cruelty or neglect. I watched the kids bonding with those horses and decided we had to fix this situation. *God gave us dominion over all the creatures of the earth!* "Let's get back in the car and go talk to the ranch owner."

A well-maintained gravel driveway skirted blackberry bushes covered with the dark purple fruit leading us toward a faded red barn. A family of quail scuttled across the road, the chicks trailing behind like the tail of a kite. Curious horses that appeared to be healthy and well fed stretched their necks over the fences to ogle us. Two mixed breed dogs chased us carrying on a cacophonous conversation with Lobo. As we approached, a man in a cowboy hat and denim vest stepped out of the barn. His hair was light brown and tied into a ponytail trailing down his collar, a wispy moustache spread above his lips. He appeared to be smiling, but since he draped a lever action rifle across his shoulder, I was wary. I reached under my windbreaker and released the safety on my Glock. I opened my door and stepped out, "You guys stay here while I talk to him. And don't let Lobo out!"

He leaned the rifle against a bale of hay and stuck out a calloused hand, "Good Afternoon. My name's Noah. How can I help you?" His voice was soft but firm.

I took his hand and introduced myself while I studied his face. Wind burned cheeks nestled below sad eyes. I pointed toward the two skinny horses near the road, "The kids and I were wondering about those two out there. They seem to be in pretty bad shape." I wanted to give him the benefit of the doubt, so I buried my anger, "What's going on with them?"

His shoulders slumped and he sat on a hay bale. He gazed out toward the horses, "Those two are my nightmare. A woman dropped them off for boarding over a year ago. She paid for the full year and promised to send money for alfalfa and grain to supplement the orchard grass that comes with the boarding fees. That money dried up six months ago and the woman keeps making excuses about their neglect. She's put me in a bind! I'm barely making ends meet with the income from the other horses and I can't afford to feed them properly much less give them vet and farrier care." He took off his hat and hung his head and I could hear the pain in his voice, "I wanted to take them to a rescue facility on the other side of the island, but they won't take them without proof of ownership. The sheriff says I can put them down if they're on my property but have been abandoned. My mom's up at the house crying her eyes out, because that's where I was heading when you showed up."

He held his head up and squinted through red-rimmed eyes at me, "The white is Shi-Shi and the chestnut is Maddie. They're really sweet horses and I just can't sit here and watch them slowly starve to death. I spent three years in Afghanistan, I killed men and I'm not proud of it, but this is the hardest thing I've ever had to do."

Charlie's scream pierced the air behind me and suddenly she was kneeling before the rancher, "Please mister, please don't!" Tears streamed down her cheeks and she jumped up to run to me, "Please Mr. Zeke, can't you help? I'll get a job and help pay to feed them!"

The other kids were wailing and Lobo was jumping from the front seat to the back. I took Charlie's hand and pulled her over to a bale and made her sit, "Don't worry Charlie, we'll work this out." I went over to Noah, sat beside him and put my arm around his shoulders, "It's okay. I think we can work something out. I'll pay for their feed and vet bills, and" I pointed at Charlie, "this young lady will give them love and curry them"

She jumped up and hugged me tight around the neck. Her tears were gone and she bubbled, "Oh thank you, thank you, thank you, Mr. Zeke! I love them so much." Max and Mike jumped out of the car and ran to us. Max squealed, "We'll help too!"

They started for the pasture, but I called them back. I looked at Charlie, "Hold on! First, we'll have to clear it with your mother. We're less than a mile from town so you can ride your bikes over to take care of your new friends. It's a big commitment and takes a lot of work and time. Are you sure?"

Charlie wiped her eyes, stood up straight with her shoulders back, "I love those horses. They're so sweet. I promise to take really good care of them."

"Okay then, there's one other thing you'll need to do." Question marks formed in their eyes and I smiled and looked at Noah, "You want to tell them?"

Noah's quizzical look disappeared and he smiled knowingly. He walked over to a wheelbarrow and picked up a manure fork and walked both over to the children, "I put the horse apples in a pile at the bottom of the property. I sell it by the truckload to some of the farmers around here to use as fertilizer." He walked over to one of the pens and scooped up a fork full of manure before dropping it into the wheelbarrow.

When the odor from the disturbed droppings reached the kids, a light came on and they cried "eeewww" in unison. But Charlie recovered quickly, lifted her head high and chortled, "No sweat. I can do it" and ran off with the other two toward the pasture.

I sat on a bale, pulled a straw out and set it between my teeth, "If you'll tell me where the closest place is for feed I'll run down and get some right away."

Noah looked at my car and chuckled, "You haven't been around horses much have you? They aren't called 'hay burners' for nothing. You won't be able to carry enough alfalfa and grain in that cute little buggy to last a day. I make a run to Freeland once a week and I'll get some then. In the meantime, the other boarders supply their own feed so I'll borrow some from their larders and replace it later. They won't mind." He stood up and shook my hand, "Thank you Zeke! I'm not sure I could have gone through with it. Let me run up to tell mom. She'll be ecstatic. Then I'll show you around."

We wandered around a well-maintained ranch and swapped stories. It was hard to tell but I estimated that he was around five years younger than me and following college spent eight years in special forces with three tours in the Middle East. After his first tour as a grunt, the army trained him as a drone operator. He would deploy with the teams and give them an eagle-eyed advantage. He was pretty burned out by the end of his second enlistment but a 'Dear John letter' cinched it so he used his savings to buy this ranch for himself and his widowed mother. The work was hard and the income slight, but he said it brought him peace. He currently boarded nineteen horses and hoped to expand by leasing the field next door.

I followed him into a large shop. An older but well-maintained diesel F-250 and a weathered Boston Whaler filled most of the space, but along the wall was a long wooden workbench holding four different aerial drones. He explained that his experience as a drone operator was providing a second source of income. The local agencies on and around the island contracted with him for search and rescue and he hoped to expand and provide his services to the utility companies for powerline inspections.

While we meandered back to the car, I pointed down the road to the fancy facility that we'd passed, "Pretty heavy competition over there?"

He laughed and shook his head, "We're worlds apart. Place is owned by some corporation. They raise thoroughbreds for the hoity-toity. They travel all around to shows and trade horses back and forth with breeders here and in Canada."

I yelled for the kids and Lobo as we walked back to the car and they came running, laughing and chattering. Charlie ran up to Noah and hugged him tight across his waist, "Thank you, Mr. Noah! I promise I'll take care of them." He tussled her hair and smiled, "Looking forward to the help, young lady. Why don't you call me Noah. 'Mister' seems awful formal."

I shook his hand and he promised to take me fishing for salmon when the season opened. I bent down to sit in the car when a melodious voice cried out, "Hold on for a minute!" I turned toward a smiling elderly lady with cherubic cheeks and a wide smile. She handed me a pie dish that emanated glorious scents, "This three-berry pie is for you and your children. I can't thank you enough. I was heartbroken by what my son was having to do. He's a strong man, but he's also gentle and pulling that trigger would have hurt him deeply. I insist that you and your family come back soon for a home-cooked meal." She reached up with her crepe-skin arms and pulled me to her in a hug.

Max shouted 'shotgun' and they piled into Karla for the ride home. I carefully placed the pie on Max's lap and started the engine. We waved and shouted our good-byes as we navigated the driveway and turned up the road just in time to see a doe and her fawn disappear into the woods. I slowed so I could look at the kids and announced, "I think Noah has a good idea. If it's alright with your mother, how about you call me Zeke?"

Mike and Charlie nodded but Max reached over with a grin and covered my hand resting on the gear shift with hers, "I'm still gonna call you Daddy if that's okay?"

I enveloped her little hand in mine, "Warms the cockles of my heart, sweetie."

———•———

Anne, being a mother, had her own thoughts about our plans, "Absolutely not!" she said when Charlie told her I said it was all right to call me Zeke, "I may be old fashioned, but children need to respect their elders. It may not be cool, but it's the proper way to act!" *She sure doesn't seem old fashioned to me!*

After some discussion, we agreed that 'Uncle Zeke' would be more appropriate. The plan with the horses took a little more convincing. Anne insisted on meeting Noah and his mother.

When we arrived at the ranch, Noah cast an appreciative gaze at her while she exited the Ghia. They showered her with warmth and walked her around the ranch. They described the safety procedures that they enforced and assured her that they wouldn't allow the children into any unsafe situation and would always be present when the kids were visiting. Shi-Shi and Maddie were the ones that tipped the scales, however. They nuzzled her with their heads as she fed them apples, "I always wanted a horse when I was growing up, but our family could never afford one. My heart breaks for these two. It's a good thing that you and the kids are doing." Her posture relaxed and she smiled, "And I've always heard that young girls with horses tend to stay out of trouble."

Louise, Noah's mother, insisted we come in for coffee and then proceeded to ply us with slices of warm pie fresh from the oven, apple this time. Noah sat in one of the big easy chairs in the sitting room and Louise sat in the other. That left a small sofa for Anne and me. I was acutely aware of her proximity as her leg brushed mine. Louise chattered on about her garden and the chicken coop out back, promising us a dozen eggs. While we talked, she sipped her coffee and watched us. Then she reached over placing her hand on Anne's knee with a foxy grin on her face and tittered, "You two make such a sweet couple. How long have you been together?"

I'm not sure which of us turned a brighter shade of crimson. We both cleared our throats and paused to respond, but Noah came to our rescue and interjected, "They're not a couple Mom. Their kids play together, and Zeke helps with home schooling."

The twinkle in Louise's eye didn't extinguish a bit, "Well, situations change all the time, don't they honey?" She patted Anne's knee and got up to clear our pie plates. I used that as an excuse for us to escape before she had us walking down the aisle.

The ride back to the shop was quiet, each of us lost in our own thoughts. I sneaked a glance and saw her staring at me, an enigmatic smile on her face. Then she turned and stared ahead.

CHAPTER 6

A FEW WEEKS LATER THE APARTMENT remodel was complete. Silas' friend had come through and pulled strings to get the project done in record time. The carpeting had been pulled up to expose natural wood planking polished to a high sheen. The kitchen was populated with new stainless-steel appliances and solid wood cabinets. A thick marble slab covered the island with a deep sink in the middle. She repainted the entire apartment in a pleasant off-white and it smelled fresh and clean. A new leather sofa and two plush chairs populated the living area.

Max and I spent a day on the mainland picking out bedroom furniture. The salesperson was especially helpful in selecting just the right pieces in just the right colors. At least that's how it worked with Max's bedroom. By the time we were through with selecting her stuff, my eyes were spinning. The salesperson took pity on me and after telling her my basic requirements e.g. King size bed with memory foam and dresser she promised to pick out a nice ensemble. She didn't let me down, both Silas and Anne said my bedroom looked nice.

We settled into a routine. Lobo and I would typically rise by five and either swim or practice Tai Chi on the beach. Deputy Terry would usually tap her horn or stop to chat if she happened to be in the area.

I'd shower, dress and have breakfast ready by the time Max rolled out of bed. Our morning meals were light, usually cereal or oatmeal, toast and fruit. Occasionally, I'd stop by the bakery for croissants or muffins. Then we slipped downstairs to the bookstore to greet Silas. Max would grab her latest book off the shelf and hunker down at the table she, Mike and Charlie had commandeered as their own while Silas and I performed the necessary rudimentary tasks required before opening the doors to the store.

Charlie and Mike would wander in and join Max while Anne would visit for a while with Silas and me. Her presence lit up my soul every time I saw her enter and I made certain that I got that rush every morning. Then, Silas, the children and I would begin our home-schooling tasks.

Today, after she left, Silas and Charlie wandered to a far table for lessons in literature. They were deep into a heavy discussion about *The Catcher in the Rye*. I'd read it at her age and thoroughly enjoyed it because it helped me understand that other adolescents had feelings similar to mine.

I could hear Charlie across the room animatedly discussing Holden Caulfield's travails while I tried my best to help Max and Mike understand number systems. After a while we switched and introduced a little algebra. Both kids, as well as Charlie, were well above grade level and easily grasped the concept of variables and equations.

After a few hours the youngsters were heads down and ardently attacking their homework assignments. Mike munched on an apple while Max nursed hot chocolate. Charlie was sitting by the window with a copy of *Catcher in the Rye* on her lap. She looked out at the gray sound with a wistful gaze, thinking those teen thoughts that none of us adults would understand.

I took advantage of the lull in action to wander up the street and eat an early lunch at Hank's Bar and Grill. I'd never been there and was curious about their cuisine. Or that's what I told Silas when I left. His eyes twinkled and he smiled knowingly, chuckling, "Say hello to Anne for me." *Busted!*

A mix of odors including cigarette smoke and rancid grease greeted me as I opened the door and entered the dark room. Booths upholstered in tattered red Naugahyde populated one wall and a long bar scarred with glass rings, cigarette burns and carved initials filled the other. Lopsided picture frames of 'famous' patrons shared wall space with beer advertisements. The obligatory pool table filled the center of the room, its green felt faded and ripped. Liquor bottles of various contents and sizes fronted the mirror behind the bar and beer taps loomed above stainless-steel sinks. The surface of the mirror was freckled with colorful decals from various military units stationed at the navy base on the north side of the island. A couple sat in a booth near the back windows enjoying baskets of fish and chips. Two old geezers sitting at the bar nursed coffee and stared at a muted television broadcasting ESPN and a beefy guy in his thirties with tattoos covering both arms sat behind a tall beer bottle at the end of the bar smoking a cigarette. The two at the bar turned and checked me out as I walked in and then went back to their curling tournament. The guy at the end of the bar stared while I pulled out a barstool and sat near the cash register.

The surprised look on Anne's face melted into a warm smile when she came from the kitchen, "Hello there. I wondered when you might stop in." She pulled a laminated tri-fold menu from a holder and slid it to me, "Can I get you something to drink?"

I asked for iced tea and when she returned with the frosted glass back, I ordered the fish and chips. After she gave my order to the cook, she came back and sat on a stool across the bar from me and we chatted while my order was being prepared. I told her about Sister Kathleen and Jessie and how special they were. I described my youth growing up in a convent and she smiled when I told her how good those two had made my life. I talked about Max and how she had entered my life and an understanding smile crossed her face when I described how smart she was and how she filled a hole in my heart that I wasn't even aware existed.

In between taking care of customers Anne told me a little bit about herself. She'd married while still in college, Charlie's impending arrival had hurried their nuptials along, and after graduation had traipsed along with her husband during his career as a navy pilot. They were transferred to Whatley Naval Air Station and were enjoying a happy life. Mike was due in three months when that happy life came crashing down. Her face turned sad as she described the day the chaplain and another officer had knocked on her door to tell her that her husband died in a collision with another plane during a training operation.

She had no family remaining, so here she was. "I love Whatley and our lifestyle, but there isn't much call for a degree in American History. The widow's stipend doesn't go far enough toward expenses." She waved her arms about the tavern with a wry smile on her face, "It's not much, but I can make more here with tips than anywhere else around. And the location and hours are compatible with wanting to maximize time with Charlene and Michael."

A party of four came in and Anne spent a few minutes settling them and taking their orders. She came back, refilled my iced tea and we carried on an easy banter about the kids, Whatley Island and life in general. She was intelligent and easy to talk to as she scooped maraschino cherries and carved limes for the bar well. I was just getting ready to leave when beefy guy yelled at Anne, "Get your ass back to work! I need a beer and I'm not paying you to fraternize."

Anne looked nervous and murmured, "Okay, Hank," and pulled a long neck from the cooler, flipped the top off and walked it down to the end of the bar.

She slid the beer toward him and his hand shot out and grabbed her wrist pulling her toward him, "How about you pay a little attention to me?"

Anne tried to wrench her arm free with a little cry, "Stop it you're hurting me! I told you I'm not interested!"

He reached across the bar and tried to grab her neck, "Dammit, you work for me and you owe me."

His hand shot out toward her face and that's when I caught his wrist and twisted his arm behind his back pushing it up until I heard him grunt, "The lady said stop. So just let her go and finish your beer."

Hank cried out and dropped Anne's wrist. I waited until she was out of striking range and then slowly released his arm. He turned and glared at me, spittle forming in the corner of his mouth. Rubbing his shoulder he hissed, "You don't know who you're dealing with hotshot! Get out of my bar before I call the police!" And then he spun around to face Anne, "And you're fired you little tease. I'm gonna spread the word, no one's going to hire you in this town."

Anne's face fell and she struggled to keep the tears from her eyes. I stood between her and Hank while she gathered her coat and purse. When she was ready, I put my arm around her shoulder, and we walked out. Before we reached the door I turned around, "She doesn't have to worry. She's already got a job lined up and was going to give her notice today anyway." I turned around, she held her head high, took my arm and we left.

We walked down the street. I knew Hank was too macho to let it go, so I went into full alert mode. When I heard heavy footsteps pounding down the pavement, I moved Anne to the side and spun around and into a defensive stance. From the corner of my eye, I noticed a flash of khaki coming around the corner, but just then Anne screamed as a pool cue swung toward my head. I turned into it and let the blow glance off my arm and then helped Hank on his forward motion. He was off balance and stumbled, dropping the pool cue until he caught his balance. The guy was my height and maybe twenty pounds heavier, but he was pretty quick. He came around and threw a hefty punch that caught me on my cheek. The blow stunned me for a second and Hank tried to take advantage, charging at me. It was a dumb move. I ducked under his arms grabbing his wrist, turned and let his momentum carry him into a hard fall on to the pavement. As soon as he was down, I ground my knee into his spine, pulled one arm up until I felt some ligaments popping and twisted his head around, "You're done pal. Give it up."

Hank squirmed and kicked, but he wasn't going anywhere. Just then, I felt a hand on my shoulder, "Okay, Mr. Jones. I've got it. You can let him go." I turned and looked into the pretty blue eyes of Deputy White Feather.

She let me get up and then motioned me over to the sidewalk next to Anne. Hank rolled over, jumped up and roared, "Arrest that son of a bitch! He assaulted me."

He started toward me but Terry used her body to block him and then pushed him back. For such a pretty thing she had a hell of a commanding voice, "Back up right now or I'm going to arrest you."

Hank screamed and spittle flew from his mouth, "What are you talking about! That bastard is the one who needs to be arrested! He almost broke my arm!" He feinted to the right and came around Terry charging with his head down toward Anne and me. *Guy's a slow learner!*

I moved into a defensive stance in front of Anne, waited and then smashed my fist into his exposed face. *Sometimes the old Mike Tyson routine was called for.* He crumpled into the asphalt, blood spurting from his nose.

Officer White Feather watched him fall, shook her head and walked over to us. She smiled at Anne and then turned to me with her professional face, "I witnessed everything that happened on the street. What I want to know is what led up to the fight."

I rubbed my bruised hand while we described the situation in the bar, and God bless them, the two old codgers confirmed what we told her. They were animated as both shook my hand. One smiled through missing teeth and week-old whiskers and murmured, "Good job, son! 'bout time someone took that feller down. He's been bullying people for years. Lon and I are taking our business down the street where there's less excitement."

Terry talked to the couple from the booth and then came over to us, "Everyone validates your version of events. Would you like to press charges?"

Anne and I both shook our heads.

"Okay, you guys can go, however, you've made a dangerous enemy, Mr. Jones. Hank fancies himself as one of the town fathers. He and the sheriff are tight and I'm pretty sure they won't let this rest. Watch your back." Her eyebrows arched up a bit as Anne took my arm and she watched us walk down the street. Hank was awake and was sitting up. He began shouting at Officer White Feather and threatening to have her job.

Anne was clutching my arm tightly and softly crying as we walked toward the bookshop. She murmured that she didn't want to upset the kids so I took her up to the apartment where she could have a good cry. She plopped down on the couch and blurted out, "Oh crap, now what am I going to do. I really needed that job."

I set a box of tissues in front of her, put the kettle on for tea and sat across from her, reaching out for her hand, "You shouldn't have to put up with that kind of abuse just because some jerk is abusing and holding you hostage with threats of being fired."

She took my hand in both of hers and squeezed my fingers, whimpering, "You're very sweet, but you don't understand. I need that job. There are just no other options in this little town." Her tears had stopped and she blew her nose before looking up at me with those drop-dead blue eyes and a little smile snuck onto her face, "You were very brave! I'm sorry to sound ungrateful, but I'm at the end of my rope."

I took my hand away reached into my pocket to re-trieve my phone, brought up *Nextdoor Oyster Cove,* and scrolled down to the want ad that Silas had placed for an assistant. I handed her the phone and chirped "Seems like solving your problems might solve ours as well. Silas in-sisted that the candidate must have a BA. He also insisted that we offer a starting salary that is commensurate with a living wage. How about joining the team?"

Anne stared at the phone for a long time, a slight tremor in her hands. After a while, tears began pouring from her eyes. Her mascara was running down her face when she looked up, grabbed me around my neck and pulled me to her. She kissed my cheek and hugged me tight, "You are a good man, Mr. Jones! Where the heck did you come from? Those women did right when they brought you up."

A hint of lavender enveloped me and electricity shot through my body from her kiss. *Oh wow!* We stayed together like that for a few moments and then she pulled back. Her face had a slight blush and a devilish grin when she cocked her head and gazed into my eyes, "I hope Silas doesn't have a rule against employees fraternizing with management." She jumped up and headed for the bathroom, "I must look awful. Give me a few minutes to freshen up and fix my face."

I didn't know what she was talking about, she looked pretty good to me.

While she was gone, I busied myself with the tea, setting the cups and a selection of flavored tea bags on the coffee table before putting the tea pot on a trivet. I was standing at the window and turned when Anne walked out of the bathroom. Her face was pink from the washing and her puffy eyes were still streaked red from crying. Her voice was soft, "Can we sit here for a bit? I don't want the children to see me like this and get upset."

I smiled and gestured for her to sit. After she chose a tea, I poured the hot water into her cup and went to set the pot down when she laid her hand on my arm, "I apologize for being so forward. I'm not normally like that". Her pink cheeks had turned red.

I set the tea pot down and gently took her hand in mine. I grinned, "Please don't apologize. I'll be honest, I was wondering how to approach Silas on that subject myself." My cheeks were getting a little pink, too. I squeezed her hand and went to the bathroom to retrieve some anti-redness eye drops for her.

Our voices were low as we sipped our tea and made small talk. Soon I had her laughing with stories about life as a boy in a convent. Thirty minutes later we made our way down to the bookstore.

———•———

The kids were curled up in their chairs, deep into their books when we entered the shop. Lobo was stretched the floor snoring softly. Max looked up and gave us a little wave and a smile before getting back to a copy of *Little Women.*

We pulled Silas to the love seats at the front of the store, gave him a sanitized version of the events and I apologized, "I'm sorry Silas, I should have consulted with you first, but after learning about Anne's education and experience I thought she'd be a perfect fit."

Anne pursed her lips, blurting out, "It's alright if you're not okay with it, Silas. I'll understand." She lifted her head, "I certainly don't want charity, either. I'm pretty sure I can get a job up in Oak Harbor…" Her voice trailed off.

Silas stood, straightened his cardigan over his neatly pressed slacks and a huge grin spread across his face, "Miss Anne, I'm thoroughly delighted! I wrote that want ad with you in mind and hoped that you would apply. I didn't want to meddle, but I've been worried sick about you having to work for that ogre." His face fell slightly, "Sorry, I don't mean to speak ill of anyone, but that bar was not a good environment for you."

Anne wrapped her arms around his neck and kissed his cheek, "I'm so blessed. I don't deserve one knight-in-shining-armor and yet I have two."

Anne glanced at me and I cleared my throat, "There is one other issue that we need to resolve." I hemmed and hawed and a pink flush crept up Anne's face. I wasn't sure how to broach the subject with him but, Silas glanced from my face to Anne's and a broad smile grew across his face, "Oh my, that's wonderful! I've seen the two of you stealing glances at each other and I hoped that something might come of it. As far as working together all I can say is Robbie and I were able to maintain a professional relationship separate from our personal lives for many years, and I have full confidence that you two will do the same."

Silas and Anne spent a while discussing her new position while I helped a customer and checked on the children. Mike was reading *Where the Red Fern Grows* and I helped him with the turn of a phrase. While we were talking Max scooted next to me and reached up to my cheek touching a tender spot, "What happened Dad, your cheek is puffed up and black and blue."

I'd promised that I would never lie to her so I moved us away from Mike so he wouldn't become upset and explained the scuffle, trying to downplay the incident. Fat chance. Max was too smart for me and peppered me with questions. When she was satisfied that she understood, she looked across the store to where Silas and Anne were talking, "She's really nice, Dad. I'm glad you stood up for her." She stretched up, planted a kiss on my cheek, tousled my hair and giggled, "Do I have to follow you around to keep you out of any more trouble?" We chuckled and I got up to help another customer find an obscure book by a local author before returning to sit with the kids and gaze out at the roiling sea. Gray clouds turned the water black and gusts of wind stirred up the water creating scores of whitecaps resembling a fallow cotton field.

Silas and Anne eventually strolled over and we broke the news about her working in the bookstore. Mike and Max were visibly happy and each of them hugged Anne in turn. Charlie's response took me by surprise, though. She rolled her eyes and whined, "Oh great, now I have a helicopter parent! Jeez!" She buried her head in her arms and wailed. Then suddenly she looked up with a huge belly laugh and poked her mom in the arm, "Just kidding! I think it's great. No offense to Mr. Silas, but I would like to get a fresh perspective on some of my literature assignments. Did I tell you I want to be an actress?"

Her goofy face was just the right antidote for Anne and me. We finally relaxed and joined in the raucous laughter.

CHAPTER 7

MY NEW SWIMMING SPOT WAS a couple of blocks away, adjacent to a much-used boat ramp. The water seemed exceptionally cold during my swim the next morning. The wind was gusting, and woolly clouds raced across the sky. I peeled off my wetsuit, shooed Lobo off the towel and dried off. I performed a comical dance while I hopped on one foot struggling to slide my jeans over my damp legs. I had just pulled a tee shirt over my head when I heard the chirp of a police siren. I grinned as I looked up expecting to see Terry White Feather. Instead, I was confronted with a thick set man scowling at me, feet spread wide apart. Broad shoulders and bulbous biceps stretched his khaki uniform shirt, but so did two inches of gut hanging over his belt. A blade of grass hung from his mouth and he crooked his finger at me, "Step up here with your ID."

Lobo growled so I put her into a sit and stay position. I took my time arranging my towel and wetsuit in my bag and then retrieving my wallet. I stepped up in front him, handed him my driver's license and smiled, "What can I do for you, Sheriff?"

He glanced at the license, "Mr. Jones, I have a citizen's complaint that you assaulted him. You need to come with me to the station."

An older couple was watching from across the street and I saw Anne and the kids walking down the hill on their way to the bookstore. Anne spotted me and the three of them stood off to the side watching the action.

I looked at his name tag and spoke loudly enough for the onlookers to hear me, "Sorry Sheriff McGraw, but I didn't assault anyone. I thought this was already cleared up by the other officer with multiple witness statements."

More onlookers were gathering, and I spied a second patrol car rolling to a stop across the street behind the Sheriff. McGraw shouted, "It was a shabby investigation. Those two old geezers aren't reliable witnesses and the other witnesses were tourists just passing through. Hank Scott is one of our town leaders and he tells a different story. You're coming with me now! Get in the cruiser!"

He reached for me and I pushed his hand away, "Your deputy did a fine job with her investigation, and I've done nothing wrong so unless you're arresting me, I'm not getting in your car. I'll be happy to come to the station later after I've changed clothes. And please don't touch me again."

His face scrunched up and grew beet red, "We don't put any credence in 'Pocahontas'. She's a token minority who was shoved down our throat. Now I'm arresting you for striking a police officer on top of the other charges. Get down on the ground, face first."

He reached for his gun when a slender brown hand tightened around his fingers. Terry whispered in his ear just loud enough for me to hear, "I really like the new nickname chief, but I witnessed the fight with Hank, and" She nodded her head at the crowd, "these fine citizens are watching this. Maybe you should just back off. Election's coming up soon."

The sheriff looked around, swore under his breath and yelled, "Okay folks, nothing more to see here. Just move on." He pointed a beefy finger at me and spit out, "Watch your step! You're on my radar and this ain't over. And get that damn dog on a leash!"

An elderly woman with a silver Q-tip hair bob and carrying a Pekinese marched up in front of him and spoke up, "You leave this young man and his nice dog alone, Clifford. You know darn well no one has their dogs on leashes in Oyster Cove." The little dog yapped as she walked away. *Bless her heart!*

The sheriff spit the grass stalk from his mouth, har-umphed and squeezed into his patrol car before driving away.

Deputy White Feather helped disperse the crowd and then turned to me, a small smile made dimples blossom in her cheeks "Seems you can't keep out of trouble, Mr. Jones. Now you've made another enemy."

"It must be my magnetic personality. Thanks for the help. I'm not sure that would have ended well if you hadn't shown up. Stop by later and there's a glass of wine with your name on it at the shop."

"Hmmm? A full-service bookstore, I like that. I'll swing by after my shift." Her dark eyebrows knitted together, and a serious look captured her face, "Zeke, you really need to be careful. That man's dangerous. Try to stay out of his way."

Anne, Charlie and Mike were still watching from across the street. Terry smiled and walked over to them, "Hey Anne, how's it going? We still on for tennis on Saturday?" She tousled Mike's hair and gave Charlie a little hug, "How's your team doing this year Mike?"

Mike pumped up a little from the attention and chirped, "We're three and two so far! I got a single and a double in the last game. We have another game on Friday. Can you come, Aunt Terry?"

"I wouldn't miss it for the world, tiger. I'll be in the front of the bleachers cheering you on! How about you, Charlie. What are you doing for fun?"

Charlie chortled on about Maddie and Shi-Shi and then went into a lengthy dialogue about the latest book she was reading, "I'm so glad you convinced me to read *Jane Eyre*. It was a struggle at first, but it's such an amazing story."

The two of them talked a bit about the plot before Terry waved at us, climbed into her cruiser and headed down the street in the opposite direction from where we headed.

Max greeted us as we entered the bookstore, and all three children ran off to their chairs while Mike and Charlie filled her in on the brouhaha. Silas smiled as he listened to their stories and then turned to me with a serious look on his face, "Master Zeke, you must be careful. Robbie never trusted the sheriff. In fact, he was doing a little investigating of the sheriff's office when he died. He thought there was a lot of corruption there."

He and Anne busied themselves with opening the store while I went upstairs to shower and dress.

———————

I spent the morning dusting shelves and running errands for Silas. Around eleven, I sat with Max as she read to me from her latest literary selection, *The Adventures of Tom Sawyer*. A frown clouded her face and she looked up at me, "We're not supposed to use the 'N' word. It's horrible and demeaning. How come it's in this book?"

"You're right sweetheart, that word is bad. But, when Mark Twain was alive, people didn't think that way. They were wrong to use racial slurs, but sometimes it takes a generation or two to set things right. However, we need to realize that is the way things were back then and Twain's depiction of life back then would not be realistic if the characters were only allowed to use language that's currently acceptable."

We read for a spell longer, then I left her with Silas for a penmanship lesson while I went upstairs to prepare peanut butter and jelly sandwiches with a side of sliced apples for our lunch.

We had just finished our culinary delight and I was sipping my coffee when my phone buzzed with a text from Noah saying he was stuck with the farrier and asking if I could run to the feed store for a few supplies that he listed.

I texted an affirmative reply and conferred with Anne and Silas before inviting the kids to join me. Mike had ball practice, but Max and Charlie were anxious to visit the ranch and the horses. Lobo jumped into the back and Max called shotgun. The four of us piled into Karla and headed down the back roads to the feed store in Freeland. The sun was getting lower in the sky and the air had a crispness to it as we wheeled along two-lane roads shadowed by fragrant pines. Traffic picked up as we approached the small town, cottages crowded the road with chickens and goats populating their front yards. Lobo traded barks with a huge brindle English mastiff standing just inside a gate beside a tan and white Pomeranian creating a cartoonish canine *Mutt and Jeff* scene that made the kids giggle.

The feed lot was dominated by large metal structures full of bales of hay and alfalfa and sacks of grain. Coils of chicken wire and hurricane fencing shared the lot with metal feeding troughs. We walked into the store and I immediately lost the kids to tanks holding baby chicks and rabbits. I noticed one section that offered clothing and called Charlie over pointing at a display of boots, "You shouldn't be walking around those horses in only tennis shoes. Go pick out a pair that you like." Max joined her and they browsed through the selection while I picked up two halters, fly spray and some treats for the horses.

My arms were full when I returned to the girls. Charlie was checking out a pair of tan suede boots adorned with pretty pink and blue flowers in the mirror. She turned and flashed a shy smile, "These are really pretty, but they're kinda expensive." She picked up a pair of plain boots and handed them to me, "These are much cheaper and they'll do the job just as well."

Sitting down, she began to pull the flowered boots off when I sat down beside her, "I think those are very pretty. And…. I think Maddie and Shi-Shi would love them. Leave them on and we'll try them out when you get to the ranch."

She whispered, "Thank you Uncle Zeke, I really love them," and then let out a loud laugh when Max came around the corner wearing a ten-gallon hat that was two sizes too big resting almost on her shoulders.

She peeked out from under the brim, "This is the only size they have. I'm thinking I'll grow into it. What do you guys think?" She twirled around and did a little dance, put the hat back on the rack and joined us at the cash register.

The late summer sun warmed us as we drove along the coast headed for the ranch. The green-blue waters of the *Straits of Juan De Fuca* sparkled and a fine mist filled the air. Terns scrambled along the shore pecking at the sand in hopes of finding a morsel. Screaming gulls soared above finding lift in the thermals and then diving toward unsuspecting fish.

A brackish lagoon replenished by high tides lay on the other side of the road, its shoreline covered by dense reeds and cattails. A blue heron stood rigidly still in the shallows focused on some unsuspecting prey. We startled it when we turned inland and it awkwardly pumped its wings to gain flight, screaming bird curses at us.

We crept along the lane leading to the ranch to keep the dust settled and as soon as Shi-Shi spotted the car she began whinnying. Maddie ran back and forth along the fence line. We were still moving when Lobo spotted a squirrel and leapt out of the back seat to give chase. Noah stepped into the sun and raised his hand to welcome us as we pulled up to the barn. The girls clambered out of the car and ran to the horses while Noah wandered over, shook my hand, and helped me unload the small trunk of the Ghia.

I followed him into the barn where he put everything away except the halters and then led me out to join the girls, "Maddie and Shi-Shi are getting frisky now that they're getting enough food. We need to put these halters on them so we can control them when we need." He handed me a couple of apples and said, "Lure one of them over and I'll put this halter on." Shi-Shi trotted over and nuzzled me for a bite, almost catching a finger while Noah slipped the halter around her snout, over her head and ears and buckled it. Maddie was a little leerier and we chased her around in vain until Charlie's coaxing brought her near and she decided that the halter wasn't an instrument of torture.

Noah checked a few fences on the way back to the house where we sat on rockers. The screen door squeaked as Louise ambled out with a platter of persimmon cookies and a pitcher of iced tea. She set them on the table between us and wrapped her arms around my neck and gave me a big hug, "Hello Ezekiel. How are you today?"

I stood and hugged her in return, the sweet fragrance of soap and carnations filled my nostrils, "Hello, Louise, it's nice to see you. I'm doing well." I held her at arm's length and proclaimed, "You're looking ravishing today. I'm surprised there isn't a line of suitors wrapped around the house hoping for your favors."

She slapped my arm softly, her face lit up and she cackled, "Now stop!" Then she got a wicked smile on her face, "I only entertain suitors on Wednesdays when Noah's not around. I could make an appointment for you, but I think pretty Anne has your eye."

Her face turned serious and she blurted, "Now seriously, I heard you got into a bit of a brouhaha in town. You need to be careful. That Hank is a nasty one and he's in cahoots with that sorry sheriff of ours. They're up to no good and it's best to steer clear of them." She patted me on my shoulder and walked into the house leaving Noah and me chuckling.

We settled into an amiable tranquility as we watched Max and Charlie mucking out the horses' paddock. We could hear the murmur of their voices as they conversed. Every so often a giggle or hoot would pierce the air.

Noah sipped his tea and then pulled a joint from his shirt. An earthy musky odor mixed with lighter fluid wafted up as he pulled out a zippo and lit it. He pulled a deep drag and held it out to me.

"Thanks man, but now that I'm responsible for that young lady running around out there, I've cleaned up my act and am trying to be a good role model."

Noah shrugged and took another drag from the joint before setting it into an old clam shell, "Got it. I can't imagine taking on that responsibility." He let out a laugh, "Mom and her sewing group's gossip moves faster than the internet. They learn things almost as quickly as they happen."

He sat up and leaned toward me with a somber face, "Mom's got a point, though, Hank and Sheriff McGraw are bad people. This county has a huge drug problem with opioids and fentanyl and that's attracting a lot of riff raff to the area. Yet I don't see the sheriff doing anything about it. Meanwhile, Hank sits on the town council and votes against any measures to clamp down on the situation and his cronies at the county do the same. They claim more enforcement will hurt the tourist trade, but they're never clear on how that's so."

I picked up my tea, sipped it and dried the ring the glass had made on the hewn wooden table before setting it down, "Sounds nasty, but I'm just going to keep my head down and stay out of their way."

Noah snickered "Good luck with that! You're on their radar." He stood up and pointed at a sheriff's cruiser passing by, "Speak of the devil, there goes your new friend." We watched as the cruiser turned into the drive leading to the thoroughbred facility next door, "Clifford spends a lot of time over there. And Hank's there a lot, too. Trying to hang with the rich guys I guess."

He scratched the side of his face and picked up the joint for another hit, "They sure are a strange lot though. Lights on late at night all the time, trucks going in and out. Cameras, motion detectors and an armed security patrols roaming the perimeter. I found out the hard way when I went looking for my dog that had run off. Had me surrounded inside of ten minutes. Didn't rough me up, but they made it plain that I shouldn't do it again. I know those horses are expensive, but sure seemed like overkill! I was tempted to put up one of my drones just to see what they're up to, but I figured they wouldn't appreciate it."

Something tickled the back of my mind that I wasn't ready to share yet, so I just smiled, "I suppose," I reached down and grabbed a cookie, "But, I bet the food isn't this good." *Yummy!*

After a while the girls ran back to the porch, grabbed cookies, and scooted toward the barn. Max managed to squeak out through a mouthful of crumbs, "We're going to check for eggs!" before disappearing around the corner. Lobo came up and laid down beside me with a grunt. I reached over and ran my hand across her silky hair, "Those girls are running you ragged, aren't they old girl." She looked up at me with those brown orbs, licked my hand and promptly fell asleep, snoring softly.

We fell into an easy conversation, and he talked about some of his experiences in the Middle East. He'd been wounded twice and lost a good friend to an IED while on patrol. He still mourned the loss. I told a few stories about my life as an NCIS agent and shared the story of losing my partner and the injury that ruined my knee. He was easy to talk to and I felt a comradery blossoming, so I shared a bit of my life as an orphan in a convent. I grinned while I described Sister Kathleen and Jessie and how their love had saved me.

The sun was getting low and the light filtering through the pines softened, so I stood, "Tell your mom thanks for the delicious cookies. I'm not sure how you remain so slim."

I called for the kids and they came running, whooping and giggling. Max blurted, "One of the eggs hatched. The little chick is soooo cute. But when I got near the rooster charged me and pecked my shoes. He was kinda scary, so we just let them be."

Noah laughed, "That old guy is pretty protective of his harem. He probably thought you were going to hurt the hen and her baby. Next time you're out here we'll distract him so you can play with the chick."

We strolled to the car where Charlie gave Noah a hug, before proclaiming 'Shotgun' and jumped into the front seat. Lobo hopped over the door and into the back seat while Max and I said our goodbyes got into the car and headed down the shadowy lane.

CHAPTER 8

THREE DAYS LATER A FAST-MOVING front, cool bordering on cold, made it a perfect day for hunkering down in the bookstore. Clouds in varying shades of gray claimed the sky occasionally giving way to brief slivers of the blue sky beyond. Light rain spattered against the windows off and on. The bay was churning with whitecaps racing before the wind while sea birds shrieked and struggled to maintain their position above unsuspecting prey. Boats strained at their ropes in an attempt to escape their anchors. A golden eagle perched upon a piling at the end of the pier scanning the sea for dinner.

The store was doing a brisk business with clientele crowding in for a respite from the blustery outdoors. Silas was busy at the front desk, operating the cash register and carefully wrapping books in tissue paper before slipping them into brown paper bags with handles and displaying the store's name and logo. He patiently smiled and answered questions about the latest best sellers as well as where to find a decent cup of coffee or which restaurant offered the town's signature oysters.

Anne had her hands full guiding customers through the shelves and helping them find a particular author or title. Her literary insights and warm demeanor helped many of the customers buy more than they had originally intended.

She suggested books to complement the customers' focus and when the title in question wasn't available, she helped find suitable replacements.

Mike was sitting on a burgundy leather wing-back chair legs tucked beneath in the corner reading *The Call of the Wild*. I'd give him a hand whenever he struggled with a word or expression.

Max sat on a plaid loveseat working on an English assignment her free hand resting on Lobo's back sitting beside her.

Charlie and I were sitting at a table fronting the windows and struggling with a trigonometry lesson. An elderly woman with white cotton candy hair, bobbed above a wrinkled yet pretty face, hovered nearby listening to our conversation and finally came over, "Excuse me, I couldn't help overhearing you two. My name is Eunice. I'm a retired high school mathematics teacher and I would love to help your daughter if it's alright." While Charlie corrected her on our relationship, I silently breathed a sigh of relief and asked her to sit next to Charlie, "Thank you, I'm afraid I'm a little rusty in this area. Your help would really be appreciated." I sat back and marveled at how a skilled teacher could remove the mystery from a subject that seemed dry while making it seem interesting and even exciting.

———

When the lesson was finished and Charlie had mastered the complexities of degrees and radians Charlie gave me a fist bump and hugged Eunice around her waist, "Yay! Thank you so much Miss Eunice. You made it so much easier." She did a side-eye at me and grinned, "I think Uncle Zeke learned a lot too."

I stood and tousled Charlie's hair, letting out a guffaw, "She's right Eunice, my math skills aren't what they used to be. I don't think we could have done it without you. And there's no way I could have made it as stimulating as you did. Is there any way we can show our gratitude?"

She began to reply when another lady came over and stood beside her. It was hard to discern but she seemed to be about the same age as Eunice. She wore overalls above a checkered shirt and her bouffant was gun metal silver with a tinge of blue. Eunice smiled and introduced her, "This is my sister Clair. We live on a farm just south of town." I shook her hand and was surprised by the strength of her grip.

Eunice continued, "We are in the same sewing circle as Louise Davis, Noah's mother. She told us all about you. She said you're some kind of federal agent. And of course, everyone heard about your run in with Hank. That man's such a thug and the sheriff had no right to harass you! Anyway, we know that your uncle did investigative work on the side and since you haven't removed the sign from the window of the store, we were wondering if we could hire you."

Max was sitting nearby and jumped up, "Oh boy! Our first case!" She walked over to the ladies and smiled, "I'm Maxine. My Dad and I are partners in the Dragon Island Detective Agency. How can we be of assistance?" *That's my girl!*

I came close to blowing my coffee through my nose and we all cracked up drawing stares from a few of the customers. I put my arm around Max's shoulders, "We certainly owe you for the help with the mysteries of Trig."

I turned to Charlie, "Will you get some tea for the ladies?" Then I smiled at Eunice and Claire, "Please have a seat and tell us what's going on and we'll see if we can help." I pulled a blank sheet of paper from Charlie's notebook and slipped a pen from my breast pocket.

Eunice took a deep breath and began to stammer when Clair put her mottled hand on Eunice's arm and interjected, "That's okay hon, I'll explain." She turned to me with a sad look, "You see, Mary Helen has run off and we don't know where she's gone. We both love her, but Eunice is especially close to her. We're afraid that she's been taken and in trouble." Her voice broke and tears began to puddle in her eyes, "She's been gone for more than week." I handed each of them a tissue just as Charlie and her mother returned with the tea.

I frowned and waited for them to calm down before asking, "How old is Mary Helen? Have you spoken with her friends to see if they might know where she is? Have you filed a missing person's report with the police?"

Clair looked confused at first, but then a light came on and she uttered, "Oh my! I'm afraid we haven't been clear, dear boy. You see Mary Helen is our cat. She's five and has never been gone overnight before. She gets to go out during the day to play in the yard and we always bring her in by four. We've always known that there was danger, what with the coyotes and such, but we need to know that she's not injured and in need of help." She paused to blow her nose while Anne and Charlie sat on each side of the ladies trying to comfort them.

I was pondering this important revelation when Max piped up, "That's really scary. I know how you feel. When I was younger, my mom and I had a cat who disappeared for three days before coming home. We think she was chased up a tree by a dog and it took that long for her to feel safe enough to find her way home."

Her voice quavered when she turned to me, "My Dad has years of experience as an investigator. We can help them, right Dad?" *Great, no pressure there!*

I cleared my throat and leaned forward, "Of course we can. But we need to set realistic expectations. There's always the possibility that Mary Helen um …" I hesitated to be the one who pointed out the high possibility that Mary Helen might not be alive.

Eunice reached over with her small, calloused hand, squeezed my fingers and sniffled, "Of course dear. Clair and I have lived on the farm for our entire life so we understand the cycle of life. We would just like closure if possible."

I raised my pen to the paper and began to take notes, "Hopefully, we'll be able to track down the wayward Mary Helen. Let's get a few facts down and we'll get started on your case. First, do you have a photo that we can use?" I winked at Max and continued, "And we'll need your address so my partner and I can get started."

Eunice dug around in an over sized purse, "It's here somewhere. Oh yes here it is!" She handed me a photo of a small gray cat with mottled orange undertones. Clair piped in, "She's very sweet but a little jumpy. You may need to take some of these kitty treats to coax her to you", handing me a bag of chicken morsels. From the picture it looked like Mary Helen really enjoyed the treats, but then again, I'm not an expert on cats.

While they were finishing their tea, Eunice wrote her address on a slip of paper and handed it to me with a trembling hand, "We're a quarter mile south of Louise and Noah, backed up against the nature preserve."

We chatted for a few minutes and promised to meet them at the farm in an hour. As they got up to leave Max gave each a big hug, "Don't worry, we'll find her."

While we walked upstairs to prepare for our sleuthing, I explained to Max that we shouldn't set our clients expectations too high, "You know honey that we might not find Mary Helen." Her eyebrows bunched together and she grimaced before nodding. I continued, "Even though I hope we can find her, I think we can only promise to do our best. We can't guarantee results. That way our clients' expectations are grounded in reality and, if things don't pan out, they may be disappointed, but they'll be prepared for that eventuality."

Her lower lip quivered, and she pouted for a second and then smiled and took my hand, "I think I understand. I guess I was hoping for a good outcome, but hoping for something doesn't mean it will happen." She pulled on my arm to reach up and kiss my cheek and chortled, "You're pretty smart for an old guy!" Then she giggled and ran up ahead of me and through the door of the apartment.

While Max changed into jeans and a yellow and gray, long-sleeved tee shirt and pulled on her ankle-high hiking boots, I pulled bread and bologna out of the refrigerator to make sandwiches. I spread mustard across the top half and broke off a lettuce leaf before slapping them together and slipping them into plastic baggies. I pulled a couple of backpacks from the closet and placed the sandwiches, a bag of chips and a pear into the front sections. Just in case it got cold during our search, I grabbed an old gray sweatshirt emblazoned with the Marine Corps' Eagle, Globe and Anchor for me and a pink 'Hello Kitty' sweatshirt for Max and stuffed them into the bottom of the packs followed by bottles of water.

Gray clouds were threatening so I rolled up waterproof windbreakers and threw them in, topping off the contents with two flashlights before donning my hiking boots. Finally, I grabbed Lobo's leash off the hook by the door and we headed out the door and down the stairs to Karla. The clouds were parting, letting the sun peek through, so I unhooked the clamps holding the rag top and pushed it to the back. Lobo sprang into the backseat before Max opened the door and plopped down on the passenger seat.

And, off the three of us went on our adventure.

We drove up the hill and past the Masonic Lodge on the right and an Italian restaurant on the left. Traffic backed up at the town's only stop light that controlled traffic for the highway. Turning left onto the highway we passed the town's sole gas station that served the town and surrounding area. A well-maintained bike path paralleled the highway with cute little stop signs for the bicyclists at each intersection with the back roads along its path.

Two miles later Max's navigation app told us to turn left onto a paved country lane just in time to spot a red-tailed hawk swooping down to grab an unsuspecting chipmunk. We slowed to a halt, giving the hawk time to grab its prey and take off, its big wings battling gravity and finally getting the necessary lift. The lane dipped down the hill and curved around through tall lodgepole pines and past small homesteads barely visible through the woods and undergrowth. Glimpses of the blue waters of the sound appeared to our right and then disappeared.

We turned left on another narrow lane and headed up a small hill. Max lost internet connection, so we slowly crept up the grade searching for the ladies' driveway. Lobo grumbled a half-bark and we slowed again to allow a doe and her mottled fawn to step across the road and into the foliage on the other side. Lobo considered a chase but decided a growl would suffice. Squirrels and chipmunks were more to her liking.

As we crept along, Max finally spotted a blue sign bearing the ladies address attached to a post holding their weathered and moss speckled mailbox. The red flag was still up indicating the day's mail had not been delivered. The entry was narrow, and the gravel two track road was pitted with an occasional pothole full of muddy rainwater. The pine boughs crisscrossed above us, plunging us into an arboreal tunnel. Trying my best to weave around the larger potholes, we came around a bend where the forest opened to a two-acre cleared area.

Ahead lay a log home, the gray chinking contrasting with the yellow pine and the green metal roof. A wrap around porch sported two rocking chairs and blazing red, green and yellow flowers in boxes along the railing added homey warmth to the pleasant Norman Rockwell sight before us.

Red and yellow roses were planted along the front and bordered a small grass lawn. Two rhododendron bushes anchored the corners of the lot, their flowers wilted and drooping after a week of color.

Hummingbirds battled for territorial rights near red feeders hung from the eaves. The driveway led to a parking area and a spur led to a barn situated next to a fenced pasture, a fat dairy cow stood feeding at the trough, her bloated udder sagging beneath her. Her large brown eyes looked up to check us out, hay sticking out both sides of her brown snout, before she went back to her meal. Chickens scratched at the soil for grubs near a coop painted red to match the barn.

A vegetable garden lay on the opposite side of the house, a veritable cornucopia of lettuce, broccoli, tomatoes, strawberries and other lush vegetables laying in rows behind a chicken wire fence meant to keep the rabbits and deer at bay. Stalks of corn were proudly displaying their half-ripe ears. A creek, crowded with ripe blackberries and blueberries, gurgled at the border of the clearing.

I instructed Lobo to stay until we made sure it was okay for him to wander around. Max and I jumped out of the car just as Eunice opened the screen door and waved to us. She shouted "Welcome!" and pointed at Lobo "It's alright for your dog to join us. Our milk cow 'Petunia' is used to dogs and will be happy for a visit." I released Lobo and she bounded into the trees after some unknown prey while Max and I stepped onto the porch.

Claire came out and joined us and asked, "Would you care for some iced tea, or I can make a pot of coffee? How about a soda for you, young lady?"

Max politely declined, "Thank you Miss Claire, but I just had lunch and I'm pretty full. Maybe when we get back."

I thanked her and said we should probably get going before it got too dark. I bunched my eyebrows into what I thought was my private investigator look and drawled, "Can you show us the places where Mary Helen usually hung out? It might give us a starting point."

The ladies led us around the cleared area pointing out various spots. Lobo followed behind and squatted to mark a few bushes. I noticed a couple of game trails leading into the woods and Lobo sniffed the ground, barked and ran down the one that appeared to be the most used. She wasn't a tracker, but she was extremely intelligent and usually picked up my vibes. We certainly didn't have any other hints about where to start.

I turned to Clair and Eunice with a grin, "Lobo seems to like that trail. We'll follow it and see where it takes us. We'll be back in a while."

———•———

Lobo jogged ahead and we pushed through the wet bush soaking our pants legs. Lush ferns sprang up alongside juniper, lupine, and nightshade. Discs of miner's lettuce enjoyed shady spots, but stinging nettles threatened anyone foolish enough to stray from the narrow path to gather them. Overhead, stands of fir and cedar competed with the pine providing hints of the blue sky. Every so often, Max would shout out, "Here kitty, kitty, kitty" or "Here Mary Helen."

After trudging along for about ten minutes, we intersected with a hiker's trail that provided relief from the wet brush. Lobo had run ahead and took the trail to the right and we followed. Wherever the sun could break through the canopy, dandelions and wild oats fronted bunches of blackberries and Oregon grapes, their fruit glistening from the early rain. I had just warned Max to be careful of the tree roots that rose across the path and threatened to trip anyone who wasn't watching their steps when one caught my toe and I stumbled wrenching my knee. Max started to giggle but changed to a sympathetic murmur when she realized I was in pain.

We sat on a fallen log while I massaged my throbbing leg. I pulled a water bottle from my pack and opened a bottle of ibuprofen, washing a two down. We passed the water back and forth sipping while lost in our thoughts.

Max had a worried look on her face and tittered, "Does it hurt a lot? Maybe we should go back."

I reached over and tousled her hair before standing, "I'm good, sweetie, It happens occasionally, but we can't let a little 'owee' keep us down. It's already much better, let's get going."

Lobo walked up and licked my knee, looked up as if to say *Come on old man!* turned and started down the path. I let Max go ahead so she wouldn't see my limp and we headed farther into the woods.

After meandering through the lush foliage for another twenty minutes Max let out a squeal and ran down a small spur leading to a fenced off area, "Look Dad, it's a gravesite!"

The fence encircled a twenty-by-twenty-foot area with a monolith set upon a gravestone in the center. As we walked up to inspect, I noticed a small cross outside the fence, "That looks like another grave. Be careful not to walk over there."

We walked to the fence and peered over trying to read the inscription. The stone was severely weathered and a patina of lichen and moss made it impossible to read all but a few of the words. We were able to discern that it was the grave of a Native American chief and that he had died in 1879. A small plaque attached to the fence boasted that the grave was cared for by a local tribe but the state of the grave meant it hadn't seen any recent care. Dandelions and other weeds sprouted everywhere. *Too busy with their casinos, I guess.*

In contrast, the grave outside the fence appeared to be well cared for, clear of weeds. A withered bouquet lay at the base of the cross. But years of Whatley Island weather had completely eroded the markings leaving us with a mystery. Max and I stood reverently before these markers and whispered a brief prayer. She snapped a few photos before we headed back down the trail behind an impatient Lobo.

After trudging along for another ten minutes I could make out glimpses of a structure ahead and we quickened our pace to find Lobo running back and forth in front of a large barn that had seen better days. A few slats were missing from the ash gray siding and the door to the hay loft swung slowly back and forth in the breeze.

Max cupped her hands and called out, "Here kitty, kitty! Here Mary Helen" while I checked the structural integrity, pushing on the walls.

I asked Max and Lobo to stay outside while I lifted a board resting across two J-shaped brackets that held the door closed. I pulled on the handle and the hinges shrieked when they broke free of the corrosion and the door swung open. Brushing aside cobwebs I stepped into the dim light. A small animal skittered across a hard packed dirt floor covered with a layer of dust and animal droppings. Piles of old hay lay in the corners and the faded scent of manure lingered in the air. Two stalls were situated below the loft, a feed crib situated beside them in the corner. A dilapidated door hanging by one hinge was centered on the back wall.

After kicking a few beams to further ensure it was safe, I shouted for Max and Lobo to come in. Max slowly crept in, her eyes wide, but Lobo darted past her and ran to the far stall. She sat down, stared into the dark recess and then back at us with a little yip.

We headed over and as we approached a soft 'meow' called out to us. Max darted ahead kicking up puffs of dust. Peeking into the crib, she gave out a shout and stepped in and then went to her knees, "Oh wow! It's Mary Helen and two adorable kittens! They're soooo cute."

Peering over her shoulder I could see Mary Helen laying on an old burlap bag atop an old bale of hay and two tiny bundles of fur stumbling about with their eyes closed searching for a teat. One kitten's fur matched Mary Helen's but the other was pitch black. Mary Helen looked exhausted, and she looked up and softly 'mewed'. I dug into my backpack and handed Max the bag of kitty treats, "I think Mary Helen's probably hungry. Why don't you see if she'll take some of these while I try to find something to carry her and the kittens."

Max held a handful of treats out to the cat and softly cooed. Mary Helen nibbled on a few and then laid her head back down on the rough burlap so the kittens could begin suckling. Max softly stroked the new mom's head and murmured, "Good girl. You're such a good mother!" She pulled a water bottle out and poured a little into her cupped hand and offered it to the new mom. Mary Helen greedily lapped at the moisture and Max added more, patiently humming an unintelligible song with a grin plastered wide across her little face.

I quietly slipped out and began searching for an adequate transport. The light was muted and the shadows obscured any details so I pulled the flashlight from my pack and flicked it on. Broken boards were scattered about the area but nothing that would suffice as a carrier was apparent. I peeked into the other stall and the only thing visible was another ruptured hay bale and more scattered detritus.

I left the stall, headed to the door in the back and was reaching for the rope handle when Max shrieked. Swinging my light around I spied a black cat hissing and prancing sideways toward the stall, his back arched and crooked tail pointing straight up and into an inverted L. He was pitch black with an inch long scar above his yellow eyes and a shredded right ear. Lobo stood and wandered between the cat and Max. Just when I thought there was going to be a skirmish, Lobo surprised me by sauntering over to the cat and licking its head. Immediately, the cat de-stressed, purred loudly and rubbed his head against Lobo weaving through her legs. *Wow! Lobo the peacemaker, who knew?*

I grinned at Max, "Looks like Daddy cat's home! He's a pretty good Dad though, he was ready to do battle to protect his family."

The new cat followed as Lobo sauntered over to the stall and lay in front of Max. She tittered, "He's pretty beat up, but kinda cute. The poor thing is awful skinny and scarred. Do you think he'll let me pet him?"

I suggested, "Hold your hand out, but don't touch him. Let him come to you. Cats are really fast and he'll scratch you if he feels threatened."

Max extended her arm slowly and the cat reached up and sniffed it and when he was satisfied that Max wasn't a predator, he licked her fingers and rubbed his scarred noggin against the tips begging for a good scratch. I could hear his loud purr from across the barn. I continued, "He's friendly and isn't skittish so I'd guess he's not feral, but probably domesticated. His owners probably lost or aban- doned him. He sure likes you and Lobo. Let me check around some more and maybe we can get Mary Helen, the kittens and old 'Scar' back to the ladies. I'll be back in a bit."

Max rubbed the cat's head and giggled, "'Scar.' I like that!"

I returned to the broken door and gave its rope handle a good tug ending with a tattered hemp rope in my hand, the door still wedged partially shut. I reached up and grabbed the door's side, lifted slightly and pulled. The wood groaned and finally released in a puff of dust, allowing me to gain an opening big enough for me to enter.

Swatting at cobwebs as I entered, I pulled my flashlight from my pocket and swept the beam around the dark room. A workbench straddled the back wall, some drawers open haphazardly, and others absent. Hay hooks hung from a slat nailed between the open wall studs. A rusted pitchfork, one of its tines broken, leaned against the bend. A spade shovel, absent its handle, lay in the dirt, covered by a thick layer of dust.

The arc of my light caught an old produce box leaning against a wall, its label advertising the name of the orchard or farm faded and indecipherable. When I reached the box and started to turn it over, a large rodent skittered away. *Dang, I hate rats!* I peered inside and found an old nest made from straw and strands of burlap embedded with droppings. Gingerly picking the container up, I hauled it outside and shook the detritus out. A pine bough served as my broom to sweep out the remaining residue. After a few minutes of sweeping I turned it over. One slat along the bottom was broken and hanging loose so I pulled it off and tossed it to the side. The other three slats were intact and sturdy enough to hold the weight of the cats so I pulled my sweatshirt from my pack and folded it inside making a cozy bed.

I walked in with the box and Max scooped her hands below the mother and gently placed her onto the makeshift litter. Mary Helen softly mewed until Max placed each of the kittens at her belly. They blindly stumbled about until they found what they were looking for and began nursing.

Scar jumped onto the box and softly cleaned each of the babies and mom. Max ooh'ed and aah'ed, "Look at them. They're so sweet! Miss Clair and Miss Eunice will be so happy!"

Max donned her pack and I threw mine over my back before picking up the box. Scar wasn't comfortable with the wobbly situation and jumped to the ground, running over to Max and putting his paws on her leg. She cooed as she leaned down, pulled him up and cradled him in her arms, "That's okay Scar. I'll carry you."

A woodpecker's rat-tat-tat filled the silence above as we headed off with Lobo in the lead. Now that we knew the way the going was much quicker but unfortunately my bum knee was on fire, slowing us down a bit. Scar would alternate between Max's arms and hopping down to help Lobo as point guard.

Twenty-five minutes later we entered the ladies' yard and headed to the porch. The screen door slammed open giving Scar a start when Eunice rushed out, "Oh goodness, you're back. Did you find…." She put her hand to her mouth and squealed, "My goodness! Mary Helen look at you." Then she caught sight of the kittens and gasped, "Clair, come quick, Mary Helen has a family!"

Scar was hiding behind my leg as I delicately placed the box on the porch and I reached around to pet him to assure him that he and his family were safe, but it was Lobo who convinced him by giving him a lick and sauntering up to the woman. Scar slowly crept forward and

Eunice sat on the porch steps and stroked his back eliciting a purr and a head rub against her leg. Eunice softly whispered, "Hello little fellow. Aren't you sweet. But my, you look like you could use some food and a bath."

Clair hustled around the corner of the house, spied Mary Helen and the gray and black furry balls stumbling around the box and cried, "Oh dear Mary Helen, you little scamp." Kneeling, she picked up a gray kitten and murmured, "Look at you sweet thing, you're just adorable." Turning the kitten onto her back she exclaimed, "This little sweetie's a girl. Let's check the other." Gently setting the female kitten down, she reached for the black bundle, but Mary Helen nudged her hand so she stroked her fur until the mother began purring, "I'm sorry honey, I was so excited I forgot about you. Are you okay? I bet you're starving." The cat licked her hand and uttered a small meow.

Unable to keep her curiosity at bay any longer, Max reached in and lifted the black kitten in both hands and delicately turning it over, "This one's a boy! That's so cool, one of each! What are you going to name them?"

Eunice stood up with a small groan, reached down and stroked Scar's head and headed in the door, "We'll have to give that some thought, but right now I'm going to call the vet who lives across the road. I just saw his truck pull into his driveway so I'm sure he'll be right over. Then I'll open a couple of cans of cat food for these two."

As soon as she was inside, Clair grinned and in sotto voce crooned, "Eunice and David are sweet on one another, but don't tell her I said so!"

Eunice cried out from within, "Now you hush Clair! You know I can hear you!"

A few minutes later she came through the door with a dish smelling of fish and a bowl of water, setting them near the makeshift cradle. As soon as Mary Helen and Scar caught the scent they scrambled over and began munching away, low grunts emanating from their jaws.

Clair went inside and came out shortly after with a tray of molasses cookies, glasses, a can of root beer and a pitcher of lemonade. She picked a bag of frozen peas off the tray and handed it to me, "I noticed you massaging your knee and I hope this helps."

I thanked her, placed it on my aching knee, sighing with relief as the cold immediately soothed the pain. Just then, a pick-up truck rumbled into the yard, its brakes squealing as it came to a halt in front of the porch. A metal utility chest covered the truck bed. It was three feet high and populated with drawers and shelving.

An elderly man with salt and pepper hair and a white handle-bar moustache jumped out, pulled out a black kit bag and wandered over with slightly bowed legs, "Afternoon Ms. Clair, Ms. Eunice, what's this about kittens?" He held out a calloused hand to me, "Howdy, I'm David Jacobs, though most people around here call me Dave or Doc."

He clamped my hand with a firm grip, and I introduced myself. Max walked up to him and held out her hand, "Hello Mr. Dave, my name is Maxine Jones. It's nice to meet you. My partner and I just rescued these kitties. I hope you can get them healthy." *Partner??? What happened to 'Daddy'?*

Dave cast me a sideways grin, bent down to take her hand and guffawed, "Well, Ms. Jones it's mighty nice to make your acquaintance. Let's go take a look at these little critters." He handed the bag to Max, "Could you give me a hand with this and maybe help me examine these critters?"

Max's grin spread from ear to ear as she took the bag and followed Dave to the porch, "You can call me Max, everybody does!"

While Max and Dave checked out the cats, the ladies and I quibbled about the fee for finding Mary Helen. I insisted that Eunice's help with trigonometry was more than enough compensation, but they wouldn't have it. They insisted on paying my going rate for detective work even after I told them that I hadn't set a fee schedule. After debating for a while we settled on Eunice helping with Charlie's math problems when needed and a batch of some of their amazing cookies.

Dave and Max finished their examination, stood up Dave pulled of his rubber gloves, smiled and said, "Mary Helen and the kittens are in good shape. But Mary Helen needs to get back to a healthy diet so she can keep up with the nursing."

He nodded toward Scar who had curled up around Lobo and scratched his head, "Surprisingly, that tom cat is pretty healthy as well. There are no fleas or ticks, probably because he's been bedding down in cedar and pine which are deterrents. He is undernourished, but that can be handled with a better diet. All those scars have healed nicely. He must be quite a survivalist!"

He looked at Eunice and Clair, "That said, Mary Helen and Scar need to be neutered or they'll wander off again. We'll take care of the kittens when they're older. I can take Scar with me and do the deed tomorrow."

I got up from the chair and shook his hand as he headed to his truck for a crate. We said our goodbyes and Lobo jumped up into the back seat and curled up. Scar followed right behind and nestled in the space between the dog's legs.

Max squealed in delight and exclaimed, "Looks like we've got a new member of the family!" She turned her pretty blue eyes to me, "We can keep him can't we Dad, please?" *Oh great, a cat!*

I was just ready to burst Max's bubble and say no when Scar jumped from the back seat onto my lap and pawed at my arm begging to be petted. I stroked his back and he settled into a ball and purred. *I'm outnumbered! But he is very cute.*

I growled and then acquiesced, "Only if you take care of him and that includes cleaning out his cat box every day!" I turned to the grinning trio of Eunice, Clair and Dave, "I think Scar has had enough trauma for the day. How about we let him get settled at our place for a while and then we'll bring him out in a few days?"

Dave nodded, the ladies giggled and Max wrapped me in a hug. I started Karla and we headed home, waving as we passed under the towering trees. *Zeke's Clan was growing in ways I never expected!*

Scar made himself at home immediately. He and Lobo would curl together on Lobo's bed or on Max's or my lap in the evening. But he preferred the bookstore during the day, either sleeping on one of the cushioned chairs or sitting regally at the cash register and gathering praise and rubs from the customers.

After a few days I figured he understood that we were his family, so Lobo and I drove him to the vet for his emasculation. He yowled when we attempted to leave until Lobo curled up next to him and stayed for comfort and support during the surgery. Doc called later that day and reported that the surgery had gone well and after a more thorough examination he declared Scar to be fit and in good health. Max and I drove over and picked up the loopy fellow. The foam cone around his neck made him look somewhat like a male lion. He slept the rest of the day in the apartment and after a couple of grumpy days he was back to normal.

CHAPTER 9

NOAH JOINED ME FOR A swim a few days later. White caps raced across the bay in the gusty wind. Gulls screamed as they fought to maintain their airspace while cormorants sat on sailboat booms, their wings spread apart to dry them in the gusts. The formidable current proved to be a hard taskmaster and we were both breathing heavily when we finally made it to shore. Shivering in the brisk wind we dried off quickly, threw on our clothes and headed for the warmth of the coffee shop.

I spotted Terry White Feather sitting at a table by the window and waved before placing our orders. Noah decided on a medium Café Latte and a bear claw while I opted for an Americano and a cinnamon twist. After receiving our order, Noah followed me over to Terry's table.

She smiled up at me as I greeted her, "Hi Terry, mind if we join you? This is my friend Noah. He and his mother live just outside town."

Noah reached to shake her hand and said hi and they both appraised each other. Not to use a cliché, but sparks flew. They held each other's gaze and hands a bit longer than might have been necessary.

We both sat and Terry completely ignored me, murmuring, "Nice to meet you, Noah. I don't think I've seen you around before. Where have you been hiding?"

Noah's grin stretched across his face and he blurted, "I have a horse boarding facility just south of here. I usually go into Freeland to shop," his smile grew even wider, "but I think I'll come up here more often."

Terry's smile matched his and she leaned forward, "I love to ride, maybe I'll stop by and check it out."

I was pleased that they'd connected and they fell into a casual conversation at the exclusion of yours truly. I obviously was the proverbial third wheel so I began to get up and make a graceful exit when Terry frowned and looked over at me, "Where are you going Zeke? I need to talk to you for a minute." She reached over and touched Noah's arm, "Can you give us a few minutes to talk business? But please come back. I want to hear more." Her hand still lay on Noah's arm in an intimate gesture.

Noah looked thoughtful, smiled and squeezed her hand, "No sweat. I need to visit the men's room and get some of this sand off me and I'm ready for another coffee. Anyone care for a refill?" His eyes never left Terry's and I'm pretty sure he wasn't asking me. Nevertheless, we both said no and he got up and headed to the front of the café.

Terry's face changed from soft to serious as she turned to me, "I like your friend. He's nice. I'm glad you introduced us."

"I can tell! Looks like you've made a friend!"

A pink blush crept up Terry's face as she watched the amusement in my eyes, "Well, we'll see." Then she became all business, "The reason I wanted to talk to you is to give you some information and to get your support. I've checked you out and everything I've learned is that you're the real deal. The Navy, ATF and the FBI all vouch for you."

She leaned closer, "What I'm about to share with you must remain confidential. Will you commit to that?"

She had certainly caught my interest. I nodded. She smiled and continued, "I'm not exactly who I said I was before. I mean I am a deputy sheriff, but the circumstances of my position are different than I let on. To make a long story short, I'm working undercover for a joint task force of the FBI and DEA along with the Washington State Bureau of Investigation." My eyebrows shot up with surprise while she continued, "I was planted in the Sheriff's office because there's a significant pattern of drug smuggling mixed with human trafficking in this area and the sheriff seems either unable or unwilling to address it. We believe that he and others in his department are dirty and working both sides."

I rolled my neck to release some of the tension while weighing this information. I was afraid I knew where this was going and wasn't very comfortable with that thought. I looked at her and asked, "That's interesting, but why are you telling me this? I'm a civilian now with a busted knee."

She scowled and her eyes turned fiery then she growled, "We both know that's not true. I know that you resisted the retirement they forced on you, but the bureaucrats forced you out!" I started to protest but she held up her hand, "And everyone we interviewed said that, even with a bum knee, you were more than fit to perform your duties!"

She continued, "Anyway to answer your question, because of the proximity to the base in Oak Harbor the drug situation is beginning to affect their personnel. The Navy has agreed to temporarily reinstate you as a team member of the task force. We want you to be our eyes on the ground because your position as a business owner provides a perfect cover."

I frowned and objected, "That might have been true before my dust-up with Hank and run-in with the sheriff. That doesn't exactly paint a picture of a meek shop owner. And I think there's something you haven't told me yet."

Her lips stretched into a thin smile, "They said you didn't beat around the bush and wouldn't tolerate half-truths. They are worried that my cover can be blown and believe you would be perfect to watch my back. They also want you involved in any operations when we decide to move. As far as the sheriff and Hank go, I believe that dust-up was a perfect cover. They would never suspect someone undercover would draw attention to themselves the way you did."

Her smile turned genuine before she gave me a plead-ing look, "And to be truthful, I'm out here on my own and scared to death. I really want you on my team. I've seen you in action and, added to what everyone tells me, I'll feel a lot safer with you covering my back." I was uncom-fortable with the praise and my face must have shown it. She whispered, "Please!"

My voice came out as a growl, "I appreciate your faith in my abilities, but I have a family now and I can't put my daughter in danger. I'm the only family she has! Besides, I find it ironic that the same Navy that booted me is now asking for my help."

Terry leaned forward, matching my scowl, "I under-stand. I have a sister who's Max's age. Both of our parents died from opioid abuse. My aunt and I care for her, but my aunt's getting on and when she goes I'll be the only one to care for her. So, I've seen, up front, the misery these drugs are creating in our community. And, ever lurking in the background is the human trafficking where children, even as young as your daughter or my sister, are thrown into an unimaginable hell that no one should endure."

I listened closely to her words, seeing the truth in them. I cocked my head to the side trying to release the tension that was building. Sister Kathleen and Jessie had instilled a sense of service in me. That was why I'd joined NCIS, so I could do some good against the evil in the world. There was no way I could walk away from this and hold my head up. *Damnit!*

Terry was squirming and her face had fallen in anticipation of a negative answer. I gritted my teeth, sighed and gave her a half smile, "Deputy White Feather, you have a second career waiting for you as a salesperson. You made a good case so here's my answer. First, you must know that I would have watched your back anyway. All you had to do was ask." She smiled and I continued, "That said, I'll join your team so we can clean this malignancy out of our community. But there are two conditions. Since you know so much about me, then you know that I don't always play by the rules. I will do what's necessary to protect the team and successfully complete the mission. That doesn't mean that I'll go rogue, but I won't be constrained by bureaucratic dictums. Therefore, I'll help as a consultant under my private investigator license. But I must be a true member of the task force. I need to be completely read in. No secrets!"

Terry's face broke into a broad grin that brought out her pretty dimples and she chortled with relief, "We were warned that you might take that position and it's already been approved. You have some good friends in high positions." Her grin dissipated and she squirmed with anticipation, "You mentioned a second condition?"

"I know you've sworn me to secrecy, but I must be allowed to bring others into my confidence so I can be effective. One example is my old boss, Jessie McCormack. She's retired but still the best agent I've ever known." I pointed across the room at Noah who was studiously stirring his coffee, "Your new friend is another. I know him well enough to trust him and he's got some resources that may prove invaluable. He already does some work for the local agencies so it shouldn't be a problem vetting him for the team if we need him." I couldn't help myself and bounced my eyebrows up and down, "I think you may want to get a little closer to him as well."

Her cheeks turned crimson and she swatted at me, "Let's not rush things, but you're right. I could use all the help I can get. I'll check with the higher-ups."

"Now let's talk about how to operate. It might raise suspicions if you and I spend too much time together, so we've set up a contact for you who won't raise eyebrows. He's a long-retired army warrant officer from the Viet Nam era who fancies himself a book aficionado. His name is Christopher Sloan. He'll contact you at the bookstore. But let me give you my private number in case you need immediate access to the team."

I handed her my phone so she could enter the information and we chatted a few more minutes about details and then I motioned Noah over. Before he reached the table, I whispered, "Good luck!" I got up and shook Noah's hand, reminded him of our appointment the next day and said my goodbyes. When I reached the door, I looked back and they were leaning across the table in an animated conversation. *I didn't realize I was a matchmaker!*

Lobo and I ran errands in Oak Harbor for a large part of the day and when I returned, the store was pretty empty, a typical weekday afternoon. Anne and the kids were off on a hunt for seashells for Mike's art project so I told Silas I could cover the rest of the evening and sent him home. Tourists wandered in and out and an elderly gentleman sat in the back overlooking the bay reading a copy of *War and Peace*. A crumpled black beret lay on the table in front of him. His back was ramrod straight and his salt-and-pepper hair was cut high and tight. Surprisingly, Scar was curled up beside him sound asleep as he stroked his back.

I wandered over and he looked up with a slight smile, "Mr. Jones I presume." He stood and shook my hand with a vise-like grip, "My name is Christopher Sloan. I believe we have a mutual friend."

His friendly face was marred by a jagged scar along his lower jaw and I saw a steeliness in his pale gray eyes. I withdrew my hand resisting the urge to massage it to get the circulation going, "Nice to meet you Christopher, I believe we have a few things to discuss. Can I interest you in a dram or two of brandy?"

His face lit up and he laughed, then snorted, "Hell boy, don't be miserly, let's make it a good pull! And I prefer Scotch if you've got it."

I reached into a small cabinet near the desk, pulled out a bottle of *Lagavulin*, poured three ounces into a whiskey glass and held up an ice-bucket in one hand and a seltzer bottle in the other in a silent question. He shook his head, "It's a sin to pollute good whiskey. Make mine clean."

I handed him the glass and walked into the storage room, retrieved a bottle of Stella Artois from the small refrigerator for myself, popped the cap and plopped down in a chair beside him. Lobo sniffed Christopher's pant legs eliciting a pat on his head before curling up on her dog bed in front of the window and falling asleep.

I looked around to make sure our discussion wouldn't be overheard. There were only two couples left and they were obviously not interested in us. I turned to Christopher and nodded, "I think it's safe to have our discussion here. Our mutual friend left a lot of questions. I'm hoping that you can clear them up."

He sipped his whiskey and smiled, "I'm certainly glad that you're a man of good taste. This scotch may convince me to take up residence here. What more could a man ask, good whiskey and a treasure trove of literature. However, I'm just a conduit and no longer actively involved in the operation side of the business." Pointing at a file folder laying on the table in front of him, "That dossier should answer most, if not all, of your questions. I've read it and it's quite intriguing. I only wish I were twenty years younger so I could be more actively involved. You should read it before our next tete-a-tete. I also included my phone number for your use." He took a long pull on his drink and then asked, "Tell me little about you. I'm curious as to why a bookseller got involved in this investigation."

I told him about my background and why I was now the owner of the shop. He looked sad when he told me he knew my uncle and that the two of them had a long friendship over their love of books. We sipped our drinks in silence staring out across the graying sound before he drained his glass smacked his lips and stood, "Thank you for the fine whiskey. I should get home; the missus is waiting with dinner. Give me a call after you're up to speed and we'll discuss the best way to conduct our clandestine relationship." He doffed his weathered beret, turned and headed for the door. I noticed a slight hitch in his step, but his back was still perfectly erect and his head was high.

———•———

After he left, I put the folder into a drawer and busied myself with the mundane duties of waiting on the few customers. A while later I heard a cacophony of laughter as Anne and the kids flew in the door carrying a bag dripping with sea water. Max ran up and gave me hug. Mike trailed behind her and shoved the bag in front of me, "Look at all the great shells we picked up Uncle Zeke. Aren't they cool?"

We pulled a towel out of the storeroom door, placed it on a table and emptied the assortment of shells onto it. Clam shells made up the majority, with oyster and mussel shells intermingled. For the next half hour, Mike engaged me in conversations about them and how he planned to use each one for his project. The girls threw in their two cents worth every now and then while Anne sat across from me watching. I looked up to see her smiling and she blushed slightly when she caught my glance.

Max put her skinny arms around my neck and reminded me, "Dad, remember I'm going with Mike and Charlie tonight." She was bubbling with anticipation for her first sleepover. She literally bounced.

I pulled her to me. "There's no way I'd forget a big event like that. I'm going to be soooo lonely tonight without your chatter. She giggled and slapped my arm then ran to the front door, "Come on, Charlie, help me get my stuff." And the two of them ran out the door.

Ten minutes later they returned. Max's backpack enveloped her backside, stuffed with who knows what and topped with her favorite stuffed bear. She carried a large sleeping bag in her arms somewhat covering her face, but her huge grin was apparent as she and the other children ran ahead on the way to Anne's house, Lobo trotting along by her side.

I couldn't help myself and half whispered to Anne, "She looks adorable. Are you sure you can tolerate all three? You'll call me if there's any problems?"

She smiled and touched my arm setting off an electric shock all the way to my toes. "It's not going to be a problem at all. She's a joy to be around and this adventure will be good for her. Try not to worry 'dad'."

We arrived at Anne's little cottage and the kids ran inside. Anne turned to me and stepped close; I caught the hint of lavender. She looked into my eyes and I put my arms around her waist and pulled her into a hug, but she turned her head up and our lips met for a brief kiss. And then she was gone and headed down the path leading to her front door, leaving an emptiness in a spot I didn't know existed. Halfway down the path she turned and smiled, "Good night, Zeke. We'll see you tomorrow." And then the door to the cottage slowly shut, leaving me to touch my lips and gaze drunkenly at her house before Lobo and I headed back down the hill to the store.

●———————●

I let myself in and busied myself with locking up. When everything was secure, I pulled the folder from the drawer, walked outside into the waning light and locked the door before heading upstairs to the apartment, Lobo quickly did her business before following closely behind with Scar scampering ahead.

I turned the lights on, threw the dossier onto the coffee table and stepped into the kitchen. Lobo followed closely behind and patiently waited while I filled her dish with kibble, rinsed her water bowl out and refilled it with fresh water. I opened a can of cat food and placed it on the mat in the corner. Scar jumped down from the counter and purred loudly while scarfing the food down.

I pulled the refrigerator door open and perused its depths, finally deciding on a plastic container of left-over meatloaf and asparagus. I slipped them into the microwave pushing, reheat and went into the bathroom to freshen up.

The timer was beeping when I returned and I checked to see if the food was warm enough, decided it needed another minute and poked the appropriate buttons before setting a placemat and utensils on the coffee table. I grabbed a beer from the refrigerator, popped the top and had just placed it on the table when the timer beeped again. I grabbed the food and set it down before plopping onto the couch to eat and read my homework. The dossier addressed two areas: the suspected corruption in the sheriff's office and the high incidence of drug trafficking in our area and the belief that both were related.

The first issue went into detail about the Puget County Sheriff's lack of arrests and apparent obstruction of investigations by other law enforcement agencies. It went into detail about specific instances where the sheriff had misled or obfuscated these operations. Much of it was anecdotal, but the sheer numbers of the cases painted an unmistakable trend. The report identified both the sheriff and one of his deputies as suspects.

There was a lot of data supporting the second issue. It went into detail about numbers of arrests and shipment interceptions compared to neighboring counties. But the arrests only grabbed the lowest elements of the operation. And these low-level dealers were not helpful in trying to get to the inner workings, much less the head of the operation. They only dealt with a mysterious go-between who had been careful to keep his identity hidden.

The Task Force was certain the shipments were coming across the porous Canadian border but were unsure how. The dossier described their suspicions that 'Oyster Cove Thoroughbreds' might be the distribution center for the drugs, but they didn't have enough evidence for either a search warrant or arrest warrant. The dossier went on to explain the suspicious activities, late night shipments, Canadian business connections, armed guards and sophisticated surveillance. My hackles went up. *This is the ranch next door to Noah's.*

The dossier tied it all together by pointing out that previous multi-agency operations targeting the ranch had included the sheriff and mysteriously had resulted in no success, as if the ranch had been tipped off. Hence, this latest operation that explicitly excluded the Puget County Sheriff's Department.

I got up and washed the dishes before taking Lobo out for one last walk and a chance to do her business. As we walked up the street my mind was focused on what I had just read, letting the thoughts percolate. Suddenly, Lobo stopped and growled. I knew this growl, so I immediately slipped into the shadow between two buildings and unhooked the strap of my shoulder holster. I reached down to assure Lobo and gave her the signs to sit and quiet her growl. I heard voices from the street ahead of us and stooped down to look around the corner of the building. Hank and Sheriff McGraw were standing outside the Bar and Grill and deep into a heated conversation. The sheriff was pushing his face close to Hank's, waving his arms and talking in an elevated whisper. Spittle flew out of his mouth. We weren't close enough for me to hear their entire conversation, but the sheriff's voice rose enough for me to hear what he said just before he walked to the patrol car, got in, slammed the door and sped up the street, "Damnit Hank, you need to get control of your end of the operation. We're losing too much revenue and the boss is getting antsy. Things are going down soon and we can't afford any loose ends. Just take the guy out and be done with it. He's a liability."

Hank muttered to himself before he opened the door to the bar and disappeared inside. When I was certain that we wouldn't be seen, I whispered 'heel' to Lobo and we stepped down the street in the opposite direction.

•———————•

When we got back to the apartment, I slipped Lobo a chicken jerky treat, rubbed her face and praised her for her vigilance. Once again, she'd proved to be a valuable partner. She and Scar climbed onto the couch as I sat down, opened my PC and wrote up notes on what I had just seen and heard.

I had just finished reading what I had written and making a few minor changes when my cell phone rang. Jessie's face and number filled the screen.

Before I could even say hello, her voice came through the speaker loud and clear, "Zeke, what the hell is going on? I got a call from the FBI verifying your veracity and my sources that are still in service say that someone's done a full background check on you. What kind of trouble have you gotten mixed up in?"

I quipped, "Hi Big Sis, nice to hear from you."

She almost broke my eardrums, "Come on Zeke, I'm worried. Don't get sassy with me!"

I squeaked out an apology and proceeded to tell her everything that was happening, from Deputy White Feather recruiting me, my meeting with Christopher Sloan and the conversation I had just overheard between the sheriff and Hank. I summarized the dossier and told her the dossier had confirmed my suspicions about the thoroughbred ranch. I also threw in my thoughts that Hank was probably involved somehow. I then told her that Terry had agreed that I could read her in and call on her for support if necessary.

After I finished, she was silent for a few minutes and then declared, "Oh baby, I thought you might stay out of trouble on that little island of yours, but here you are neck deep in a covert operation! Can you trust this Terry White Feather?"

I assured her that Terry was the real deal and that it wasn't just my opinion but her being trusted to go under-cover by the task force confirmed it. But Jessie wasn't satisfied, "Still, it's just the two of you. I need to finish up a few things here and then I'll fly up early next week."

I started to object and pointed out that she had her new business to run, but she interjected, "I'm already bored with this PI stuff. It's mostly insurance scams and cheating spouses." She let out a small laugh, "Besides what you're doing is a lot more exciting. So, I'll be there to watch your six just like always. You're my little baby!"

I thanked her and we talked for a bit longer before she hung up.

I sipped my beer and stared across the sound. *Damn, it's good to be loved!*

CHAPTER 10

WE'D JUST FINISHED A LESSON, Anne with Mike and Max while Louise helped Charlie with the ongoing mysteries of mathematics. I just stayed out of the way and tried to follow the lesson. After Louise left we gave the kids a midmorning snack of carrots and peanut butter celery. The kids' heads were down in concentration as they studiously did their homework. The bell on the shop door tinkled and I glanced in its direction to see Noah slip inside and head my way weaving around the customers and browsers. He had a friend who owned a seaplane and had arranged for a tour of the islands from above. There was a bounce to his step, and he looked like a new man, smiling from ear to ear. I told him I was ready and resisted the urge to tease him as we said our good-byes to Silas, Anne and the kids before walking out into a gentle breeze that was blowing the clouds away making room for a bright sun.

We hiked down the street past the shops and cafes and then out onto the wharf. I spotted a Cessna floatplane bobbing in the blue-gray water atop white floats attached to the struts. A slender man was removing a fuel line as we walked up. His face was creased and weathered, the top of his head was devoid of any hair and sprinkled with large brown freckles.

Noah reached out and shook the man's hand, "Lou, this is my friend Zeke. He owns the bookstore in town and is a fellow vet." He let out a laugh and crowed, "He also spent time as an NCIS agent, but we'll forgive that transgression!" That's when I noticed the Navy Aviation tattoo on his right forearm, "Zeke, Lou flew rescue helicopters in the Persian Gulf during the second Iraq war."

I reached over and shook his hand and Lou smiled shyly, his voice so low it was almost a whisper, "Nice to meet you Zeke. You ready for the grand tour?"

He started up the ramp to the marina office to pay for his gas and I tugged gently on his arm, "You're very kind to spend time with us and I insist on paying for the fuel."

He looked at me with a grin and murmured, "You're on, but Army boy over there has to buy the beers in Friday Harbor."

As I returned from the office, Lou cranked the engine filling the air with the sputtering of the rotary engine. He unhooked and threw off the mooring ropes. Noah climbed into the backseat and let me ride shotgun while Lou pushed off and climbed into the pilot's seat. We fitted the earphones over our heads as he went through a checklist that was attached to the console with Velcro. With his checks complete, he revved the engine, guided the plane out into the bay, turned into the wind and we bounced along until the airspeed was sufficient to lift us into the bright blue.

We threaded through the space between Whatley and Camano Islands and turned northwest along Skagit Bay. Lou guided the plane slightly inland past a large marina on the left and a small town on the right. "That's Shelter Bay on the left and the town of La Conner on the right. The weather seems to accommodate the Tulip industry."

He nosed the plane down and flew above acres of bright flowers. He continued, "They have a Tulip Festival every year if you're into that sort of thing."

Noah and I blurted in unison, "Thanks, I'll pass!"

The three of us sniggered then Noah got a whimsical look on his face, "Might be something to take a lady friend to, though." I looked over at him and grinned.

The plane's nose turned up to gain altitude, continuing along the bay and then turned southwest through a narrow straight between two rocky cliffs. Lou spoke into his microphone, "This is Saratoga Passage." He pointed ahead at a picturesque arched bridge, "That's Deception Pass. It separates Whatley Island from Fidalgo Island." The cliffs on both sides of the pass were covered in tall pines and the scene was reminiscent of Big Sur along the California coast, but maybe a little more majestic. Boats were huddled in small coves and kayakers scooted along the shores. Seabirds rose and fell effortlessly with the thermals.

We climbed and flew north over a mid-sized town, its harbor sporting numerous marinas accentuated by the tall masts sweeping arcs in the air as the ocean swelled. Lou grunted, "That there is Anacortes. All the ferries through the San Juan Archipelago originate here. There are over 170 islands in the group and the ferries only service a few. There's also a ferry to Sydney, British Columbia on Vancouver Island."

"I'm going to fly north to the Canadian border and then we'll turn south and take in some of the islands in the chain. After that we'll stop at Friday Harbor on San Juan Island for refreshments." He pointed the nose down until we were a couple of hundred feet above the sparkling blue water.

After a few minutes, Noah patted me on my shoulder and pointed down and to the right where a pod of dolphins was frolicking in the cerulean water. They would breach and one would occasionally somersault, flying high into the air and landing with a splash.

We banked and headed back south when Lou brought the plane into a shallow dive and announced over the intercom, "Look just ahead and ten degrees to the left."

We both strained our necks to look and I finally spotted a pod of humpback whales cruising along below us. I pointed and shouted to Noah, "There!" just as one of them breached and seemingly rose from the water before splashing down on its back. We flew in circles around the pod watching in wonder at one of God's beautiful creations until they finally dove into the depths and disappeared.

We hadn't gone far when I spotted an island ahead of us. It appeared to be about two miles wide and half mile across. At first glance it appeared to be just like the other islands we'd passed until I noticed a runway. Along the runway was a fenced pasture and a dozen horses gamboled along the fence when they heard the plane's engine. A monstrous home sat in the bluffs above a sheltered cove where a long wharf jutted like a finger into the ocean. A breakwater extended even farther. Anchored in the man-made bay one of the largest super yachts I'd ever seen bobbed in the swells. There appeared to be a heliport located on the aft and a swimming pool graced the forward deck.

I was just about to ask about this beautiful estate when Lou banked and began to climb. I glanced over with a questioning look and he spit out, "That's Will Island. It's privately owned by one of our state senators. Any other island I would fly right over it, but the senator pulls a lot of weight and throws it around if we 'violate his personal airspace'. I unknowingly flew over it once and the local 'gendarmes' were waiting for me when I got back. They strongly suggested that I shouldn't do that again if I wanted to keep my license. I got the message and have avoided it ever since."

Something nibbled at the back of my mind. I looked around at the smaller islands a few hundred yards offshore from the big one we'd skirted, "Pretty nice place. How far are we from the border?"

Lou poked his thumb behind him, "I'd say it's no more than 3 miles as the crow flies, give or take. Why?"

I scrunched up my face in thought and mumbled, "Oh, no reason. Just seems like they might cross over to do some of their business rather than go all the way to Washington. Probably make trips on a regular basis."

I glanced back at Noah, and he was grinning and nodded. I got the feeling he was on the same page as me. My eyes focused out the window as we flew south and the island became smaller in the distance.

•————————•

We flew over barely exposed reefs that interrupted the sea with sprays of mist shooting into the air. Lou would weave around small islands dropping down to scope them out and giving us views of granite cliffs covered in pine trees rising from the blue abyss. After a few minutes I spied a large island shaped somewhat like a pair of saddlebags ahead. Lou came over the intercom, "That's Orcas Island, the largest in the chain. About five thousand people live there. Like all the islands the only public access is via personal watercraft or the ferries." He pointed down at a green and white ferry just pulling into an ungraceful landing at the southern tip of one of the saddlebags. Cars were queued up along the side of a narrow road that ended at the seashore. We buzzed the ferry and wiggled our wings as the passengers waved.

Banking left to avoid another small island immediately ahead, we then bore southwest to slip between that and another island. Lou quipped, "Shaw Island on the right and Lopez island on the left and up ahead is Friday Harbor. That's where we'll stop for a breather and Noah can buy us those beers."

Lou spoke on the radio to the ground crew at a large marina and we slipped down and gently skimmed across the water of the protected bay. We idled up to a pier at the marina. Lou jumped out, greeted a red-headed young woman dockhand in cut-off jeans and a tank top by name, threw some bumpers between the plane and the dock and helped secure the plane to the cleats.

The lady asked Lou if he wanted to gas up and Lou shook his head, but I touched his arm, "Let me show my appreciation for a great tour." He started to protest but, I reached across him and handed a credit card to the woman, "Don't listen to him. He's got his head in the clouds!" She grinned, gave me a sassy salute and headed to the fuel station.

Lou led us up a path toward a ferry terminal that sat at the end of the main thoroughfare leading up a hill. One of the green and white behemoths was just pulling in and the captain sounded his horn to announce their arrival.

We followed Lou up the main street for a couple of blocks while he gave us a quick tour. Most of the businesses were tourist shops, restaurants and coffee shops. A few hotels dominated the hills on the side streets. We crossed the street and headed back down toward the harbor when Noah and Lou ducked into a shop specializing in Port wine while I kept walking. I noticed a bookstore and entered to see if I could get any new ideas for our shop. The unmistakable aroma of the books invaded my senses, somewhat grassy with a hint of vanilla. The front tables were dedicated to the latest best sellers and local authors, but the books along the back and covering rows of shelves drew me and other customers in.

I chatted with the owner, an older woman with silver hair pulled into a tight bun, about the bookselling business. She said she knew my uncle and expressed her sympathy about his passing.

We were exchanging contact information when my two compatriots joined us carrying bags of bottles that tinkled as they bounced together. Noah announced that he had picked out a perfect Tawny Port for me that would do well in the bookstore along with a humidor of Cuban cigars. "I could probably get into a Tom Clancy adventure for an afternoon with that combination." Lou guffawed and the lady got an uncomfortable look, so I thanked her for her time and ushered my friends back out to the street. *Can't take these guys anywhere!*

Lou led us down to a stylistic restaurant sitting directly above the marina with stunning views of the harbor. A pretty hostess with a nose stud and four hoops in her left ear grabbed three menus and the drink list before leading us to a table shaded by a forest green umbrella near the edge of the deck. An armada of all sizes and shapes shared the panorama before us with the sparkling bay and a ferry just departing, leaving froth in its wake. The distinctive odor of marine fuel mixed with the tang of salt water wafted up from below.

The waiter walked up to take our order as I perused the menu. Noah smiled at the waiter and said, "Put all of this on my tab. I'm ordering the Dungeness Crab Tots and the Salmon plate for us to nosh on while we enjoy our beers. And I'm going for the Sierra Nevada Pale Ale."

Lou went with a non-alcoholic beer and explained, "I never drink when I'm flying. Need to keep my head about me." I joined Noah with the ale, and we sat back enjoying the view and relaxing in the warm sunlight, each in our own thoughts.

I was daydreaming when the waiter interrupted with our beers. We picked up our bottles, toasted each other and tapped our bottles together with clinks. A short while later we were treated with a platter of smoked salmon and discs of toasted bread accompanied by cream cheese, capers and thinly sliced red onions. Another platter held large, deep-fried balls of riced potato mixed with panko breadcrumbs, spices and fresh crab. We were quiet as we dug into these delicious treats.

After tasting the crab tots, I complimented Noah's choice, "These are the best twist on tater-tots that I've ever had. I could probably make a meal out of a plate full of them. And the smoke on the salmon is just right, not too heavy, but with a wonderful kick." Lou nodded and Noah just grinned through a full mouth.

After we finished our snack, Noah paid the bill while Lou and I visited the restroom to empty our bladders for a comfortable trip back to Whatley. Then, the three of us wandered down to the pier and climbed aboard the freshly fueled conveyance gently bobbing against the white bumpers lining the wharf. I let Noah have the shotgun seat and climbed into the back. The red-headed dockhand helped Lou untie from the cleats and then threw her arms around his neck, whispered something, and kissed him passionately on the lips. He jumped into the cockpit with a sheepish look and began his pre-flight checklist. Noah reached over, ruffled his hair, and crowed, "Yeah, the flyboys get all the pretty girls."

And off we went, bouncing along the waves that had been churned up by a passing trawler covered in gill nets and pursued by screeching seabirds.

As soon as we cleared Lopez Island, Lou brought the nose down and we flew low over the azure sea. Noah and Lou carried on a banter in the front so I fell into thought. My tummy was happy and my thoughts drifted to everything Terry White Feather had told me. Something kept pulling me away from these thoughts and I cleared my mind in hopes of getting a grasp on it. As my rumination kept bouncing between drug running and human trafficking suddenly my head popped up with what it was that bothered me, that mysterious island and Noah's neighbor. Just as that thought entered my mind we touched down and began motoring to the Oyster Bay dock. I tucked my suspicions away for future examination.

———•———

I thanked Lou and the three of us talked about getting together for a beer in a few days before I said my goodbyes and headed up the hill to the bookstore. The sun was low in the sky and partially hidden by thinly layered clouds turning the sky into a palette of majestic oranges, pinks and reds to the southwest.

The little bell tinkled as I walked through the door. Lobo ran up and nuzzled me for a pet. Silas smiled and greeted me warmly, "Good afternoon, Master Zeke. How was your tour?"

We chatted while I described the trip and suggested he might want to do the same. His brows drew down and he proclaimed, "Oh goodness no! I'm deathly afraid of flying and those little planes seem like death traps. They're so flimsy and seem to be ready to fall apart with their rattling while bouncing from side to side. No sir, I'll stay right here on old terra firma!"

I chuckled, "I understand, but you don't know what you're missing."

Max was in the back curled up with a book on her lap sound asleep in one of the big armchairs. I suspected there wasn't much 'sleeping' on her sleepover and gently picked her up. She buried her head into my chest and mumbled, "Hi Daddy. Did you have a good time?" before slipping back into dreamland.

CHAPTER 11

THE LOUDSPEAKERS GROUND OUT SOMETHING that was supposed to pass as music, but it was overwhelmed by the din created by the chatter, babel and clamor of the hundred plus kids that wandered about the field house. Charlie stepped out onto the veranda and watched as groups of the other, older kids surreptitiously passed bottles and joints among themselves. Since the chaperones were focused on the 'teen dance' inside, many of them didn't even try very hard to hide their actions.

Danny stood beside her and they watched a couple making out and pawing each other near the corner of the porch. Danny was sweet on her and she sorta liked him too but they both figured they were too young to be anything more than friends. She liked it that way.

The dance was supposed to end at ten and her mom had insisted that Lobo join her after she had begged to attend. She and Uncle Zeke had said that Lobo would be a good escort. She reached down and scrubbed the dog's head. Lob licked her hand and gave a little woof. Charlie didn't mind having her along, in fact she enjoyed it. Lobo was her friend and she actually enjoyed her company over the other kids'. Hers and Danny's that is. They were just so juvenile!

Charlie turned to Danny, "This is boring. I'm not sure why anyone would enjoy it?"

Danny face broke into his sweet smile, and he nodded, "It is pretty messed up. Maybe we should head home."

Charlie looked at her watch and shook her head, "It's only eight thirty and we don't have to be in until ten. I'm going to ride over and visit Maddie and Shi Shi. I didn't get a chance today and I'm sure they miss me. Want to come along?"

Danny barked out a laugh, "You sure do love those horses. But I think they're neat, too. Let's go!" He jumped on his bike and shouted, "I'll race you."

Charlie squealed, "No fair!" She jumped on her bike and raced after him, Lobo loping behind.

———

The moon was three-quarters full and lit their way along the country road for the mile to Noah's place. Charlie could see the glow of light from Noah's house nestled in the trees as they pulled up to the fence and dropped their bikes. She heard Shi Shi nicker as she hobbled over to the fence. Maddie was more cautious and stayed back until Charlie pulled an apple from the basket attached to her handlebars and held her palm open for Shi Shi to nibble at. Charlie turned to Danny and whispered, "Get one of the apples and feed it to Maddie but be careful to hold your palm flat so she doesn't catch your fingers. It really hurts when they bite."

Maddie wandered over, bit the apple in two and Danny began giggling as the horse chomped away at the fruit, pulp and juice dribbling out the sides of her mouth "She's making applesauce!"

They were stroking the horses and getting ready to head home when the flash of a vehicle's headlights lit up the trees above as it turned into the neighbor's driveway. Loud voices joined with the rumble of a diesel engine as the truck moved inside the gate and continued toward a large outbuilding. Danny grinned and held his finger to his lips and whispered, "Let's go see what they're doing!" and then slipped into the darkness of the trees.

Charlie was worried, started to tell him not to go, but he had disappeared. She sighed heavily and followed behind, Lobo at her heels. She had to crawl under a low-lying branch and then spotted him as he stepped on the bottom strand of barbed wire, bent over, and slipped through the gap. He waved her forward, "C'mon!" he whispered, holding the wire for her to crawl through. Lobo sidled under the wire and joined them.

Charlie had a bad feeling about this, and she pulled Danny to her and mumbled into his ear, "This is crazy, we're going to get caught."

Danny smiled and sputtered, "Let's get behind this log where they can't see us. I just want to see what's going on."

They both crouched down behind the rotting trunk of a fallen tree and poked their heads up. The halogen yard lights lit up the area as if it were day. The truck had turned around and backed up to large open doors of the metal building. Men were running into the building and then emerging with boxes. Based on the hunched over shoulders and grunts from the men the boxes must have been heavy. They watched as one of the men tripped and the box tipped its contents onto the ground; brick shaped packages wrapped in cellophane. The man cursed and crammed the spilled contents back into the container.

Charlie pulled Danny back into the darkness of the trees and sputtered, "I don't know what they're doing but it's not good. Let's get out of here." Danny nodded while Charlie pulled her phone from her jacket pocket and snapped a picture of the truck.

They slowly crawled to the barbed wire, Danny opened a gap and crawled through and held it open for Charlie when Lobo growled and three men rushed her. She shouted, "Run Danny" just as one of the men grabbed her. Lobo immediately attacked the man and clamped her jaws around his ankle. The man screamed and loosened his grip just enough for Charlie to turn and thrust her knee into the man's crotch, just like her mother had taught her. Then she hit him as hard as she could with her phone. But it wasn't enough. Another man grabbed her by her hair and threw her to the ground. The air burst from her lungs as she hit the ground and her phone flew from her hand and into the brush. Gasping for air, Charlie watched as the third man grabbed Danny by the hood of his sweat-shirt, swung him around and slammed him to the ground. Danny fell to the ground, hitting his head hard, his body going eerily still. Lobo fiercely attacked Charlie's attacker, but a shot rang out, followed by a yip and howl.

Charlie struggled to get away from the man who held her hair in his grip and heard one of them shout, "Bring them both. They'll make a nice addition to our collection. The boss will be pleased. Some of his customers like it both ways. Never mind the dog. She's finished." Charlie screamed and swung at the man holding her and suddenly a fist slammed into the side of her head. The last thing she heard was Shi Shi whinnying in the distance before every-thing went dark and she crumpled to the ground.

CHAPTER 12

M AX WAS IN A SNIT because I wouldn't let her join Charlie at the teen party, so I treated her to one of her favorite meals, a nice dinner of spaghetti and meat balls. The food helped lighten her mood and we ate bowls of fresh strawberries, lightly sprinkled with sugar, while settling in for a screening of 'Monsters, Inc.'. When the movie was finished, I fixed hot chocolate for her and black tea for myself while she brushed her teeth and donned her 'Hello Kitty' pajamas.

It was late and her head was nodding before she finished her cocoa and she finally leaned over and fell into a deep slumber, her head resting on my lap. I gently picked her up and lugged her to her room. *Man, she's getting big!* I laid her on the bed and pulled the covers up tight to her chin and kissed her forehead when she wrapped her arms around my neck and murmured, "Good night, Daddy. I love you.", before turning on her side. I watched her chest rise and fall, a gentle snore slipping from her mouth. *I hope we can resolve all our spats with dinner and a movie!*

I slipped out the door, back into the living room, grabbed a copy of *A Stillness at Appomattox* and plopped down into the easy chair. Scar rubbed against my leg and jumped into my lap, his motor purring softly. I reached down and stroked his head, "You miss Lobo too, don't you? Don't worry she'll be back tomorrow after her chap-erone duties."

The book was interesting, but my eyes kept blurring and finally my chin dropped to my chest and dreams of drug busts gone bad invaded my mind.

———•———

Drool was oozing from the side of my mouth when Scar jumped up and hissed. I heard loud steps running up the stairs outside, stood and reached into the drawer of the side table, sliding my Glock from its holster. I pulled and released the slide driving home a round into the chamber. I then brought up the surveillance camera on my phone. Just as the image cleared to display the landing in front of the door, Anne pounded on the glass, shouting, "Zeke, I need your help!"

I opened the door and Mike stumbled in wearing a jacket over his pajamas and softly crying. Anne was right behind, wearing jeans and a sweater. Her hair was dishev-eled and her eyes red. She stumbled in and began sobbing, her words jumbled, "Charlie. …. gone. Can't… fi. Dan… Help. Please."

I guided her to the couch and made her sit, went to the kitchen, and poured a glass of water, bringing it to her. Her hands were shaking as she took the glass, spilling some. I gave her shoulder a slight squeeze and turned to her son, "Mikey, why don't we bed you down in my room." I took his hand and led him down the hall and lifted him onto the bed. I pulled back the covers, pulled off his shoes and pulled the covers over him. His sad eyes looked up at me and he gurgled, "Mom's real upset. Charlie didn't come home, and I'm scared."

I pulled him into a hug and rubbed his back, "Don't worry big guy. We'll get to the bottom of this. Why don't you lie down and close your eyes. I'm going to help your mom."

Anne was rocking back and forth and mewing when I returned. I filled the teapot and placed it on a burner before sitting beside her and draping my arm around her shoulder. She turned into my chest; her sobs muffled by my shirt. I stroked her head and softly whispered, "It's okay. Tell me what's going on whenever you're ready. I'll help however I can." Reaching to the side table I pulled out a wad of tissues and handed them to her.

She cried against my chest for a few minutes, then shuddered, blew her nose and sat upright, "Charlie didn't come home from the teen party at the rec center. The dance got over at ten and she was supposed to come right home afterwards. You know because you let Lobo go with her. At first, I thought she was a little late but after half an hour I began to get worried. I called around to her friends and they said she and Danny had left together on their bikes. They didn't know where she had gone, but Alice said she thought she heard them talking about the horses. I called Danny's folks and they're worried, too. Danny isn't home yet either."

Just then, a slight knock on the door drew our attention. Anne turned to me, "That's probably Danny's parents. I hope you don't mind but I told them I was going to ask for your help and asked them to meet me here."

I got up and patted her shoulder, "No problem. We may need their help" and then trod to the door. As soon as I opened it, a small woman wrapped in an overcoat and a beefy guy in jeans and a plaid work shirt barged in. The woman ran to Anne and squeaked, "Have you heard anything?" Anne shook her head and the two of them began sobbing. The man stood there, shoulders hunched with a dejected look on his face before turning to me, "I'm Phil Svenson and this is my wife, Faith. Sorry to barge in like this, but Anne thought it would be all right. She seems to think you can fix this."

His hands were trembling as I took his arm and led him to an armchair, "I'll do whatever I can. Please sit." The teapot was whistling and I went to the kitchen, turned the burner off, grabbed a fistful of mugs, teabags and the teapot before placing them on the mat on the coffee table. I poured four steaming cups and threw chamomile teabags into two and Earl Grey into the others without asking. I reached into the kitchen and snagged the sugar bowl and spoons setting them on the table.

Before sitting in the other armchair, I fixed one of the chamomiles with one sugar, the way I knew Anne liked hers, picked up the mug and forced it into her hands. I urged the others to fix their tea and then started, "Okay, bring me up to speed. Of course, I know Charlie, but who is Danny? How old is he? Has he or Charlie ever done anything like this before?"

Everyone started talking at once so I held up my hand and pointed at Phil, "Let's do this one at a time. Phil, tell me about your son."

He looked up, his eyes red and blurted, "Danny and Charlie are the same age. They've known each other for almost ten years. He's a good boy and we've never had any problems. He gets straight A's in school and plays on the regional soccer team. He's an altar server at Mary, Mother of Mercy. I know that I'm his father and you'll think I'm prejudiced in my opinion, but I don't think he would purposely worry us like this. He's a good boy."

Anne lifted her head and her sunken eyes bore into me, "Phil's right. Danny and Charlie are best friends and neither one has ever missed curfew. It's just not in them!"

Phil stood up, began pacing around the room and continued, "He has other friends from school and soccer, but we've called all of them and they don't know where they are. He's not answering his phone either." His face turned to me pleading. "He's our only boy and I'm at a loss."

I nodded and turned to Anne, "Did anyone call the police?"

She scoffed and spat out, "They aren't interested! They said teens do this all the time and that they'll be home whenever they're ready." She moaned, "They told us we have to wait seventy-two hours before filing a missing person's report." Her voice raised to a keen, "That's three days! I can't wait that long. Something bad has happened! I can feel it! Please Zeke, please."

Just then my cell phone rang. I recognized the number as Noah's.

I answered and, before I could say anything, Noah shouted, "Zeke, you've got to get over here! Lobo's been hurt. I heard a shot close to the house and went out to investigate. Lobo was laying on the ground with a wound in her fore quarters. Lots of blood but I packed it and she's alert. I don't think it's major but I called Dave just in case and he's on his way over."

I asked him if he'd seen the kids, but the question confused him so I gave him a brief description of the situation. He got silent for a moment before answering, "I didn't see them but I was pretty much focused on Lobo. I can go check."

My voice was tight, "No, it sounds like it might be dangerous. You need to wait until I get there." I paused, "And Noah, you better arm up."

I told him I'd be right over, hung up and then turned to Anne and Danny's parents, "Lobo's at Noah's. She's been hurt. She was with Charlie so this might help us find her. I'm going to head over there."

•————————•

Anne jumped up, "I'm going with you!"

Phil chimed in, "Me too!

Turning to Anne and Phil I shook my head, "We don't know what's going on over there. It might be dangerous. And someone needs to wait at home for Charlie and Danny in case they show up."

Anne stood ramrod straight and cried, "There is no discussing this! Charlie is my child and I'm going with you." Phil stood next to her nodding emphatically.

Faith stood and murmured in a voice that was barely a whisper, "You can't leave your child here alone either, Zeke. Please go wake the children. Anne lives two doors down from us so I'll take Mike and Maxine to our place. I'll leave a note on Anne's door for Charlie in case she shows up. Now please give me your cell number so I can contact you." *Strong woman!*

I recited mu number, donned my holster and slid the Glock into it and started for my room when Anne stopped me, "If you have a shotgun in your arsenal, bring it to me. I'm quite good with one." I looked to Phil and he just pulled his coat back revealing a revolver in a leather holster. It looked like a 357 Magnum. *Good, we'll have some heavy firepower.*

I rushed to my closet, opened the gun safe, grabbed my Go-Bag, checked the contents and grabbed two more magazines from the shelf, stuffing them into my jacket pocket. Reaching into the back of the safe I pulled out my double-barrel shotgun with the barrels sawed off at barely the eighteen inches required by law. I felt around and grabbed a bandolier stuffed with shells filled with buckshot. I headed to the kitchen and grabbed three tactical flashlights and three bottles of water.

I handed the shotgun and bandolier and one flashlight to Anne and the other flashlight to Phil. I stuffed the water bottles into side pockets of the Go-Bag.

I headed to Max's room while Anne bundled up Mike. She was already awake and looked at me when I entered, "What's going on Daddy? I heard shouting. Why are there people here?"

I sat on the bed and explained the situation in terms as mild as possible trying not to frighten her. She stood and began getting dressed and turned to me, "I need to go with you and keep you safe. We're partners and you said you'd never leave me."

I pulled her to me and whispered, "You're right sweetheart. We are partners, but right now, I need you to take care of Mike and be my point of contact at Danny's in case they show up. The situation might be dangerous and not a place for children. I promise I'll be careful. Besides, Noah's got my back so you don't have to worry."

She hugged me and pulled my head down to her level, "Okay, but you better come back," before kissing me on my cheek. She got up and pulled out some jeans and a pink and yellow Taylor Swift sweatshirt. She pulled it over her curls, shook the hair from her face, turned to me, her face lined with concern, "I know you said that we shouldn't make promises that we may not be able to keep but, you need to find Charlie. Please promise." Tears were pooling in her eyes.

I pulled her to me and murmured, "I promise to do everything in my power."

She looked into my eyes, nodded and headed for the door.

Ten minutes later, Anne, Phil and I were speeding toward Noah's, my Go-Bag on the backseat next to an upright Anne, bandolier across her chest and shotgun between her legs.

CHAPTER 13

T HE LIGHTS IN NOAH'S HOUSE were ablaze along
with the big halogen light hanging from the rafters of
the barn. Even with those lights and Karla's headlights on
high beam, the few ruts along the driveway were hard to
discern as we bounced along. Pulling into the gravel turn-
about, I spied the vet's old pickup in front of the house,
one of the cabinets in the pickup open. I pulled up behind
and we all piled out just as Noah opened the door and
waved. There was a holster attached to his side filled with
what appeared to be a Colt M1911. *That's more firepower!
These Whatley Island guys don't mess around!*

Noah opened the door wide so we could all file in
and I made quick introductions before rushing to Doc's
side where he knelt before a prone Lobo. I bent down and
she looked up with a grin on her face, lifted her head and
slathered my face with her tongue.

Doc nudged me aside and fussed, "Sorry, but you're
blocking the light. I've just about finished stitching her up.
Hold her head still for me."

I stroked Lobo's head and murmured dog praises to
her until Doc finished up and turned to me, "She's a lucky
girl. Another inch and the bullet might have crushed her
shoulder or hit an artery. See here," and pointed to where
he had shaved her fur around a nasty gash covered with

stitches and orange antiseptic. He continued, "She needs to rest and not move about too much so the stitches can do their job." About then Lobo, whined and started to get up. We gently laid her back down and Dave covered the wound with a thick gauze that he held in place with tape. When he finished with the wound, he pulled a donut-shaped pillow from his bag and attached it around her neck, "This will keep her from licking and worrying the wound, but I can tell she is devoted to you and will follow you. I can give you some sedatives to help keep her inactive if you wish."

The thought of drugging my best friend turned my stomach and I quipped, "I'd rather not. She'll stay if I tell her." I gave her a down command followed by 'stay'. Her eyes were sad and she whined, but she didn't attempt to get up again.

I stroked Lobo's head once more before standing, "Noah, can you show me where you found her? We'll use that as a starting point in our search for the kids." We started for the door and Lobo sprang up again and limped in front of us and headed for the door. Dave's face was grim and his eyes were filled with kindliness, "Seems like Lobo is too invested in finding her charges and she's not going to be left out of the search. She can probably be a big help." He reached into the bag, pulled out a roll of adhesive strips and knelt down in front of Lobo, "These adhesive strips will help keep the area around the wound from pulling at the stitches and also keep it from getting too soiled. Just try to minimize her activity." He unhooked the donut and removed it from around her neck.

•————————•

Lobo turned and licked my hand before turning to the door with a small bark. I brushed her head with my hand and knelt, "You're a tough old girl, aren't you? I should have known better than trying to keep you out of the action." I opened the door. Lobo limped out and led us down the drive toward the pasture.

The light from the moon lit our way until a cloud shrouded it, leaving us in darkness. I turned on a flashlight. Lobo crossed over to the pasture and squeezed under the gate and continued on while we unhooked the gate's clasp and scrambled through. Noah's voice was barely above a whisper, "She's heading toward the spot where I found her."

Maddie and Shi Shi nickered, walked to us and Maddie rubbed her head against Noah. He stroked her nose before turning and shining his flashlight at an area where the grass was depressed, "I found her right over there. You can see the blood on the ground."

We stopped and shined our lights around and one of the beams picked up a reflection near the road. Phil rushed over, tripping and nearly falling when a fallen limb snagged the toe of his boot. He shouted, "It's their bikes! They were here!"

We shined our flashlights around the area near the blood and I saw traces leading toward the border fence. Lobo was on her feet and limping in the same direction. She yipped and headed farther away, turned and yipped again before disappearing into the brush.

I turned to Phil and Anne, "Check the area around the bikes and see if you can find anything else." I had a tingling sense of danger and wanted them out of harm's way just in case. I motioned to Noah to follow me and started after Lobo.

I could see drops of blood on the ground in the direction the dog had disappeared. We pushed through the bushes, blackberry stickers grabbing at our clothes and nettles turning my bare arms to fire. I could just see the fence separating Noah's property from the equestrian facility so I motioned to Noah and we both doused our lights and crept forward, my hackles up and on full alert.

We crept to the fence and I saw that Lobo had already slithered under the bottom strand and was waiting near a fallen log on the other side. Noah came up silently beside me and I whispered, "Lobo's found something. You stay here and I'll check it out." Noah nodded and stepped on the lowest strand of the fence and pulled the middle strand up for me to duck through.

As I stood on the other side, I noticed a piece of blue cloth attached to a barb and fluttering in the slight breeze. I pulled a square of nylon with jagged edges from the fence and examined it, "This looks like it was torn from a jacket."

Dawn was a soft hint in the eastern sky, and we used the dim light to examine it. Anne and Phil traipsed up. Anne whispered, "There was nothing that we could see around the bikes. We may be able to find more when the sun finally comes up. Have you found anything?"

I held up the two-inch piece of cloth and Phil sucked in his breath loud enough for us to hear and grabbed the fabric from my hands, "I'm pretty sure this is from Danny's windbreaker. It's the right color and material."

He started to climb through the fence but I put my hand on his shoulder and held him from going any farther. My sixth sense was screaming danger! "This is private property, and I don't want anyone else to get into trouble. I noticed what appears to be a camera on that tree over there and a motion detector on that fence post. Let me go see what Lobo's found and check things out. If I find anything and it's safe, I'll signal and you can come forward."

I crept forward to the downed log where Lobo was patiently sitting. The grass around it was crushed as if many people had been walking in the area. A bare spot on the ground held an imprint of a small shoe, maybe from a sneaker. I duckwalked to Lobo, "What have you found girl?"

Lobo let out a small yip and advanced her front paw under a fern surrounded by scrub brush. I got on my hands and knees and peered around, but couldn't see anything in the weak light, so I reached under the bush and felt around. *Hope the critters are friendly!* I was just about to give up when my fingers brushed against something hard that didn't seem natural. I stretched my arm farther and my hand enveloped a hard plastic case. I knew what it was before I had extricated it and I spoke in a loud whisper, "It's a phone." I pulled the device from the bushes, stood with it in my hand and immediately recognized the purple cover. I had seen that phone in Charlie's hand many times back at the bookstore.

As I carried the phone over to Anne, she let out a small moan, took it from my hand and turned it on. The screen was cracked, but it powered up to show a screen saver depicting Maddie and Shi Shi's long faces peering back. Anne's hand was shaking, and she began crying, "Oh my God, it's hers. Where is she? Why did she leave her phone? Where's my little girl?" She sank to the ground silently sobbing.

Phil put his arm around her shoulders and tried to console her, but the tears forming in his eyes exposed the panic and sadness the two of them were sharing. Noah stood there looking on not knowing how to help.

I went back to the log and snapped a picture of the shoe print that I'd discovered before shining the light around the area. Something glinted at the edge of the beam. I pulled out a handkerchief, reached over and picked up a bullet casing and examined it. The flashlight provided enough illumination so I could read the caliber. *Forty caliber, probably from a Glock. A lot of law enforcement agencies use them.*

I walked back to the fence and handed the casing, wrapped in the cloth, to Noah, "Hold on to this. It's probably what they used on Lobo. We may get lucky with a fingerprint, but even if we don't, we'll have the ballistics."

Noah nodded and slipped the shell into his jacket pocket, "We can give it to the sheriff and maybe they can expedite it."

I shook my head and pointed to Anne, "She already tried to get help from the sheriff's office, and they blew her off. I already think the guy's dirty and for all we know he's mixed up in this. When we get back, I can call in a few favors at the agency to get it processed."

Anne stood up and walked over, her jaw set. She held the phone out to me, her hands trembling, "It still powers up. I Know her password, but I don't see any recent phone calls or texts. How did it get here? I don't understand what she was doing out here so far from the horses."

I whispered, "Check her social media, like Facebook and Twitter or whatever it's called now."

Scrolling through the phone for a few minutes, she finally shook her head, "Nothing on either of those accounts. I even checked to make sure she wasn't signed up on one of those nasty ones like Ticky Tacky or whatever it's called." She bent over the phone and then cried out, "Wait! There's a couple of photos that appear to have been taken just a few hours ago. Look, it's a photo of a truck in that driveway over there," pointing at the Thoroughbred facilities, "and there are people either loading or unloading the truck." She handed the phone to me and I glanced at it just as Lobo began a low growl from deep in her throat.

I handed Anne the phone and put a leash on Lobo, handing the end to Noah, "Someone's coming, take Anne, Phil, and the dog back into the trees. You need to protect that bullet casing and the phone. Stay out of sight and don't let them know you're here! I'll handle this."

Three shadows emerged from the direction of the facility and rushed toward me. All three were carrying M-4s and one of them rushed me shouting, "This is private property. You're trespassing!"

He didn't wait for an answer before lifting his rifle and bringing the butt-end toward my head. I went low and ducked under the blow that glanced off my shoulder. I grabbed his arm and used his momentum to flip him onto his back where he landed with a grunt and a whoosh as the air left his lungs.

Pulling the rifle from his hands I swung around just in time to receive a haymaker to my jaw. Stars lit up my vision and I stumbled, barely able to remain on my feet. The guy thought I was almost finished and stepped up to finish me off.

That was his mistake! I pounded my fist into his midriff and when he bent over, I brought my extended fingers up and into his neck. He fell into a heap, just as I heard the slide on a pistol slamming home.

"Get down on the ground, face first with your hands extended in front of you." I complied and the man behind the gun kicked my legs apart, then rasped "Now use two fingers to pull your weapon from its holster and throw it over here." *This guy's a professional.*

He put his knee into my spine and the barrel of the pistol into the base of my skull, growling, "I recommend you don't do something stupid. This has a hair trigger."

"Not gonna move an inch," I promised.

"Smart boy," He hissed and wrenched my right arm behind my back and looped a zip-tie around my wrist pulling it tight enough to cut off circulation. Shifting the gun to his other hand he did the same with my left wrist and pulled the ties to where they bit into my skin.

He got up and stood above me for a second before slamming a boot into my kidney. I grunted as the pain shot through my torso. He aimed one at my head and I turned to avoid taking one in my eye. Stars filled my vision and nausea overcame me.

He laughed and aimed another kick toward my abdomen, but just as he pulled his foot back an explosion ripped through the dawn and leaves fluttered down from a tree overhead.

Anne's voice was crystal clear, "If you don't stop right now, you'll be eating double-aught buckshot! Now back away! And drop that gun while you're at it."

The man looked up with a wicked smile, hesitated and there was another explosion, a branch falling onto his head. The gun dropped to the ground and the man stepped back, "This guy is trespassing."

I heard Anne open the breach of the shotgun and drop in two more shells, closing it with one swift motion. A siren sounded and I could just make out blue and red strobe lights through my peripheral vision. I half mumbled and shouted, "Go back now before the police show up. Have

Silas call Jessie. She'll know what to do!" The branches of the trees rustled and the barrel of the shotgun disappeared.

The guy standing above me picked up his gun and gave me one more kick to the ribs before snickering, "Your friends can't help you. The sheriff is going to give you a real good time."

The brakes on the police cruiser squealed as it came to a halt and the door opened. Boots stomped up and appeared near my head. I heard Sheriff McGraw ask, "What do we have here Ed?"

Ed, who was apparently my captor, chuckled, "This guy was trespassing. He beat up two of our guards when they asked him to leave. There was someone else over in the bushes, but they ran off when they heard you coming."

McGraw leaned over and grinned at me, "Well, well, well. What do we have here, Mr. Book-man? I figured you and I would cross paths again. Seems you like accosting innocent people."

He grunted as he straightened up and tried whispering, but they were close enough that I could hear their conversation, "Thanks, Ed. I'll take it from here. Everything okay back there?"

Ed croaked, "Everything's on schedule. Hank's here already and got everything lined up. One more shipment tonight and we're clear."

Since they weren't too concerned with keeping their conversation a secret, they figured I would either be in jail or dead and not screw up their operation. *Sure hope Jessie works fast!*

Walking over, the sheriff gave me a kick in the kidneys and pain shot through my system. Wrenching my shackled arms up he snarled, "Get your ass up book-man. You're headed for a long stay, courtesy of Puget County."

My arms and shoulders were nearly wrenched from their sockets when I finally got my feet beneath me and was able to stand. I mumbled through my sore jaw, "I was just looking for some missing kids."

Ed came behind and punched my other kidney. The pain was almost unbearable as I tried to maintain my footing. He stood in my face close enough for me to feel the spittle flying from his mouth and barked, "Ain't no kids here! Just some mongrel I shot earlier."

I straightened, looked into his eyes and growled, "You made a big mistake! Nobody messes with my dog, asshole," and slammed my knee into his crotch with a vengeance. He doubled over and fell to the ground screaming, just as the sheriff yanked me toward his cruiser.

Opening the back door, he shoved me in without protecting my head that smacked the roof, blood dribbling down my face, "If that wasn't so much fun to watch, I should have shot you for resisting arrest." Walking around the vehicle he shouted, "Ed, you dumb ass, get up and get back to work."

Starting the car he revved the engine, drove out the gate and turned in the opposite direction from Oyster Cove. He glanced at me in the rearview mirror and vented, "Now what the hell am I going to do with you? Seems like there's no one around to get you out of this, so maybe we'll take the long way to town. And just maybe you'll have an unfortunate accident."

I looked over as we passed the driveway to Noah's ranch and saw his truck pull behind the cruiser, Phil riding shotgun and Anne seated in the middle, a cell phone stuck to her ear. They continued to follow through back roads and into the darkness of trees. We were on a rutted road in the middle of nowhere when McGraw leaned forward, looked in the rearview mirror and cursed, "Looks like we have company. They friends of yours? I guess this is your lucky day and you'll be spending time in one of our cold, dark cells." He laughed, turned right on a paved road finally headed in the direction of Oyster Cove.

CHAPTER 14

THE SHERIFF'S OFFICE WAS TYPICAL, desks crammed together end to end and the odor of stale coffee mixed with sweat and a little bit of urine. The sheriff marched me up to the bailiff making sure I didn't get away by wrenching my arms hard behind my back, my stretched tendons shooting pain into my shoulders.

The bailiff was almost as round as he was tall, the donut in his hand and the powdered sugar dripping from his skimpy mustache hinted at the possible reason for his not-so-slim figure. His head was completely devoid of any hair and his stained uniform shirt strained against the buttons. He grinned broadly through a mouth sparsely populated with crooked teeth and croaked, "What you got here Clifford, another poacher? Looks like he must have tripped a few times." He let out a raspy sound that might have been a laugh.

The sheriff cut the zip-ties from my wrists then pushed me forward, "Not this time Hal, this here's that book-man that sucker-punched Hank the other day. He's charged with trespassing and assault and battery. Caught him red-handed over at the Thoroughbred Facility."

Hal guffawed, "I heard about that. Ol' Hank sure got himself a new nose job from that one." He turned to me and growled, "Okay sport. Empty your pockets into this basket." I complied and he scribbled the contents on a form and shoved it and a pen at me, "Sign here and get over against the wall so we can take a few pictures."

I picked up the pen and contemplated which three moves I would need to take out the sheriff and this clown. *Patience, Zeke. This is just the beginning. Just let them think they've got the upper hand.*

I started toward the wall and stumbled when the sheriff kicked me in the back of my bum knee. I caught myself and went to a wall marked with black horizontal gradients to depict suspects' height fronted by a camera on a tripod.

Hal barked, "Stand up straight book-man!" The flash brought stars to my eyes and then I was harshly jerked around for a profile shot.

Next was fingerprinting. The sheriff pushed me toward the desk containing an inkpad and a cardstock with ten boxes, one for each of my digits. Hal twisted my wrist with more zeal than necessary to position each of my fingers over the appropriate box.

When he finished, the sheriff walked up punched, the side of my head, "Get moving, book-man! We ain't got all day. Time to introduce you to your new home." He pushed me toward a hallway where three deputies were standing along the wall. As I passed, each took a shot at me, one in the ribs and two to the gut. The bigger of the three was probably six-three with hands like hams. He guffawed, "Not so tough now are you book-man!"

My bottom lip had swollen and my words were ragged, "I get one phone call."

The big guy looked down at me and a grin formed across his face before he buried his fist into my stomach forcing me to bend over, "Book-man wants to call his lawyer! What do you think guys? Let's show him where the phone is."

The sheriff watched as the three deputies began punching, kicking and laughing like hyenas. I was beginning to think I should have taken them out earlier when Terry White Feather's sweet voice broke through the din, "What's going on here? Let him up!"

The men pulled back and I heard one of them hiss, "Oh great, it's Pocahontas. Can't have any fun with her around."

My ears were ringing when I heard Sheriff McGraw's voice bellow, "Ain't nothin' going on. These boys are just helping our prisoner to the phone. Seems like he stumbled and he's having a hard time walking. White Feather, why don't you help him make his call and get him to his cell? He goes before the magistrate at one. See to it he gets cleaned up before then. He's a mess. Come on boys, we got the public to protect."

Terry took my arm and led me down the hall with dingy yellowed walls and stained linoleum floors to a black telephone hanging on the wall. She stepped away to give me privacy and I dialed Jessie's number. She picked up on the first ring, "McCormack!"

I squeaked through my swollen lips, "Hi Big Sis."

Her voice boomed, "Zeke, are you okay? Dammit, can't you stay out of trouble? I got the call from Silas, but he didn't have a lot of details. What's going on?"

I whispered, "Still in jail and can't talk – the walls have ears. Call this number. She's a friendly and can fill you in a little more." I recited Terry's burner phone number, "I need to get out of here ASAP. Are you working on it? And I'm going to need backup."

"The lawyer's on the way. I had to charter a helicopter for him to get out to your island in time for the hearing. Seems the ferry is down to something called 'one boat service' and it's backed up with a two hour wait. What the hell is that all about? Silas said someone named Noah would pick him up and take him to the courthouse. My flight lands in Everett in two hours. Silas said somebody named Lou would fly me out there in his seaplane. Seems like you've made some useful friends, but why the hell can't you get into trouble in a more accessible place? You know how I am about flying and now I've got to get into a flipping seaplane!"

I thanked her and let her know that I would fill her in as soon as I got bailed out. Then I told her that she was the best sister anyone could have before hanging up. I motioned Terry over and whispered to that her Jessie would be calling. She nodded and took my arm to lead me down the hallway toward the cells, stopping before a restroom, "Go on in there and clean yourself up and then I want to hear what the hell you've gotten yourself into. You're not exactly keeping a low profile."

I stumbled into the lavatory, leaned against the sink, peered into a small mirror, and took stock. One eye was almost swollen shut and blood crusted under my nose and around my puffy lips. I lifted my shirt and examined the bruises along my torso from my ribcage to my kidneys. *Not too bad! Those guys are really lightweights when it comes to giving a beating.*

The hot water spigot wasn't yielding anything except a rusty drop and a small spider that was upset for being disturbed so I cranked open the cold and splashed my face. The water ran red for a few minutes and finally cleared. Pulling a handful of paper towels from the dispenser, I dabbed the gashes along the side of my face until the blood slowed and began to coagulate. I was worried about damage to my kidneys, but when I urinated the liquid ran clear. I felt I had cleaned up as well as possible and opened the door to a scowling Deputy White Feather, "Okay Jones, what gives?"

I put my finger to my lips and pointed to the walls and my ears to indicate that someone may hear us. I scanned the walls for any cameras and when I didn't see any, I moved my finger across my palm in a writing motion letting her know I needed something to write with.

Sighing heavily, Terry pulled a pad from a pocket in her vest and a pen from the pocket of her shirt. She shoved them at me, "This better be good," she hissed.

I scribbled,

Charlie and Danny Svenson are missing. Believe abducted at Thoroughbred Facility. Something's going down tonight!

Terry read over my shoulder and looked at me with wide eyes and sputtered, "Why the hell didn't you just notify the police?"

It irked me that she was still talking. I scowled and again I motioned to the walls and to my ears and wrote,

Don't know who's listening. 72 hours before police even interested! Can't wait!

She grabbed the pad and pen from hand and rapidly scrawled,

Okay. The Task Force is zeroing in on that place. I'll contact them and let them know. It may take a day or two.

I shook my head violently, the motion making me slightly nauseous,

No time! We're not waiting! Those kids are in danger! Going in with or without the TF.

She stared into my eyes for a few moments, struggling with her decision before nodding, taking the pad and writing,

You're right, we can't wait. I'll let the TF know and maybe they can mobilize more quickly. But you're not going anywhere until the judge sets bail and you're released.

I nodded and she took my arm, shuffling out a door to another hallway that led to the cells.

It was a typical holding cell, floors so sticky they threatened to pull your shoes from your feet and walls covered with more graffiti than paint. The smell of stale vomit and urine invaded my olfactory senses. The twenty-by-fifteen room was crowded with five fellow miscreants whose charges ranged from drunk and disorderly to domestic abuse. One of the cellmates was coming down from a high, his hands shaking and his head jerking violently.

No one seemed interested in me, so I found a bunk in the corner, sat on the tattered mattress and waited. A while later, a cop called my name from the front of the cell, "Jones, your lawyer's here. Step up and I'll get you to the interview room."

I stepped up and he cautioned the other prisoners before unlocking the door and leading me down another begrimed hallway to a small eight-by-ten room with a table and two chairs in the center. A tall man dressed in a three-piece suit, with closely cropped salt-and pepper hair and steel rim glasses covering green eyes, walked up to me with his hand extended, "Mr. Jones, my name is Merritt

Nash. I've been retained by Ms. Jessica McCormack to represent you in this matter."

I shook his hand, and we sat opposite each other at the table. I gave him the 'Reader's Digest' version of the events ending with "I'm pleading not guilty, but I need to get out as soon as possible."

He nodded, "Of course, we should be able to arrange that most expeditiously." He leaned over and scrutinized my face, "It seems that there are three witnesses who claim you attacked them on private property, but you seem to have received the worst of it. Do you wish to make a countercharge?"

My smile split my bottom lip, "If it comes to that I have that many witnesses who will tell the truth, but I don't think there will be anyone to press charges in a few days."

His eyes widened slightly, he straightened his tie and cleared his throat, "I hope you're not considering retaliation. As a member of the bar, I can't be a party to that."

My smile widened, cracking open more of my split lips, "Don't worry counselor, I'm not going on some sort of vendetta. What I have in mind is perfectly legal." I grinned again, baiting him a bit, "Or it should be."

The twinkle in his eye told me he wasn't too concerned, "Very well then, I'll see you in court in a few minutes."

Twenty minutes later two deputies came to the cell, cuffed all of us prisoners and led us downstairs to the basement, through a maze of unpainted hallways and back upstairs to a room with a window looking into the courtroom.

<hr>

The judge was twenty minutes late. I was last in line on the docket, so I had to wait for my cellmates to complete their hearings. I was getting anxious by the time my case was announced two hours later. The prosecutor was a wispy man with a hook nose and pinched mouth surrounded by a salt-and-pepper goatee. He presented the case in a dry formal manner before sitting down.

When the judge finally asked how I wished to plea, it was close to one o'clock. I responded, "Not guilty." And my attorney took over to arrange bail.

I almost fell out of my chair when the prosecutor argued for a ridiculous amount of one hundred thousand dollars. He cited the fact that I was armed when I illegally entered private property and accosted three men.

Merritt stood and walked around the defense table. He stopped in front of me and pointed to my swollen face, "Your honor, my client was distraught and concerned by the disappearance of two innocent children. Yes, he admits that he was on private property, but there was no posting anywhere around. And yes, he was armed but never drew his weapon. And, when this case reaches trial, we'll demonstrate that Mr. Jones did not instigate the altercation, but was only defending himself. As you can see from the injury to his face, the three men whom he is accused of attacking obviously got the better of him."

He continued, "My client is a respected member of this community and owns a business in town. His daughter lives with him and he poses no flight risk. It is unconscionable that such a punitive bail amount be imposed in what was clearly a misunderstanding that got out of hand. I move that the charges be dropped or at the very least be reduced from a felony to a misdemeanor." *I don't know where Jessie got this guy, but he's a keeper.*

The prosecutor began to rise from his chair when the judge motioned him down, "I understand your point counselor. Mr. Jones does seem to have gotten the worst of it. However, trespassing and assault are serious charges. Sheriff McGraw brought them personally and I must give them credence. I'll leave the motion to reduce the charges to the examination of all the facts prior to his next court appearance."

He pointed at the prosecutor, "As for your bail request, I also find it to be excessive and unsubstantiated. Bail is set at ten thousand dollars." I shook Merritt's hand before they shuffled me off to the maze leading back to the jail.

An hour later, I walked out the front doors of the sheriff's office and into the sunlight. Jessie stood there holding Max's hand. As soon as Max saw me, she ran to me. I scooped her up into my arms and we both hugged each other tightly until Max pulled her head back and stared at my scabbed, black and blue face, "Dad, I was so worried about you. Are you alright?" She reached up and softly caressed my swollen eye, "Does it hurt? It looks awful."

Her little fingers were just the salve I needed. I kissed her on the cheek and in sotto voce growled, "You should see the other guy," and wiggled my eyebrows, grimacing against the sharp pain.

Max wasn't in a lighthearted mood. Tears bubbled up from her eyes and she punched my arm, "It's not funny Dad! You could have been killed. You have to be more careful! Who's gonna rescue Charlie if you're not around, and I don't want to be an orphan either. Please promise me you'll take care of yourself."

I brushed the tears from her cheek, hugged her and gave her another kiss, "Sweetie, I'll do everything I can to stay safe. But sometimes things get out of our control and we need to be prepared for them. Jessie and I are going to try our hardest to find Charlie and Danny. But until then I need you to stay brave and take care of Mike. He's probably pretty scared right now. Can you do that for me?"

Jessie walked up and put her arms around both of us and proclaimed, "Max, your Dad is one of the smartest and most resilient guys I know. A few little scrapes aren't going to slow him down. We'll find your friends!"

Our group hug was interrupted by a large shadow looming over us from the stairs above. Sheriff McGraw looked down and snickered, "Well book-man, you're out for now. Your fingerprint results just came back from the FBI NICS. Seems like you used to be some federal agent. You musta ridden a desk since you can't defend yourself too good." He snorted, "Maybe you've learned your lesson not to mess with real law enforcement."

Jessie pulled away from us and stepped up to her full height, staring into his eyes close enough that he had to take a step back. The muscles in her arms were like ropes and she cut a formidable figure when she barked, "You made a big mistake, Sheriff. As they say, 'Don't poke the bear'." She pointed at me, "You messed with my baby and now you've got me. If I were you, I'd be looking over my shoulder from now on."

She took another step toward him, and he backed up again. The smirk had disappeared from his face as he sputtered, "Are you threatening me?" He looked around for some backup, but we were the only ones nearby. His hand went to the weapon on his belt, "I'm an officer of the law and you need to back up or I'll arrest you."

As quick as a blink Jessie's hand was covering his, the muscles on her forearm forming knots, as she squeezed his fingers against the metal until he flinched. A slight smile turned up the corners of her mouth "If you want to keep that hand, I suggest you let go of the pistol and get the hell out of here before I get upset."

McGraw looked at me with eyes that almost pleaded. I almost felt sorry for him. I've felt that grip, before. I grinned, "Don't look at me. Remember I just ride a desk, but I've seen her like this and it ain't pretty. You should probably leave."

Jessie released her grip and the sheriff took a step back rubbing his hand. As soon as he felt he was a safe distance away, he puffed up and tried to regain his composure, but unfortunately his voice cracked halfway through, "This ain't over. We'll be meeting again."

Jessie's face broke into a wide smile and she teased, "Good. I can't wait."

We turned and walked away. I chuckled at Jessie's antics until I spied Anne and Mike down the street. The pain written across their faces sobered my mood immediately. Phil and Faith were standing beside them, forlorn expressions painted across their faces. Jessie's eyes followed my glance before turning to me, "I hope you have a plan."

CHAPTER 15

J ESSIE, MAX AND I JOINED the four of them. Anne didn't say a word, she just walked up to me and caressed the side of my face, her blue eyes pleading with mine. I took her hand from my face and kissed her fingers, "We'll find her, I promise. Let's get back to the shop and formulate a plan together."

Jessie put her arm around Anne's shoulders and whispered, "Come on sweetheart. Zeke is the best there is. If anyone can fix this, it's him."

I looked at Jessie and blurted, "I'm only second best, but Jessie and I will solve this and get Charlie home." I glanced down at Max, "I know I shouldn't make promises, but I can feel it in my soul that Charlie and Danny are alright and just waiting for us to find them. But right now, I need coffee and a shower."

Max took my hand in hers and pulled me toward the shop, "I know, Dad, I feel it too. We better get started."

The two of us followed Jessie, Anne and the others down the hill and into the shop where Silas was waiting with a steaming cup of coffee and a grim look on his face. He turned his face sideways to examine my cuts and bruises. "Welcome back Master Zeke. I trust you were able to give as well as you got?"

The coffee scalded my lips as I took a sip and then answered, "A bit, but you know what they say, 'Revenge is a dish better served cold'. I'm going to run upstairs and clean up. When I get back down, we'll close the shop so we're not interrupted while we put together a plan of action. Max, I'm starving. Can you and Jessie go down the street and grab me a couple of sandwiches?"

Max grabbed Jessie's hand and blurted, "Sure Dad. Is anyone else hungry?" She picked up a pad and pen and proceeded to take orders from Phil, Faith and Mike. Anne declined, even though her gaunt look hinted that she hadn't eaten since this nightmare had begun.

I downed the remainder of my coffee as Jessie and Max walked out with me. I turned before I started up the steps to the apartment and declared, "Grab something for Anne. She looks like she may pass out and we need all of us to be sharp."

•————————•

The shower was blessedly scalding, and I let the water beat against my face and torso. Blood dripped down for a couple of minutes before the water turned pink and then ran clear. After ten minutes the water, slowly lost heat and began to run cold. I turned the hot handle completely off and let the frigid stream rejuvenate me and clear my mind.

After my skin was covered in goosebumps, I turned the water off and stepped before the fogged mirror. I dried off, wrapping the towel around my waist and then used a hand towel to wipe away the mist and stared at the disfigured battle zone of my face. The cold had reduced the swelling around my eye leaving only the slightest swelling of the skin around the brow. The cuts and scrapes were minor and only one above my eye required a butterfly bandage.

The darn flesh colored plastic kept folding upon itself and adhering to the other side and I had to grab a new one. I was struggling with another strip trying to apply it over my eye when a soft hand reached up and took the bandage from me. Her voice whispered, "Here, let me help you, you're making a mess."

Anne's hands were gentle and I breathed in the lavender scent of her as she squeezed the cut together and smoothed the bandage across my eyebrow and forehead. When she finished, she pulled me into a hug and snuffled, "I'm sorry you have to go through all of this but I have complete faith in you. I know you can't make any promises, but please find Charlie and Danny."

I looked down into her eyes and resisted the urge to kiss her full lips. Instead, I held her tightly and whispered, "I'll do everything I can, and with Jessie here, I'm confident we'll find them."

I held her at arm's length and stared into her eyes, "There's a lot of work to do, so I need to get dressed. Why don't you have a seat on the couch, and I'll be right out. After this is over, we'll continue this discussion, just the two of us. Would you call Noah while you wait, and ask him to join us? We're going to need his help."

My ribs were aching and raising my arms to pull on a tee-shirt followed by a lightweight sweatshirt over my head was agonizing, the collars adding insult to injury as they slid roughly over the bruises and cuts on my face. After I pulled on a pair of jeans, I applied some Aquaphor to the larger abrasions, strapped a sheath containing a five-inch knife to my ankle and laced up my boots. I walked out of the bedroom, grabbed the dossier from the desk, took Anne's hand in mine and headed downstairs.

———•———

We reached the street and were assaulted with the luxurious odor of fried food. My stomach growled in anticipation as we watched Jessie and Max stepping up the street, toting greasy bags. I grabbed the bags from Max and we stepped into the store. I was closing the door when Noah appeared around the corner, a grim look on his face. Silas cleared a table and we spread the food across the top. Everyone piled in and grabbed food while Noah went to the back and set a laptop down. I grabbed a roast beef sandwich and joined Noah on a stuffed chair in front of the window. The others brought their food and huddled around.

Just then a sharp rap came at the door. I peered over a bookcase and recognized the ramrod straight profile of Christopher Sloan behind the windows. Silas was already at the door, opened it a crack and proclaimed, "Sorry, Christopher, we're closed for the day. We're, uhh, performing an inventory. Perhaps you could come back tomorrow."

I joined Silas and whispered, "It's all right, he's one of us. Go ahead and let him in."

Silas smiled and stepped back, let the elderly gentleman in, and shook his hand before securing the lock. Christopher grinned, grabbed my hand, whispering "Isn't this exhilarating!" while I escorted him to the table.

As soon as he sat down, Scar jumped onto his lap, curled into a circle and fell asleep.

I quickly introduced him around and offered him tea, but he demurred, "The sun's over the yardarm! I hope you still have some of that fine whisky stashed away. All this excitement has made me thirsty. How about a couple of fingers?"

I pulled the bottle from the cabinet, splashed in three inches of the amber liquid and handed it to him.

Swallowing a large chunk of my sandwich I washed it down with a gulp of tea and explained, "A few days ago before this went down, I was recruited by Terry White Feather to support a task force that's looking into drug and human trafficking in the area. The information gathered by that task force is contained in the folder there on the table." Anne picked it up and scanned it while I continued, "The feds are heading up the multiagency task force including the FBI, ATF and the U.S. Marshals. The state Bureau of Investigation is also involved. It seems the authorities are convinced that Sheriff McGraw and some in the sheriff's department are involved, so they've been kept out of the loop on the task force."

Anne passed the folder to Noah, who studied it before handing it to Phil, who just shook his head and pushed it toward Jessie.

She studied it for a few moments and when she finished, Jessie looked up her face contorted with concern, "They're talking big time stuff here, cartels and the Nevada mob."

I stared into her eyes and growled, "Yep, the same bad guys we tried to take down last year. That means we're going to be dealing with professionals as well as those locals from last night. Gonna make it tough."

Christopher was quietly sipping his drink when I turned to him, "Do you have an update from Officer White Feather?"

"She wanted me to tell you that she's working the feds as hard as she can. They're getting a warrant approved and a team together. She said it may take some time."

Anne and Phil immediately started grumbling and Phil spat out, "We don't have time! Those are our kids, damnit!"

I tried to settle everyone, "Let me give Terry a call and find out more about the situation," before stepping away from the table and dialing the number of her burner phone.

She picked up on the first ring, "I figured you would call. I'm afraid I don't have any good news. We're having trouble with the warrant. The local judge may be compromised, so we are chasing down a federal judge. But she's out hunting pheasant and not answering her phone, probably out of cell range."

My temper came to the surface and I clenched my jaw before responding, "We don't have time to muddle through the judicial bureaucratic maze. Those children could be whisked away at any time. We need to move soon!"

I heard Terry take a deep breath before uttering, "I'm just as frustrated as you are, Zeke, but they don't want to jeopardize their bust so they're moving cautiously. They told me to ask you to have patience."

I could feel the blood rush to my face before I shouted, "Patience my ass, those kids are the top priority, and their bust is way down the list of importance. We're going to get those kids with or without the task force."

Terry whined, "Zeke, I'm with you two hundred per-cent. I'm friends with both of those kids and their parents. Let me make some calls and I'll get back to you in fifteen."

She hung up before I could respond. I paced the front of the store until my blood pressure dropped and I turned to Anne, "I forgot about the photos and didn't have a chance to study them on Charlie's phone. Can you send them to Noah so he can put them on his laptop's screen for all of us to look at?"

Anne fumbled around in her pocket and pulled the phone out before conferring with Noah for his contact in-formation. Her hands were trembling as she pushed a few keys, "You should have them."

Noah nodded, made some movement with his mouse and turned the laptop around so we could all see the images. Anne pointed and choked, "See, there's the truck and those men appear to be loading or offloading some boxes. The focus isn't great and they're a little far away, but one of them looks like Hank to me."

Jessie scooted beside her while Phil and I looked over her shoulder. Max leaned in from the other side. Phil tensed, uttered an oath and sputtered, "That's him for sure. I'm gonna wring his sorry neck when I catch him."

I put my hand on his arm and affirmed, "You'll get your chance …"

Jessie shrieked, "Look there in the shadows. Isn't that a cop car? You can just make out some of the unit number, it's 'something 13!' I wonder if we can find out all the unit numbers for the sheriff's fleet?"

Noah turned the laptop around and began rapidly slapping at keys. He moved the mouse, double-clicked and looked up at me with a smile on his face, "There are two patrol units whose designators end in 13. One is assigned to Deputy Noonan and guess what, the other is driven by our old friend Clifford McGraw! I wonder…" His voice trailed off as he pushed a few more keys and moved the mouse around before he smirked, "Deputy Noonan's car has been in the shop for repairs for the last three weeks. I believe we've got the SOB!"

I patted him on his back, "Good job, buddy. Now all we need to do is get in there without all of us getting shot up!"

His grin widened, he nodded and went back to the computer, fingers flying across the keyboard. While he typed on the keyboard and fiddled with the mouse he explained, "After I got back to the ranch, I was able to put the high-altitude drone up without the bad guys noticing. I flew it in the opposite direction of the facility before gaining altitude and then brought it back around and hovered it over the facility. It was high enough that no one would be able to detect the sound of the propellers. I then took both hi-res and infrared videos of the entire facility. Because I had to fly at that high altitude the images aren't perfect, but they are good enough for our purposes. This first one is the hi-res video. Let's take a look." We all huddled around his chair and watched as a grainy image appeared and shapes slowly began to come into focus.

We could make out people scurrying about, some leading horses and others performing typical ranch tasks. Two appeared to be working on a fence and another person was hefting a toolbox toward the barn. A tractor hauling a trailer came into view and headed down a path in the direction of the ocean.

There appeared to be six armed men patrolling the perimeter. We watched as they made their rounds, ducking in and out of the trees bordering the facility. I pointed to them, "These are our first targets. We need to study them to see if there is a pattern to their patrols so we can take them out cleanly."

Jessie looked around the room and growled, "There's four of us, no problem! What about surveillance?"

Noah pointed the mouse and ran the cursor along the border between his property and the Thoroughbred facility, "They have cameras and motion detectors along this edge of their property, so we can be sure they have the same on the other side." He moved the cursor to the corner of the barn, "Most of the buildings also have cameras as you can see here." He moved the cursor to other buildings highlighting small protrusions from the eaves of each, "And here and here."

His face scrunched up and he turned and looked at me, "They also have spotlights on all night. It's going to make it hard to not be seen."

Phil was standing to the right of Noah and wondered out loud, "Maybe we could take out their power, blind them for a minute while we make our move."

Jessie pondered a moment, pointed at one of the structures then blurted, "That looks like a generator shed. That means we can't take out their power. We might have five seconds before the power switches. That would give us a head start, but there's a lot of ground to cover between the trees and the compound before the lights come back on."

Max was standing in front of me peering at the screen. She took the mouse from Noah and made a few keystrokes with her other hand. The image expanded and the details of a boathouse came into focus. A sleek cigarette boat was parked outside along a pier jutting into the water.

She grunted and I leaned over to get a better perspective on what she was looking at. Nothing stood out so I asked, "What is it honey?"

She looked up with a mischievous grin as wide as the Cheshire Cat and bubbled, "There aren't any cameras on the boathouse and there aren't any trees between it and the compound. Why can't someone go in from the water? I don't see any lights around the building."

My little genius!

I smiled, gave her a squeeze and messed her hair, "That's brilliant! If we go under the cover of darkness someone can be at the compound before they realize we're there." I looked around at the others and they were all smiling.

Jessie punched my arm and whispered, "Musta got those smarts from her mother." She gave Max a hug and addressed Noah, "Sounds like a good start, but it's at least a hundred yards from the water to the compound. A frontal assault by all of us runs the risk of detection and then we'd be sitting ducks."

I nodded in agreement, "You're right. But one person could probably get up there undetected and maybe take out the security system if we knew where it was. Then we could envelop them and be assured no one could escape, or worse, take the kids out the front."

Noah began fiddling with the mouse and made a few keystrokes, "Let's try to figure it out. If there's any insulation in the roofs of those buildings, we won't be able to detect heat sources inside, but we may be in luck since most ranch or farm outbuildings don't need to be insulated. I've overlayed the IR heat sensor data onto the video. They must have one heck of a central computer and server system to handle that many sensors. And those computers put off a lot of heat. Let's see what we've got."

The IR images wavered on the screen. The barn was obvious and the heat from a dozen

large equine bodies shimmered within. Two smaller heat sources moved about the barn. Noah pointed, "Those are probably the guys who take care of the horses."

He moved the cursor over a large round structure. There were no heat sources within, and he opined, "Pretty sure that's a covered arena. See the sides are open."

Moving the cursor again, he hovered over a long building with stairs leading to the inside on one end and windows reflecting the light. Heat emanated from the entire structure. A heat source walked toward the building and its signature disappeared as it entered. Noah quipped, "I'd say that's a bunkhouse. You can see a much brighter signature from what's probably a heater in the middle." After a minute, a heat source exited from the building and walked across the compound.

He moved the cursor to another medium-sized building that Jessie had pointed out earlier. Noah yipped, "Bingo! This must be their computer center where all the servers are located. You can tell because those servers put off a lot of heat. None of the other buildings are putting out that much. There's a chimney protruding from the roof so I'd bet the generators are in the same building, which means the power distribution center is there as well. Might be able to pull off a 'two fer', power and surveillance, if we can get in undetected."

I nodded as I stared at the screen. Something about a smaller building near the bunkhouse pricked my interest and I pointed, "Look? There are two small heat signatures in that small building. One is still, but the other is moving back and forth. I think that might be the kids. We need to make that our prime target!" Anne put her fingers to her mouth and gasped as she watched the tiny glowing figures.

We watched the screen and dismissed two other small buildings as not important to our effort. While we were watching, an SUV pulled through the gate and up to a row of vehicles near the bunkhouse. Three images carrying what appeared to be rifles exited the vehicle and entered the bunkhouse.

Jessie shook her head and let out an exasperated sigh, "Great, more reinforcements for the bad guys. And we don't know how many are already in there because we can't detect them."

Noah chimed in, "There's probably one or more in their computer room, monitoring the cameras and motion detectors and maintaining the gear. They're probably armed as well."

As I watched the yellow blips on the screen, I began to formulate a plan, "We're going to need a command-and-control center and eyes in the sky giving us real-time information when we form our assault. That means Noah needs to stay back which brings us down to Jessie, Phil, Anne and me. I don't mean to offend, but Anne, you and Phil don't have the tactical experience for this operation. Phil, how about you make sure they don't escape out the front gate….and of course keep any reinforcements from coming in?"

Phil smiled and stood, "If Anne will give me that shotgun no one goes in or out!"

Christopher interjected, "I'm too old to run around, but I still fire expert at the range. I'll stand guard with Phil.

Anne interjected, "I can relieve Noah on the computers and operate the comm, but I can't fly the drone."

Max jumped up and sputtered, "Mike and I know how! Noah lets us fly them when we go over with Charlie to work with the horses. Noah says we're pretty good."

I looked at Noah and he nodded, "Both those kids are naturals. It's because kids today live with computers and video games. I can program a flight pattern so Max won't have to do much anyway. That will free me up for the assault."

Jessie stood and began pacing. She stopped and stared at the computer screen, "That still leaves us outnumbered significantly, seven to three at best. Not very good odds even with the element of surprise. And you said it looked like some of them had military backgrounds."

I massaged my sore ribs and looked up at her, "Well besides the element of surprise, they'll be in disarray for a few minutes after the power goes out." She started to say something, and I held my hand up, "That said, the chances of a successful operation are pretty low. I wonder how Terry's doing with the task force?"

We continued to formulate our plans for the assault and fifteen minutes later Terry called, "It's a no-go! Those stuffed shirts are still muddling." Her voice was rising and she shouted, "And they had the audacity to tell me to order you to stand down. The hell with that, I'm making some calls and then I'll be right over!"

We spent the next twenty minutes setting up plans for our incursion before a loud knock came from the front door. I looked out between the lettering on the door and saw Terry and three large shapes behind her. I didn't recognize anyone else, so I slipped my Glock from its holster before unlatching the lock and letting them in.

Terry had a murderous grin on her face when she turned to me, "These are my cousins. They're here to help." She turned to the very large men behind her, "This is Jeb, Lee and Petey. They all have military service, One Marine and two Army. Say Hi to Zeke."

They were all native American. One sported a mohawk haircut while the other two's heads were shaved. The three carried AR-styled rifles and towered over me, their faces somber. I shook hands with each of them, their grips firm, while Terry continued, "Jeb's sister died from a fentanyl overdose last year and Lee and Petey's sister, Suzy, went missing last week."

I led them to the back and introduced them before we sat down.

Jessie smiled and quipped, "Things are looking up. We just may have a shot at this. Let's finish the plan and get moving."

Christopher raised his glass and beamed before draining the liquid, "Oorah!"

CHAPTER 16

I T WASN'T A COMPLICATED PLAN. Christopher and Phil were to guard the gate against any ingress or egress. Jessie, Terry and Noah would come in from Noah's ranch and the cousins would enter from the other side of the property. I was to enter from the water and try to get to the generator shack without detection. Everyone was to wait until I could disable the power and security systems. Noah uploaded an App on each of our phones that communicated each of our positions utilizing the 'Emergency SOS' feature. Each team was distinguished by a different color on Noah's computer; Green for Jessie's team, Red for the cousins (they insisted) and Blue for yours truly.

Anne, Max and Mike were in Noah's barn, manning the computer and initiating a drone that would fly above. We set up a conference call with our cell phones and everyone inserted earbuds so we could stay in touch during our raid. We did a quick comm check before I headed out to the beach while Noah helped maneuver the drone away from the facility before gaining altitude and coming back to hover above.

I donned a light pack with extra ammo, a flashlight and a first aid kit before weaving through the trees to the shore. Fortunately, the tide was out, and I was able to dodge large rocks and skirt along the sand below a low bank until I was directly behind our target.

I poked my head above the bank and ducked down immediately. Two of the guards were standing twenty feet from me, smoking and talking in low voices. There was no way to get around them without detection and I was trying to figure out a way to silently take them out when one of the guards took a long drag from his cigarette and croaked, "We better get back before they miss us. Tonight's the big night and we don't want to miss out on that bonus Hank's been talking about." He flipped his cigarette butt in my direction and the two of them wandered toward the east side of the facility, disappearing into the trees.

As soon as they were out of earshot I whispered, "Jeb, two bogies coming your way. Take care. I'm on my way to the generator."

A soft 'Roger' came as a response.

There was a small swale running along the west side of the property and I was able to crouch low enough to avoid detection while staying on my feet until I reached a point two hundred feet from the shack where the depression petered out. I was going to be exposed the rest of the way. I figured I would attract attention if I just jumped up and started running. Besides my knee probably wouldn't hold up. The only option was to brazen it out and act like I belonged there. I whispered, "I'm going to walk up there. Keep your eyes peeled."

I stood and began to walk forward. Anne's muffled voice startled me, "Someone's on your left and walking your way!"

I hunched into my jacket and glanced over. A large, bearded man with an AK-47 slung over his shoulder was walking in my direction, smoking a cigarette and peering at his phone. He didn't notice me and I crouched down, my back to him, as if I was tying my boot laces.

When he was within ten feet he looked up and growled, "What the hell are you doing? Get back to your post."

I heard his steps approach and slipped the blade from the sheath on my ankle. He started to grab my collar and shouted, "Who the hell…?" when I inserted the knife under his rib cage and into his heart. He let out one surprised gasp as blood poured over my hand. Before he could fall, I hooked his arm around my shoulder, half dragged him to the generator shack and laid him in the shadow of the overhanging eave.

Removing the knife, I wiped the blood off on his jacket and edged to the door of the shack. Inching the door open, I peered inside to see a man and a woman, both wearing sidearms, sitting in front of a console containing four monitors, each split into a two-by-two grid displaying the feeds from various cameras. A panel above the console depicted the status of various motion detectors. Eight racks of computer equipment filled the wall behind the console, red, amber and green lights flashing their messages. A large generator dominated one end of the building and I could see the master power panel attached on the wall at one end.

Heavy metal music was loudly playing from a boombox lying on a table scattered with pizza boxes and soda cans. The music masked my sound as I pulled my Glock and rushed behind the operators, hitting the man across the side of his head. He slumped as I grabbed the woman by her hair and yanked her from the chair and to the floor. She let out a scream and reached for her pistol before I stepped on her hand and ground my heel into her wrist.

This time her scream threatened to break my eardrums, but she was tough, and she rolled away and reached for a red alarm button on the wall. Before I could stop her, she jammed the button and then turned on me with a snarl. A loud claxon began pulsing and I could hear shouts outside.

I shouted into my phone, "Hang loose, I'm almost there and then things will go dark." Just then, the woman plowed into my solar plexus and we both went down with a thud. She was strong and fighting like her life depended on it. Her fingernails ripped at my eyes and down my cheek. I grabbed one hand and twisted until I heard a loud pop along with another scream. Suddenly her other hand came up with a six-inch blade headed toward my neck. I rolled and the knife grazed my forearm before I landed a roundhouse into her face. Blood spurted over the floor and she dropped, eyes glazed.

Pulling her up, I ripped a data cable from the back of a computer and trussed her up, hands together and then looped it around her ankles. She wasn't going anywhere so I jumped up and over to the master panel. The large breaker in the middle was locked in place with a large padlock. We were running out of time and I was out of patience. I figured the compound had been alerted so I pulled my Glock and shot the lock. The locking mechanism flew away and I ripped the hasp off and was ready to throw the switch when the door flew open and two bad guys barreled in, guns drawn. I fired my pistol, pulled the breaker and hit the floor as everything went dark. A staccato of gunfire erupted outside.

One of the two guys at the door did something stupid, he turned on his flashlight and swept it around the room. I couldn't see him with the bright light shining my way so I just aimed where I thought center mass might be and fired.

A loud scream came from the door, "Damnit, he hit me. I'm bleeding. Give me a hand Hank!" *We meet again!*

Hank hissed, "Shut up you fool!" His voice turned toward me, "There's only one way in or out. Ain't no way you're getting out of here. And you're outnumbered. Why don't you give up now and we'll let you go."

My eyes had adjusted to the dark and I could just make out a dark form crouched behind the console. He was right, the exit was effectively blocked. I was trapped unless I could take him and his partner out.

I fired a shot and scrambled behind the generator so I could stand. Two gunshots followed me and split the wood walls behind. The fight was raging outside and I needed to get out there to help. I slipped to one side and fired a shot before rolling to the other side. Hank's shadow moved and he reached around the computer rack to fire a round. I was waiting. My shot was slightly off and hit the equipment in front of Hank, but metal flew everywhere and Hank screamed, "Damnit, my eye." Reflexively, he grabbed his eye and stood and my next shot was dead center in his chest. His mouth formed an 'O' and he dropped to the ground.

I could hear the other man moaning and slowly approached. He was very young, barely out of his teens, sitting in a pool of blood and holding his side. He looked up at the Glock in my hand pleading, "Please don't kill me. Please help me. I'm bleeding."

I walked up to him and checked out his wound. It was superficial and the blood was already coagulating. Pulling his hands behind him, I ripped out another cable and bound his hands and feet. I growled, "You'll live. Now tell me where they've got the kids!"

"They're in the building next to the bunkhouse. Please, mister, I didn't do anything. Those kids are off limits according to Hank. Said the boss uses them as a bonus for the important customers. No one is allowed near them. I'm just here to provide guard duty. You have to believe me. Kids ain't my thing. Bunch of perverts if you ask me."

The firefight outside was raging, shouts and curses filled my ears from the members of our team. I needed to get back out to help, but I had more questions for this dirtbag while he was still worried that I was going to kill him, "What about the drugs? When's the shipment? How do they get here?"

He croaked, "I can't tell you that. Those people are powerful! They'll kill me even in prison."

I reached over and jammed two fingers into the hole in his side ripping at the flesh and eliciting a shriek, "If you think the cops will save you, you're mistaken. I'm not a cop and I'm the one with power right now and if you don't talk, you won't be going to prison. You'll be dead."

The man shuddered and began crying, "Please stop! I'll talk, I'll talk! There's a shipment already in the barn waiting to be picked up tonight. It's hidden in the feed. I don't know exactly how they get the drugs here, but it has something to do with the horses coming in from Canada."

I let him go and started outside before another question popped into my mind. I yanked his hair back until he was looking at me, "And what about the kids they kidnap? Where do they hide them. Where do they take them from here?"

Snot was running from his nose, his eyes were streaked with red and he was shaking, "I'm not sure. I wasn't part of that operation, but I heard that they take them to some island where the rich people can have their fun before they smuggle them across the border and sell them."

I dropped him to the ground, where he curled into the fetal position and headed for the door.

More bad guys must have arrived between the time Noah recorded his video and our assault. Men were firing from three different buildings toward the trees on either side of the property. At least eight men wearing assault gear including Kevlar vests were firing from the barracks and the building holding the kids, laying down heavy fire in the direction of Noah's ranch, effectively pinning down Jessie and her team. Four others were hiding behind a truck and firing into a stand of trees where the cousins were situated. Another two were advancing along the side of the barn and would soon be able to fire on the cousins from the rear. But their backs were to me and I lined up a shot with my M-4.

I spoke into my phone, "Jeb, there are two bogies coming in on your right. I'm going to take at least one out but watch your flank." I squeezed the trigger and the man went down.

A voice sputtered, "Thanks, we have him." A shot rang out and the second man crumpled to the ground, "Jeb's been hit. He's alright, but out of commission. Taking a lot of fire over here."

The men behind the truck had noticed my fire and scrambled for cover behind a stack of pallets. While two of them kept the cousins pinned down, the other two turned toward me and opened fire.

I ducked around the corner of the building, wood splintering over my head. Laying in the prone position, I peeked around the corner of the building and received another volley, shattering wood and kicking up gravel into my face. I felt a stream of blood inching down into my ear and yelled, "Jessie, sitrep!"

Jessie's calm voice came back, "Welcome back, Little Baby. Everything's kosher over here. Terry took one in the thigh, but she bandaged it herself and is back in action. Tough broad, she's a keeper."

She chuckled, "On the tactical front, we're holding our own, but there's too many of them. We can't make any progress. Got any ideas?"

While I was talking to Jessie, one of the bad guys slipped around the corner and a red dot wiggled around my torso. I began praying the Hail Mary as my last seconds counted down, but the shooter jerked and fell to the ground ten feet in front of me. I looked toward the gate where Christopher stood smiling, his rifle pointed up. He used two fingers to give me a small salute from the edge of his beret and slipped back behind the columns of the gate.

I returned the salute and turned back to my next problem, "Anne, give me an assessment. We need to know where all the bad guys are."

Anne's voice was clear and without any hesitation, "We can see four people near the truck and the pallets. There's at least another six near the barracks and that other building. Another one is hiding behind the barn and firing at Jessie. If you can get to the barn, you may be able to get behind those at the barracks, but it looks like Terry's cousins need your help."

Phil's voice came across, "Zeke, we think it's time to call up the reserves. That would be Christopher and me. There's no activity out here and we can use the cover of the hedges along the front to flank the bad guys holding Jeb and the others down. Then you can go help Jessie."

Anne's voice came across, "I'll head down to relieve Phil and Christopher at the gate. I'll take Noah's truck and park it across the front of the gate. Max and Mike are better at the computer than I am anyway. Phil, I'll need the shotgun back."

We didn't have any other options and I acquiesced, "Okay, lets do it. But someone's probably got word out about our foray, and reinforcements could be arriving any time. If they show up Anne, stay hidden in the trees and take out who you can and let us know. Phil, let me know when you can provide covering fire and I'll head to the barn."

A scratchy 'Roger' responded.

I changed the clip on the M-4 and continued to trade shots with the guys behind the pallets and a ninety seconds later heard Noah's big diesel flying up to the gate and sliding to a stop. Anne jumped out, traded a rifle for the shotgun and Phil and Christopher disappeared behind the hedges.

I began peppering the bad guys in front of me with shots as quickly as I could squeeze the trigger of the semi-automatic. Phil's voice rose through the static and sound of the gunfire, "Okay, we're in position. We're ready to put down a distraction so you can get to the barn. How about you guys, Petey?"

Petey spoke, "We're ready."

I stood and tested my knee. It was twenty yards to the edge of the barn and I was sure it would hold up. I shouted "On three! One, two three!" I took off under the cacophony of semi-automatic AR-15s and hunting rifles firing as rapidly as possible.

Dirt and pebbles flew into the air in front of me as I dashed for the protection of the barn. I was five feet from my destination when my foot caught on a hidden hazard, just barely twisting my knee enough for me to fly face first into the planks of the barn. Shots impacted all around me as I crab-walked on hands and feet to the relative safety around the corner.

Max's voice chimed in, "Someone's on the opposite side of the building. They're going around back and coming up to your end."

I couldn't slip around the front or I would be exposed to the crew at the bunkhouse, so I flattened myself into a prone position and pulled the rifle into my shoulder lining up a shot about three feet high and a few inches off the corner of the barn. Sure enough a dark figure materialized in my sights. I squeezed off a shot and heard a sharp cry.

Max's voice squeaked, "He's getting away!"

I rushed to the back of the barn in time to see a small man limp around the corner. Running up to the corner, I was surprised when he was waiting for me with his gun aimed at my torso. Tucking my head, I rolled away and fired a wild shot, but it was enough to affect his aim. His round ripped through the material of my jacket and a sharp pain screamed from my bicep. I lifted my rifle toward him just as he lined up another shot. I was microseconds faster and his body jerked back as my slug hit him in the shoulder causing his shot to go wild and his rifle to drop to the ground.

But the guy was tough! He pulled a pistol and swung it in my direction before my next shot hit center mass and he crumpled to the ground.

I didn't have time to make sure he was out of the picture before the wood of the barn splintered above my head and gravel erupted from the ground. Two men were at the corner of the building where we suspected the kids were being held and rapidly firing in my direction. They must have been the horse handlers because they were lousy shots, and I was able to slip back around the corner of the barn to relative safety.

I returned to the prone position and worked my way around the corner to take a shot. I was worried about hitting the occupants of the building and wanted to be sure my shots were true. One of the shooters was hiding behind a water trough and popped up every few seconds to fire. I put the sight a foot above the penstock and waited. He came up and I squeezed. The man went down hard and the other guy must have figured he'd had enough and began a zig-zag run for the trees.

I took a quick shot at him as he fled, but capturing him wasn't our goal, so I turned my attention back to the melee taking place behind. Jessie and Terry had spread out, leaving Noah to take the brunt of the fire. He was well protected by a fallen log and I yelled over the phone, "How are you holding up, Noah?"

His voice croaked, "Couldn't be better. These guys are sure expending a lot on ammo over here. Terry and Jessie are trying to flank them. Are you in a position to help?"

I started crawling from the barn and reached a tractor twenty feet away before standing. I had a clear view of the barracks. The baddies were hunkered down along a line on the porch of the building. I hollered, "Jessie and Terry,

I'm at their six and got a bead on one of them. As soon as I take her out, they'll probably scatter. Check your ammo and let's finish these guys."

The woman was concentrating on the fight in front and never even heard the shot that took out her knee. Her scream caught the attention of the others and they all swung around to face me. I began squeezing shots as rapidly as I could and glimpsed Terry rushing the building from the left. One of the bad guys swung his rifle around to take her out, but as soon as he was exposed, I put a bullet through his neck.

Jessie let out a banshee scream as she rushed from the right, her weapon taking out two before she took a hit and fell into the tall grass. I swung my sights to the shooter who had hurt my friend, squeezed and his head exploded, fine red mist spraying the side of the building.

Noah and Terry rushed the rest while I ran to Jessie and knelt beside her, "Damnit Sis, what is it? Where are you hit?"

She raised up on her elbows and grinned at me, "Aw Zeke, I thought you didn't care anymore." And then she winced and put her hand to her side, "Went right through my love handle. Don't think it's anything serious, but it sure stings. Help me up. We still have work to do."

I pushed her down and pulled her shirt up so I could examine the wound. Blood was still oozing from a large gash, but it was slow and coagulating nicely. I pulled my pack off and ripped it open to find a first aid kit, tore open an adhesive gauze pad and slapped it on the wound. I turned my face to her, "Scared the heck out of me for a little scratch. Gonna have to start calling you Big Sissy!"

Jessie giggled and slapped my arm away, "Funny guy! Let's go!"

We jumped up and turned in time to see Terry and Noah standing over two men and a woman lying face down on the ground, their hands bound behind them with zip-ties. The woman and one of the men had blood seeping down their arms. Terry's face was covered with grime and, taking Noah's hand in hers, she smiled at us, "This is fun. When can we do it again? Two of these scumbags need medical attention. I'll call for a couple of ambulances while we get over and see if those kids are in that building."

We jogged to the building and Jessie took one side of the door, while I stood on the other, pistols at the ready. Noah walked up and kicked the door near the doorknob, scattering broken pieces of timber in all directions. A small scream came from within, and Jessie and I charged into a room dimly lit by the half-moon above. The building consisted of a single room and appeared to be a storage space. Shelves filled with small packages lined two walls. Two figures were huddled against one wall and a voice squeaked, "Please don't hurt us! We just want to go home, please!"

Terry pulled a flashlight and shined it at the figures. Two teenage girls were cowering in each other's arms and for a minute I thought one of them was Charlie, but when the light hit her face, I could tell that I was mistaken.

Terry and Noah knelt down beside them and pulled them into their arms. Noah croaked, "Hush. It's okay. It's all over. We're the good guys. We've got an ambulance on the way." He pulled a bottle of water from his pack and handed it to the girl he was consoling.

The other child was sobbing and shaking uncontrollably. Terry held her tight whispering softly "It's okay Suzy,

Lee and Petey are outside waiting for you. Her shaking diminished and she slowly began to relax.

I spoke into my phone, "There are two teens here, but they aren't Charlie or Danny."

I heard a mournful sigh from Anne, "Damnit!"

Jessie walked to the shelves, pulled out a knife and poked the blade into one of the packets, extracting a small amount on the blade and sticking her tongue to it. She turned to me with fury covering her face, "Pure coke! What's in here is probably worth $100 Million, but once they cut it the value increases significantly."

The girls began to calm so Jessie and I headed out the door to help with the remaining firefight. The gunfire from the trees where the cousins were hunkered down was subsiding and Christopher was standing over an inert body on the ground, his rifle digging into the person's neck. He looked up as we approached, "There's only one holdout in the trees and he's just trying desperately to get away. The others are all down for the count. Jeb's been hit in the shoulder. We need to get him to the hospital, but he'll survive."

A loud chirp followed by a siren came from the gate and we all began running in that direction. Before we were halfway there, the loud roar of the shotgun ripped through the air followed by glass shattering and a second boom moments later.

We slowly approached the gate crouching behind the hedge. I peeked over the hedge to see Sheriff McGraw pinned against his cruiser; the shotgun jammed into his neck. Anne's finger was close to the trigger and she was shouting, "What have you done with my daughter you bastard? Where is she?"

The tendons of his neck were stretched to the limit and his face was beet red, sweat pouring down his cheeks. He rasped, "Please, please. I don't know. Please take your finger off that trigger!"

I slowly approached them and softly cooed, "It's okay Anne. I'll take it from here. We need him alive so he can tell us everything he knows." I reached up and wrapped my hands around the barrel of the gun and looked into her eyes, "He is a bastard and he'll get what's coming to him, but we need him alive for now."

Moments passed by before Anne's grip relaxed and I was able to take the shotgun from her. As soon I did, the fool got his hubris back and started shouting at us, "You don't know who you're dealing with! I'm the sheriff and I'm arresting all of you for trespassing and assault!"

Anne grabbed the shotgun from my hands by the barrel and drove the stock into the man's oversized gut. Air and spittle whooshed out of his mouth and he doubled over. Anne brought the gun up in a violent arc contacting his jaw and he fell into a pile, motionless.

Sirens sounded in the distance and just then two black Escalades screamed up the road and slid to a stop in front of us. Agents wearing windbreakers emblazoned with FBI, ATF and DEA logos across the back piled out, pulling their guns and aiming them at us. A tall fit man with closely cropped gun-metal colored hair yelled, "Federal agents, down on the ground!"

Terry walked between us and up to the agent and calmly stated, "Knock it off, Fred! These are the good guys. You guys are about an hour too late!" She waved her arms at the other agents snarling, "And you look like the 'Keystone Kops!' Follow me and I'll show you what we've got, but our highest priority is finding those kids, so don't get in our way!"

The sheriff was sitting on the ground leaning against the gate post. Terry walked over and stood above him, "Clifford McGraw, you're under arrest for drug trafficking and kidnapping."

He looked up and spat, "You don't know what the hell you're doing, Pocahontas. You people don't even have a warrant for busting in here and shooting the place up."

She squatted down in front of him and growled, "That's Deputy Pocahontas to you. Don't need a warrant. I heard a commotion and suspected there might be illegal activities here." She waved her hand toward Jessie, Noah, Anne, Phil and me, "And these fine folks agreed to be my deputies." Turning to one of the Feds, she hollered, "Read this scumbag his rights and get him out of here before his fat mouth gets him shot."

CHAPTER 17

I HEARD HER CALLING "DADDY" BEFORE Max and Mike burst from the trees and began running toward us. I ran forward and scooped each of them under an arm and carried them back toward Noah's property and away from the carnage. Anne and Phil followed close behind. Setting them onto a fallen log, I pulled both into a hug and whispered, "Everything's okay. It's all over now."

Anne came up behind me and pulled Mike into her arms, both of them bawling.

Max pulled back from me and examined my face. She reached up and pinched an inch long splinter and pulled it from my cheek. She wiped away the blood that followed and groaned, "That was so scary. I thought for sure all of you were going to be killed. I tried to grab one of Noah's guns to come help, but Mrs. Louise stopped me and said that I need to do my job and fly the drone because it was important. So, I did but I felt helpless."

I took her face in mine and brushed the tears from her cheeks, "Louise was right and I'm glad you stayed on the drone. Every member of the team had an assignment and you carried yours out flawlessly. You and Mike were the key to us beating these bad guys. We couldn't have done it without having the information you gave us. You guys are the best."

She began to sob and buried her face in my shoulder, "But you didn't find Charlie and Danny! Where are they? What will happen to them?"

I sat on the log between her and Mike and put my arm around each of them. I looked directly into Anne's watery eyes, softly whispering, "We'll find them. I got some information from one of the bad guys and we'll scour the facility for more clues. Don't give up on me."

I stood and turned to Max, "I need to get back over there to find those clues. Why don't you and Mike head back to Louise's. I hear she makes some mean pancakes and then I need you to get back on Noah's computer to find out everything you can about 'Oyster Cove Thoroughbreds'. We need to tie this place to a face and a name or names." I nodded at Anne and Phil. They took the kids' hands and headed back to Noah's.

I jogged back and found pandemonium. Men and women in windbreakers emblazoned with their parent organization stenciled in bold letters ran amok back and forth between buildings. The ambulances were lined up in the driveway where I found Terry leaning over Jeb stretched out on a litter. Jeb's face was ashen, but he smiled when I walked up, "Hey chief, we got 'em didn't we?"

I took his big hand in mine and murmured, "We sure did buddy. How are you doing?"

Terry's face was streaked with soot, and she piped up, "Big galoot took one in the shoulder. Another few inches and it would have taken out a lung. Nicked the clavicle, but the EMTs say he'll be fine." She took Jeb's other hand in hers and stammered, "Jeb, Zeke and I have to start searching this place to find anything we can about where they took those kids. Will you be okay?"

Just then Petey and Lee slumped down beside Terry. Lee's jacket had a rip along the side and Petey's scratched face was speckled with dried sweat and blood. Lee intoned, "Don't worry Terry, we'll look after him. Just go and get those kids back."

Terry and I found Jessie sitting on the steps of the barracks, being patched up properly by an EMT. Her hair was poking in all directions and blood was oozing from a busted lip. She grinned up at us and crowed, "And here I thought retirement life would be boring. Damn, that brought back memories. As soon as my friend here is done, let's get cooking on finding those kids."

Noah walked over and handed each of us an energy bar and a bottle of water, "How do you want to do this, Zeke? Where do you want us to start?"

The four of us eagerly gnawed at our energy bars and emptied the water in our bottles with one swig. An EMT was watching us, pulled four more bottles from a cooler in the ambulance and handed them to us before cleaning and slapping a bandage on an oozing gash on Noah's arm and checking Jessie's bandage. He probably spent more time than necessary and smiled at her as he was doing it and she returned it with a slight blush.

I sipped some water and turned to Jessie, "We need to find something that will give us a clue as to where they took those kids…."

Before I could finish, Fred, the FBI guy, stomped over and announced, "You folks did a good job. We found enough drugs to put the state of New York into a stupor. Thank you for helping us but we need to lock this crime scene down. So, you guys can take off as soon as you make a formal statement. We'll take over from here and keep you informed about progress."

My blood began to boil and I started to stand but, Terry put a hand on my arm, "I've got this, Zeke." She walked up to Fred nose-to-nose, poked a finger into his chest and growled, "I'm going to give you the benefit of the doubt that you didn't understand what I said before and I'll say it nicely once more. The task force was authorized for two purposes; to stem the flow of drugs and to shut down human trafficking in the area. This is my bust and these are my deputies, and we are in charge, not you. We're going to collect clues to help find those kids and I expect you and the others to assist us."

Fred started to huff and puff, but Terry put her hand up, "Listen Fred, there's already enough evidence around here to put these clowns away forever and you can take all the credit for that. Any clues we find now won't just help us find the kids, but we may find something that will take down the higher-ups of the organization. The safety of those young people has to be the highest priority. You have kids of your own, so I have to believe that you understand."

Fred was silent for a moment then sucked in a lungful of air and nodded, "I'll gather up the team and you and I can make the assignments."

———•———

The wounded had been transported to the hospital, bodies had been carted off, the sun was approaching its apex but we were no closer to figuring out where the kids were than we had been when we started two hours previously. Suzy and the other girl who had been held captive were even more in the dark than we were and were in the process of being reunited with their families.

The bad guys who had survived had been exhaustively interrogated and couldn't or wouldn't add to our knowledge. The only information gained from them was the mention of an island by the guy I had wounded in the generator shack, and since then he and his compatriots had lawyered up.

We were searching through files in an office located in the barn. Anne and Phil had taken Mike and Max to the bookstore where Silas and Faith were keeping them occupied. They returned with sacks of greasy food, coffee, bottles of water and two laptops that were now open on Anne's and Jessie's laps while they continued to unravel the maze of shell corporations sheltering the identities of those involved with 'Oyster Cove Thoroughbreds'. Noah was hunched over a desktop computer trying to hack the password.

Anne's eyes were ringed in dark but sparkling when she looked up from her computer and shared, "Here's something interesting, Clifford McGraw is named as one of the board of directors for a second-tier shell corporation."

Jessie voiced from the other side of the room, "I've seen his name a few times in the logs. What are the other names there?"

Anne listed a half dozen names that meant nothing to any of us, but when she got to the last name Noah's head shot up, "Alastair Beaumont! Isn't he a state senator? He's from this area as I recall."

I recognized the name and rifled through a pile of papers on the floor in front of me, "You're right! Here he is at the grand opening of this facility with a bunch of other mucky mucks, telling people how good it will be for the economy. Little did they know it would be drug money spreading around the county. What do we know about the senator?"

Anne tapped away and looked up with a smile, "He seems to have come out of nowhere ten years ago and owns a car dealership on the mainland. Started his political career as mayor of a small town on the mainland before getting into the senate race three years ago with a huge anonymous financial backing. His opponent conveniently disappeared three weeks before the election. There are some articles trying to link him to a crime syndicate, but nothing has ever been proven."

There was still something nibbling in the far recesses of my mind, but I couldn't quite bring it to the forefront. "Sounds interesting. Maybe there's a connection there. Keep digging and find out anything you can about the guy."

An hour later, Jessie and I were stretching our legs outside. I put my arm around her shoulders as we walked, "Hey Big Sis, that EMT is smitten with you. Did you guys exchange numbers?" She punched me softly in my stomach and giggled, "He's kinda cute isn't he. We made tentative plans to get together after this mess is over."

Fred and another agent were walking past us as we approached the barn when Noah stuck his head out the door, his excited voice booming, "Jessie, Zeke, get in here! We might have found something."

Jessie, Fred and I darted for the barn and rushed in. Anne was sitting on a chair in front of her laptop resting on a folding card table. She looked up and smiled, "It seems the senator's ties to organized crime might be a little closer than at first glance. His father was gunned down in a gang war thirty years ago when he was a child. He was raised by his uncle who just happened to come out on top of that war. They did a pretty good job of camouflaging his past with a new name and identity, but there's a definite link there."

Noah was at the other computer and chimed in, "When we uncovered that information, we started digging into the other names from that shell corporation. It seems all of them are tied to, or suspected to be tied to, the Grazzo family in Las Vegas.

Fred had been leaning against a wall. His face lit up and he stood erect, "You're talking about the biggest crime syndicate west of the Mississippi. Those guys are into everything from running numbers to murder-for-hire. If we can make a solid connection, we might be able to take them down. Holy cow!"

Jessie's face grew dark and her eyes seemed to throw flames. She exploded with a string of expletives before growling, "We're familiar with them and this has now become personal for Zeke and me. They were behind the broken operation that took out Zeke's partner and two other agents."

Everyone erupted and began to talk at once. Anne brushed a curl of hair that had slipped over her forehead and waited patiently for the ruckus to calm down before clearing her voice, "I've been looking into Senator Beaumont's history. They did everything they could to shield him from the 'family', so they changed his name and gave him a respectable background, but he got into some trouble while he was growing up. The court records are sealed so we can't be sure but there are a few threads on the internet that imply our boy may be into sexual abuse. One anonymous thread says he raped a thirteen-year-old girl when he was nineteen. Another, hints about him and his friends' involvement in gang rape." Tears began to slide down her cheeks, "Oh my. We have to get Charlie now!"

Terry sat beside her and put her arm around her shoulders, "That's okay, honey. We'll find her and get her home safe."

Just then Noah, who had been intently studying the computer screen in front of him, let out a loud 'whoop' and sputtered, "Gotcha, you SOB!" He turned to me and said, "Zeke, do you remember when we were flying over the islands with Lou? You asked about an island close to the Canadian border that was owned by a state senator. Well, guess what! That senator is none other than Alastair Beaumont. He turned his laptop toward us to display a picture of a perfectly coifed middle-aged man standing next to a buxom blonde woman on one side and a palomino on the other.

The niggling in the back of my mind burst forward, "That's it! That island sits right at the border and would be the perfect location to sneak drugs or humans across." I jumped up and began pacing, "We've got to get there before they slip Charlie and Danny away. It will be almost impossible afterwards!"

I turned to Fred, "Get a warrant together. I know it's Sunday afternoon but find a judge to let us search that island."

Fred pushed himself from the wall and headed for the door, "I'm on it. Like you said it's Sunday afternoon so it'll take a while to track down a judge, but I'll let you know as soon as I have it."

As soon as he had stepped out the door, I turned to Noah, "Based on our last experience with the judges around here, I'm skeptical. Let's be proactive and come up with a Plan-B. Give Lou a call and see if he might be interested in some night flying. In the meantime, Jess, Terry and I will come up with a plan for getting on that island, grabbing those kids and getting back off without getting everyone killed."

Two hours later we were sitting around my apartment, still waiting for a call from Fred. Max was sitting at my side with Scar on her lap while Noah and Terry sat in the easy chairs. Lobo lay on her bed softly snoring, her bandage white against the dark fur. Lou was helping Jessie in the kitchen fix quesadillas. He had cancelled a charter trip and shown up an hour before and we were discussing Plan-B.

There wasn't much to our plan. Under the cover of darkness, Lou would fly Jessie, Noah, Terry and me to the backside of a small island a half-mile away from the senator's compound. Even though the engine of his plane was relatively quiet, he would kill the lights and the engine and coast to a water landing. The small island's silhouette would hide our approach.

Once Lou landed, Noah would launch a small drone to reconnoiter the situation at the compound and scope out a suitable place for us to come ashore. With any kind of luck there would be enough cloud cover to block the moonlight and mask our approach. Once we knew the situation at the compound, we would deploy a small four-person inflatable and paddle our way across the open sea to land undetected … hopefully.

There wasn't much more planning required other than to slip into the heavily armed compound, spread out, find the kids and slip out undetected. *Piece of cake!*

Jessie's quesadillas were warm, oozing with cheese and full of refried beans, lettuce, onions, and peppers wrapped in a heated flour tortilla. We scarfed them down, followed by coffee. There wasn't much left to do until we heard from Fred about the warrant. We would wait until darkness, but if we hadn't heard by then, Plan-B would become Plan-A.

Terry left for the sheriff's station to retrieve Kevlar vests and four small tactical radios we would need to maintain contact with each other and Lou. Noah went back to his ranch to clean up and change clothes. Lou left to prep his plane and load up the inflatable. Jessie crawled onto my bed and was soon softly snoring. Max and I fell asleep together on the love seat, Lobo at our feet.

My dreams were a kaleidoscope; My former partner, a small hole surrounded by spatters of blood centered in her chest, was sitting in front of me saying something I couldn't understand and then she disappeared to be re-placed by Sissy lying in her hospital bed, tears streaking her face. Just as suddenly, her image disappeared and was replaced by the stark images of my mother and father as they abandoned me at the convent and drove away. Every time I would shout 'don't leave' as their apparitions faded away.

I woke with a start when soft fingers brushed across my cheek and Anne softly whispered, "Wake up Zeke, you're having a bad dream." My eyes popped open and her lovely, freckled face was staring down at me. I took her hand and sat up. The sun was closing in on the horizon.

Max was sitting on one of the barstools, nibbling at an apple, "Wow Dad. You were really jerking around."

Lou and Jessie were in the armchairs, their heads together, laughing. Jessie's eyes were sparkling as she reached over and touched Lou's arm to make a point. *Hmm! I wonder if that EMT stands a chance?*

Terry and Noah were sitting close together on the floor, pistol parts arrayed before them on cloths as they cleaned their weapons. Cans of soda sat beside them as they carried on a happy banter.

Anne sat beside me and the warmth of her body felt luxurious. She murmured, "I know you don't have to do this and I thank you for caring so much. I hope you'll be careful." Her voice broke and her lower lip quivered, "Please bring my baby back to me. I don't know what I'd do if I lost her. Please, Zeke!" Tears streamed down her face, her whole body shook and she collapsed into herself.

I gathered her into my arms and broke my rule with Max, promising, "We'll get them. Don't worry." I pointed to my friends scattered around the room, "We've got a great team, and we'll have Charlie back before you know it." Her quiet sobs tore me apart and I was ready to do something … anything to comfort this woman.

It was getting late. Anne had taken Max and Mike home with her but not before Max held me in a tight hug around my neck and whimpered into my neck, "Remember you have to come back to me. You're my Dad and I need you."

I could feel her tears running down my neck. I whispered, "Don't worry little one, I'll be fine. You and I are partners and I'm not going anywhere without you. We'll be back in no time with Charlie and Danny. How about you take care of Mike and Anne while we're gone? They need someone strong to get through this."

She pulled her head back, wiped the tears away with her sleeve, forced a lopsided grin and squeaked, "Okay partner, but let's make our next cases a little less dangerous." She leaned in and kissed my cheeks before standing and walking out with Anne.

Jessie came up and put her arm in mine, "You're already a good Dad. I'm proud of you. We can't just sit here so Lou and I are going down to the floatplane. Lou wants to check everything over again and I'm going to check the gear. Give me a call when you hear anything."

Everyone was antsy and found a different way to keep their minds busy and settle their nerves. Terry and Noah left for a walk and I poured over the charts around the island compound to judge the currents. *Not that I can do anything about it.*

Silas locked up the store and came upstairs with a pot of tea and we sat together on the armchairs with our own thoughts, staring out the window at the gray sound. The tea warmed my insides but didn't help my apprehension a bit.

A short while later, Silas had headed home and I was rinsing out the teacups when Terry burst through the door, Noah trailing closely behind. Her face was contorted into a scowl, "They couldn't get the judge to sign off on the warrant. She says there's not enough probable cause. Fred and his team are pouring through everything at the facility hoping to find some more evidence to satisfy her, but it's not looking good."

I wasn't surprised by the news. Knowing that we were finally going to take some action, albeit without support, brought a calm over me and my mind switched to mission mode, completely focused. I looked at Noah and Terry and could tell they had made the switch as well and I was certain that Jessie was already there.

I made quick calls to Anne and Silas to let them know the situation before grabbing my Go Bag and heading down to the dock to join Lou and the team. When I got there, Lee and Petey were standing with the group, rifles slung over their shoulders. Petey came forward, "We want to come along. We want to help finish this business and nail these bastards."

I looked at Lou and he nodded his head, "We can handle the extra weight of one of them but not both."

I turned to Jessie and she looked at Petey before responding, "The inflatable is designed for four, but I think one extra would work, and we sure could use all the help we can get."

I turned to the cousins, "Your help is appreciated and both of you could really help. Which of you is the better hunter?"

Petey stood a little taller and Lee nodded his head, pointing at his brother, "Petey nailed an eight-point buck at three hundred yards last year."

I smiled, "You're our man."

Disappointment flashed across Lee's face, but I turned to him, "You guys are lifesavers. We've been so focused on getting those kids we haven't given thought about how to get back off, especially if we're under fire. Do you have access to a fast boat that can reach the island and carry all of us and the kids?"

Lee's frown spread into a grin. He pointed to a pretty white cuddy cabin bobbing in the small waves of the sound, "My twenty-four-foot Grady White carries ten and the two big Evinrudes make if practically fly. She's got the range to get there and it's all fueled up."

I clapped him on the back and gave him the radio frequency we would be operating on, "Don't approach the island until we contact you. Better get going."

He grinned at me and croaked, "You forgot something else." He chuckled at my confused look, "Where am I going?"

The crowd behind me burst out laughing. I was slightly embarrassed, but the humor had released a lot of tension in all of us.

Jessie handed a chart to Lee with the island circled. Lee shook our hands and jogged toward a dinghy with a small motor tied to the dock. The rest of us piled into the seaplane and we were finally off.

CHAPTER 18

WE STRAPPED IN AS THE seaplane bounced along the small waves and finally lifted off. I noted the extra time for us to get airborne and Lou confirmed that the weight was a bit over the capacity for the Cessna. He smirked, "No problem. I carried even more once, after I picked up some over-zealous hunters and the meat from too many moose." He chortled, "Little did they know I called ahead, and the gendarmes were waiting when we returned. Can't stand poachers!"

The plane only had two headsets for passengers so Jessie and I shared while Terry, Petey and Noah passed theirs back and forth while we discussed the plan and how we would utilize Petey's talents.

Jessie pointed at a map of the island, "We didn't know you were coming Petey, so we're short a Kevlar vest and tactical radio. I think that, with your marksmanship skills, you can set up outside the perimeter to give us cover while staying out of the firefight. We'll leave Zeke's radio with you; Zeke and I are comfortable using hand signals."

I unclipped the radio from my belt, handing him the device, "Let's all try to maintain radio discipline. No talking unless it needs to be said."

Petey lifted his rifle and pointed to a black tube attached above the receiver, "I like that. This is a night vision scope, so I shouldn't have problems picking targets."

Noah chimed in, "Sounds like a plan, big guy. Just don't shoot us."

We all chuckled nervously and leaned into the task of checking our gear for what was probably the hundredth time.

Forty minutes later, Lou's voice came across the intercom, "We're getting close. I'm turning off the lights and killing the engine. We'll be on a glide slope and I won't have power to finesse the landing, so it may get a little rough when we hit the water. Just in case something goes south, everyone needs to be prepared to bail out." *Cheery thought!*

———•———

Lou brought us down unscathed to a perfect location behind the little island. We all let out a collective sigh as the plane bobbed like a cork from the gentle waves. Jessie and I wrestled the rubber boat out and inflated it with a push of the inflator button. Meanwhile, Noah had his small drone sitting atop one wing while he connected with his computer and started its four little motors. He moved his mouse around, typed a few commands and the running lights extinguished. The motor sound was barely discernable when the drone lifted off the wing and climbed straight up.

We huddled around the laptop and watched split screens as Noah guided the UAV toward the compound. One screen was overlaid with a map of the island and a blue dot moved along a trajectory leading toward it. The other screen was dark until the screen lit up suddenly with a bright glow from buildings and then two small yellow dots appeared, slowly moving across a lawn. Noah pointed and whispered, "Looks like two bad guys heading toward a helipad. See the windsock?"

The sock was barely discernible and marginally puffed out with the gentle breeze. I scoured the entire image and drawled, "Those are the only baddies I see. Maybe this will be easier than we thought."

The four of us moved close to study the compound. Nestled against the hill was a bright glow from the main house. Two buildings were located on the north side. Noah pointed at them, "That's the barn and feed shed. You can tell from the appearance of the rectangular windows along the side, and I can see at least one horse in the paddock."

The opposite end of the compound contained two buildings and a boathouse. One building had windows and light seeped out of them, "That's the quarters for the hired hands. They treat their help well. Unfortunately, I can't tell if there's anyone else inside."

The boathouse was lit, but there didn't seem to be anyone around. A breakwater jutted across the mouth of the small bay to provide protection for the mega yacht that was anchored in the middle of the small bay and we saw movement on the deck. The boat had to be at least two hundred feet long. There was a small Zodiac inflatable floating alongside a pier that was used for access to the yacht. Terry whispered, "From what I can see it looks like there's only one person on the boat. There may be some below deck, but I can't tell."

A small beach with Adirondack chairs was located near the helipad and we could make out a path leading up a low bank and through low bushes toward the house. That seemed to be the best bet for getting ashore undetected.

We discussed our approach and decided we would split up. Terry and Noah would head for the house while Jessie and I would approach the bunkhouse and other building. The closer we could get before detection would add to our advantage of surprise. There appeared to be a small knoll near the house that would give Petey an unobstructed view for providing covering fire, if and when we needed it.

Lou wouldn't be able to take off without alerting the bad guys so he would monitor our progress while paddling like mad to keep his plane from being pushed against the rocks of the small island. As soon as things started popping and the noise of his engines wouldn't matter, he would take off and head back to Friday Harbor to refuel. He'd continue to monitor the radio in case he might be needed to return.

After a final weapons check, we piled into the inflatable. Petey, Noah, Jessie and I began rowing while Terry sat in the middle on the deck. The only sounds were the splashing of the oars and soft grunts as we powered our way ahead. The weather was with us, no rain and the moon was hidden behind the clouds.

We paddled around the little island and headed toward our target outlined in the dim sky.

●────────●

The crossing was relatively uneventful, a seal kept us company part of the way before being distracted by a school of fish. Seabirds floated by, not in the least perturbed by our passing. As we approached the sand of the beach, a large shadow passed beneath on its lonely passage to the depths.

We splashed ashore and began pulling the raft up the sand when we heard the distinctive 'whup, whup, whup' of a helicopter approaching the island. We scrambled up the beach, pulling the inflatable behind us to the reeds and bushes covering the hill leading to the compound. We fell to our bellies as the whirlybird passed directly overhead.

I lifted my head and watched as the Sikorsky S-76 gently touched down in the middle of the heliport, the engines whining as they slowly wound down. The rear door opened and a man carrying an AK-47 jumped out followed by two men in slacks and open collared shirts. Jessie whispered, "That's Beaumont!"

Before I could reply a woman climbed out pulling someone behind her with their hands bound. The distance made it difficult, but it looked like Charlie. A man followed leading another bound person who looked a lot like Danny. Jessie whistled silently and exclaimed "Bingo!"

Beaumont and the others jogged toward the boathouse. Charlie tried to resist and pulled at her captive. The woman grabbed her hair and yanked her along.

As the sound from the copter's engines dissipated, I heard the distinctive roar of the yachts powerful diesels starting up.

No one was looking in our direction, so we slowly rose to a crouch. I leaned toward Petey, pointed at the helicopter and blurted, "As soon as the action starts take out the pilot and disable the helicopter."

Petey grinned and nodded.

I turned to the others, "They're headed toward the yacht. If they get out to sea, we'll never catch them. Let's go but be careful that you don't hit the kids!"

We began running toward the boathouse when the dirt kicked up around us followed by the hollow-metallic sound of an AK-47. We all fell to our faces behind a berm barely high enough to protect us. Dirt kicked up across the top of the berm effectively keeping us pinned down. A bullet ripped through the canvas of my Go-Bag. I flattened myself, kissing the dirt.

I heard a grunt and Noah cried out, "I'm hit! Got me in the thigh. I won't be going any farther, but I'm okay. You guys keep going!"

I looked over and Noah had stripped off his shirt and was tearing it into strips. Terry slid over and helped him cover the wound and bind it with strips wrapped around his leg. She patted him on his cheek and rolled into a prone position and fired her rifle in the direction of the bad guy. He returned her fire and while he was distracted, Jessie rose and sprinted to a tree on our left where she knelt, rested her elbow on her knee and squeezed off a burst in the direction of the man holding us down. We heard a scream and the man stood up and fell forward from his hiding place behind a water trough.

We stood and began to run, but two rifles opened fire from the bunkhouse forcing us to scramble for cover. At least these guys weren't great shots and no one else was hit, but we were losing ground to Beaumont and the kids as they approached the small dock and Zodiac that would take them out to the yacht.

I used a hand signal to have the three of us spread out. Terry slid to the right and, when Jessie fired a burst at the bunkhouse, she sprinted to a large hay wagon, slipped behind the wheel and raised her sights, firing two short bursts at the bad guys. They directed heavy fire at Terry, and Jessie slipped around the back of the building. She inched her way to the corner while Terry and I peppered them from the front. We heard a scream and watched as one of the baddies fell to the ground and the other began running toward the dock.

Terry fell to a prone position, pulled her rifle to her shoulder and nailed him twenty feet from his goal. He fell face first and the three of us jumped to our feet and sprinted toward the dock to watch the Zodiac pull alongside the yacht where two men pulled the senator, the other man and the captives aboard. A deckhand secured the line from the Zodiac to a rear cleat and the large boat began moving toward the mouth of the little bay.

We couldn't fire at them because of the risk of hitting the kids, but I wasn't ready to give up. The yacht would need to clear the breakwater before heading out to sea. I sprinted toward the breakwater with Jessie close behind. While I ran, I shed the rifle and my Go-Bag. My knee was screaming as I scrambled over the large boulders and I prayed it would hold out just a little longer.

My foot slipped on a slick rock and pain shot through my knee, but it held. I kept running, or rather hobbling, to the end of the breakwater. Jessie was two yards behind and I screamed, "Call the Coast Guard! Call the Canadians! I'm going in!"

The yacht had turned and was nosing through the passage to open water when I hit the water in a flat dive, hoping there wasn't anything hard to split my head. The freezing cold water stunned me for a moment before I began powerful strokes through the darkness, swimming perpendicular to the boat's progress and praying I could intercept it, and not quite sure what I would do if I did.

The cold water was sapping my strength, and the effort was draining me. I watched the hull of the yacht pass five yards in front of me and stroked as hard as I could, but my hand brushed the stern as it slipped by with nothing to grab.

CHAPTER 19

I SCREAMED WITH FRUSTRATION INTO THE water and stroked helplessly after the boat as it pulled away. Slapping the water, I watched the distance grow. I suddenly felt something rub against my neck. Thinking it was a curious fish, I reached up to brush it away and my fingers wrapped around a rope snaking rapidly through the water behind the yacht. I grabbed and the rope burned through the flesh of my palm. I brought my other hand around and grabbed harder, managing to get the rope behind my elbow to help me hold on.

Now I was porpoising through the water and having trouble getting a breath. Every time I breached and tried to take a breath, I ended up with saltwater rushing into my mouth and nasal cavities. The rope was slowly slipping through my hands and I wasn't sure how much longer I could hold on when something bumped against my head. The Zodiac!

Somehow, I needed to get up into it. I doubled the rope around my left wrist so I wouldn't lose the rope prematurely and reached up with my right hand, trying to find something to grip. I finally grabbed a rope running along the top of the inflatable's rubber pontoons. I wrapped my right arm under it and let go with my left, praying I could hold on.

The speed of the boat through the water acted like a catapult and I threw my leg up onto the top of the pontoon and flipped onto the deck gasping for breath. I turned onto my stomach and wretched salt water through my mouth and nose until there was no more.

I lay face down for a few minutes, catching my breath before I reached up and unraveled my arm from the rope. Sitting up, I peered over the bow at the yacht steaming ten yards ahead. Fortunately, no one on the boat had witnessed my antics and there was only one person on the aft deck, leaning against the side, smoking and staring into the darkness.

Getting to the yacht was going to be a trick. I crawled up to the front of the Zodiac and leaned over, trying to grab the tow rope. I finally snagged it and attempted to get close to the yacht by pulling hand-over-hand, but it was no use. The yacht was moving too fast and the rope would slip through my raw fingers every time I tried to pull closer.

I sat back on one of the inflatable's benches, rubbing my sore hands and watching as the man on deck took one last puff of his cigarette, flicked it into the ocean and slipped through doors leading forward.

I had two options; Wait until the yacht reached its destination before taking down the bad guys or start the engine on the Zodiac and slip alongside before boarding. Both had problems. If I waited for them to reach their destination, I had no way of knowing how many others would be there to greet them. And, more importantly, there was no way of knowing what they were doing to those kids or if they would ever reach the destination. I couldn't wait!

But if I ran the Zodiac's engine, those on board the yacht might hear it and they could easily pick me off as I tried to get alongside. Then again, the yacht's big diesels were probably making enough noise to mask my approach … and everyone was currently inside, further reducing the chances of them hearing. *Sounds like a plan!*

I slid to the rear of the boat and looked around. A flare gun and flashlight were in a storage compartment on the transom along with a life vest and a stack of towels. A gas can lay against the bulkhead of the transom. I picked it up. It was half full. The storage spaces under the passenger benches contained more life vests. I grabbed the flashlight and crawled over to the console. Shielding the light, I checked out the controls. The key was in the ignition but before I turned it, I checked to ensure the running lights were off.

I said a short prayer and turned the key. The motor came to life with a small rumble but well below the noise of the big boat's diesels. I checked the fuel gauge and was relieved to find the tanks were three-quarters full. We might need the gas for our escape. Pushing the throttle forward the engine raced and I felt the boat move forward releasing the tension of the tow rope. Inching ahead, I slowly gained on my target.

Keeping my eyes open for anyone coming on deck, I eased the inflatable forward until it bumped against the swim platform of the yacht. I ran forward, reached across the bow and grabbed a handhold straining against the current until the nose of the inflatable slipped across the surface. I jumped across, grabbed the tow rope and tied it to a cleat, leaving a few feet for the Zodiac to float freely if it slipped off the platform.

Reaching into the scabbard strapped to my leg I pulled my knife free, hunched over, hopped over the transom to the deck of the yacht and ducked behind a mahogany chest. I peeked over the top and watched as a shadow moved in front of the windows on the third deck. The shadow moved to the port side of the boat and started down an external ladder. When it reached the second deck, an outside light illuminated a man with a pistol in a shoulder holster and carrying a Kalashnikov, one of the guards. He crossed to the other side and then started down another ladder leading to the deck where I was hiding.

I slipped behind the corner of the bulkhead and waited. He was softly whistling an unintelligible ditty and he let out a sharp cry and dropped the rifle when I snaked my arm around his throat, pulling him close with my wrist bone squeezing his larynx and cutting off his breath. Using my other hand, I pushed the point of my knife's blade into his cheekbone just below his eye, causing blood to run down his face and neck. I breathed into his ear, "One sound and you'll lose an eye!"

I kicked the AK-47 into the shadows, pulled him into a dark alcove leading to the engine control room, opened the door and dragged him inside, slamming him against a metal table. The rumble of the engines was loud in here so I released the choke hold, spun him around, jammed the knife under his chin, causing another spurt of blood, and rasped, "You get one chance to live. Tell me where the kids are and you might make it out of here alive. Lie or refuse and I'll push this knife up to the hilt." I put pressure on the knife to emphasize my point.

His eyes were full of hate, but they were also tinged with fear and he sputtered, "You don't know who you're dealing with. You're a dead man."

I added pressure to the knife and blood streamed down my wrist. He let out a yelp and tried to pull free, "Okay, have it your way. I was hoping you'd make this a little easier." I wrapped my left hand around his mouth, pulled the knife from his cheek and in one stroke sliced off his ear.

The engines were just loud enough to mask his muffled screams as he flopped around under my grip. I moved the knife back to his throat and snarled, "I'm feeling benevolent today. Last chance or it's going to get a lot more painful."

He stopped struggling and squeaked, "Enough! Please! I'll tell you."

I grabbed a greasy rag off the table and handed it to him. He snatched it from my hand and pressed it against the cavity that had been his ear a few minutes earlier, "I'm just a hired guard and I don't owe these guys anything. I sure didn't sign on for this. They're in the forward guest suite on deck 3. Kinda hope you get them out of here. Bunch of perverts if you ask me."

I slammed the hilt of the knife into his temple and he dropped to the floor. I found rope in the workshop next door and trussed him up with his hands bound and cinched tightly to his ankles bent behind his back. I wrapped another piece of the rope around his neck and tied it to an iron pipe running from the floor to the ceiling. The greasy rag went into his mouth, secured in place with more rope.

I pulled the Sig Sauer from his shoulder holster, slipped outside, picked up the rifle and headed up the stairs to the next level.

* ———— *

The lights were on in the lower lounge and I stole a look. Beaumont was sitting in a leather armchair speaking with a swarthy man with oily jet-black hair and a bushy mustache sitting across from him. Both held brandy snifters in one hand and cigars in the other. We must have slipped across the border or into international waters because they were both laughing, not a care in the world. I wanted to go in and punish them severely, but I needed to find the kids. As I watched, a door opened at the front of the room and a servant entered carrying a tray of canapes. He set the tray down on the table between the men and stood erect waiting to be dismissed. I could hear the murmur of their voices but couldn't make out the words.

The frigid water had done wonders for my knee and I was able to get down and crawl under the windows and slip forward under the expansive windows. Twenty feet later, I was able to stand erect and ran another ten feet to a door leading to the interior. I pulled it open a crack to discover a small anteroom with another door on the other side.

I crossed the room and slowly opened the door in time to see the waiter exit the lounge and step down a staircase leading to the deck below and the galley. Slipping inside I headed to the hallway that led forward toward the guest quarters. Reaching the hallway, I peeked around the corner and immediately pulled my head back. The corridor was forty feet long and at the end, two rough looking guys were seated outside the forwardmost stateroom door, pistols strapped to their sides. A tray of food was sitting on a table between them and they were each noshing on sandwiches, staring at their phones

With surprise on my side, I could probably take them out with a couple of shots, but I didn't want to risk it not knowing how many other baddies would come running. I needed a plan, but one wasn't forthcoming and I was ready to storm the two when I heard someone coming up the stairs and slipped into the darkness of the alcove. A waiter in a white blouse walked slowly toward me and I snaked my arm out and grabbed him around the neck and yanked him to me. He let out a small yelp, but I cut it off by twisting his neck sharply in a direction it was never intended to go. I slowly lowered his body, pulled off the white jacket and donned it. It was a little small but I doubted the goons would notice. I just needed to get close enough to take them out without raising a ruckus.

Slipping the Sig into my waistband, I palmed my knife, took a deep breath, turned the corner and stepped toward them. One of the men glanced up, but immediately went back to whatever was drawing his attention on his phone. I quickly closed the distance and slammed the knife into his throat.

The other goon started to rise, shouting, "What the …?". He was halfway up before I swung the Sig around to the side of his head and he crumpled to the deck. Slowly opening a door to one of the other cabins, I peeked inside to ensure it wasn't occupied, dragged the bodies inside and closed the door. The one guy started to come around and tried to squirm out of my grip. I was running out of time and really wasn't feeling charitable toward these creeps so I finished the job with a slice across his jugular. There wasn't much I could do about the blood in the hallway, so I slipped out, stepped over it and up to the stateroom door. Whispering a small prayer, I opened the door to a dark room. I reached around and flipped the light switch.

Charlie was tied in a chair her head hanging down. When she heard me come in, her head raised, her eyes grew wide and she let out a whimper, "Oh my God, Zeke. What, how…?"

I held my finger to my lips and she quieted. Convulsive sobs racked her body as she watched me cross the room. I hurried across the room, wrapped my arms around her and whispered, "It's okay. We're going to get out of here. Where's Danny?"

She moaned, "He's in one of the other rooms, but there are other girls here, too. I'm not sure where, but I saw them when we got on the boat." Tears poured from her eyes and she began to shake violently.

I hugged her tighter and growled, "Okay, we'll get them too, but if we're going to get out of here it's important for you to be calm and focus on whatever I ask you to do. Just think about your Mom and Mikey waiting for you. Can you do that for me?"

She pulled in a huge breath, her trembling slowly settled and she nodded her head.

I released her, reached for my knife and sliced through the bindings, "Good girl! Can you stand? We need to move!"

She rubbed her arms, stumbled to her feet and mumbled, "I think I'm okay. But Danny hit his head really hard. He was awake last time I saw him, but kinda groggy."

I took her hand, reached for the door, and slowly opened it a crack. The hallway was empty, so we slipped out, closing the door behind us. I left her in the hall and reentered the cabin where I had dumped the bodies, checking to ensure I hadn't missed the kids in my haste. It was empty and I moved to the next door and peeked in. Three girls were bound to chairs and their eyes grew wide when I entered. One of the girls moaned, "Please don't hurt us. We just want to go home." I turned and ushered Charlie into the room, "Don't worry, I'm not going to hurt you, I'm going to get you out of here. But the only way we can escape is for us to be very quiet and follow my instructions." I turned to Charlie, "Help me untie them while I find Danny. I'll be right back" I turned and slipped out the door and faced a brute of a man coming around the corner. He was probably six-five and well north of two hundred pounds.

He took one look at me and charged, driving his shoulder into my chest, driving me to the deck. He was quick and before I could defend myself, he straddled me, grabbing me around my throat cutting off my oxygen. I struggled and squirmed, but he had taken me by surprise and I couldn't seem to get in any meaningful punches. My legs flopped harmlessly and I was slowly running out of energy when I heard a scream and a sickening crunch before the behemoth slumped across my chest, blood streaming from a gash in his head.

The guy was so big I had a hard time rolling him off to the side before looking up to see a black girl standing over him holding a fire extinguisher like a baseball bat. She grinned and crowed softly, "That felt really good, but so much for being quiet." She squinted at me, "I'm Cillia. You okay mister?"

I rolled over and stood up slowly and muttered, "I'm good, but we probably made enough noise to alert the bad guys. The other three girls streamed out of the cabin. A pretty Hispanic girl ran up hugging me before stepping back, reaching down and pulling the giant's Glock from his holster. She pulled the slide back and checked the chamber like a pro before tucking it into her waistband. She saw the look on my face and her eyes crinkled with a smile and she chortled, "I'm Maya! Advanced self-defense classes. Required in the barrio."

We heard shouting and footsteps approaching. I turned to Charlie and uttered, "Check the other cabins and find Danny. We've got to get moving."

Charlie opened the door to the next cabin in line and disappeared just as two guys burst through the door at the door at the end of the hall, pistols at the ready. I dropped one with the AK and turned to the other, but before I could swing the rifle around, he dropped like a rock, a red splotch growing center mass. I turned to Maya, "You must have passed with honors." She grinned.

Charlie shouted from the cabin, "Danny's here, but he's really wobbly and can't walk."

I ran into the room and lifted Danny over my shoulders in a fireman's carry and yelled at the girls, "Time to get out of Dodge ladies! Let's go!" and we all ran down the hall toward the exit.

I sat Danny on a bench along the wall, held the girls back and pushed the door open to a staccato of gunfire from the stern, shattering the window above my head. Slipping back into the hall I grabbed Danny, and we ran toward the circular staircase and headed down.

The girls were following closely behind and one of them let out a yelp as the swarthy guy appeared at the top of the staircase, a wicked toothy smirk beneath his bushy moustache. He held a pistol in his hand aimed directly at me and bellowed, "Say your prayers, senor!"

That was his mistake, talking rather than shooting, my shot entered just below his left eye and the back of his head explode before he fell to the deck.

Beaumont had been standing to his side and he turned and ran back toward the lounge. As much as I wanted to go after the bastard, I had to get the kids out of there so we sprinted down the stairs, past the kitchen where a cook was cowering in the corner, through a huge pantry and into the control room where I'd left the trundled guard. He glared at me as I took the time to fire the remaining rounds of the rifle into the control panel. The engines coughed and then were suddenly silent.

Opening the door to the outside deck, I was surprised that no one challenged me. Leaving the girls in the shadows, I crouched and carried Danny to the Zodiac where I laid him in the bow. I started back to get the girls when I heard a commotion above. Beaumont was standing near the railing and berating one of the crew. I couldn't hear what he was saying, but he wasn't happy. Again, I wanted to take him out, but my shot would bring attention to our escape route. Instead, I ran back to the alcove and signaled for the girls to stay low and follow.

We slunk along the shadows to the inflatable where I lifted each of them in and grabbed the gas can sitting in the back. Crawling back toward the engines, I unscrewed the top of the can and splashed gasoline across the deck and emptied some onto the chaise lounge cushions before sprinting back to the kids and pushing the Zodiac into the water. I sliced the rope that tethered us to the cleat, turned the key, started the engine, and slammed it into reverse.

Shouts rose from the big boat where Beaumont and two others stood at the railing with rifles. I swung the boat around, shifted gears and put the pedal to the metal. Rounds flew overhead and I pushed the girls down below the gunwale. We were quickly moving out of range when a slug slammed into my shoulder knocking me to the deck.

Charlie screamed and crawled to me. My left arm was useless, but I managed to roll over and pull myself up to the seat. I pointed and yelled at Charlie, "Get the flare gun from that cabinet." She scooted over, grabbed the case holding the flare gun, scooted back and opened it for me. There were four flares, as well as the gun, in the case. It was impossible to open the gun and I talked Charlie through the opening and loading process.

Then I did the contrarian thing and, using my right hand swung the boat around and headed straight for the yacht in a zig-zag pattern. When I thought we were close enough, I pointed the flare gun at the big boat and fired. The flare arced and flew over the top. I was disappointed but now I had the range. Handing the gun to Charlie, she quickly reloaded it and I let another one fly. This one was on the money and bounced across the deck of the yacht in a flurry of sparks. Seconds seemed like hours before the gasoline covering the deck burst into flames sending the bad guys scrambling. Cillia shouted "Nice shot cowboy."

I was losing blood fast and getting weak. Maya and Charlie helped me lay on the back seat while the other girl applied pressure to the wound. She whispered, "Mr. Zeke, my name is Judy. My mom's a nurse and she taught me how to control bleeding. You're my hero and I'm not going to let you go, so stay with me."

The girls were hovering over me and I pointed to a compass located in the console and grunted, "See that compass?" They nodded and I continued, "Keep that pointer headed south, don't go too fast and if any planes or helicopters fly overhead use the flare gun."

The last thing I heard was Charlie moaning, "Oh Zeke." Then darkness set in.

CHAPTER 20

THREE DAYS LATER THE TANTALIZING fragrance of lavender invaded my olfactory senses and I opened my eyes to a redhead beauty sitting next to my bed and stroking my hand. Anne let out a gasp and cried, "Oh my God, you're back!" She stood and leaned over, stared into my eyes and said a small prayer before brushing her lips across my cheek.

For a moment I thought maybe I was in heaven and rasped through a parched throat and around a feeding tube, "Could use some water. How are Charlie and Danny and the others?"

Anne's face broke into a wide smile that reached to her gorgeous eyes as she reached for a glass half-full of water and a flexible straw. She guided it to my chapped lips and I sipped at it thirstily. When I was sated, she put the glass on the bedside table and tittered, "Isn't that just like you, worried about them before yourself. They are all doing well. Charlie has rebounded remarkably from the experience but I'm keeping an eye on her. Danny had a concussion, but he's on the mend with no aftereffects. The other three girls will need lots of therapy but are healthy and all of them are anxious to visit their 'Uncle Zeke'. They are telling the most remarkable tales about their hero. And, as soon as Max knew you would recover, she's eating it all up. She sits with you every day until Jessie and Sister Kathleen pry her away." She pulled her phone from her pocket. "They just ran down to the hospital cafeteria for lunch, and I promised I'd call if you wakened."

I tried to reach for her hand, but my shoulder and left arm were bound in plaster of Paris, my arm sticking out to the side in an L-shape, "Let's wait a minute. I need to know how you're doing as well."

Tears bubbled up in her eyes and dribbled down those lovely cheeks, "There you go again, caring about every-one before yourself." She swiped at the tears and chortled, "I was so worried that I'd lost my little girl. As soon as I knew she was safe, I considered leaving this town for somewhere safer, but then I realized two things; there is danger everywhere and, I know it sounds a little corny, but where would I go and have a knight-in-shining-armor to take care of me and the kids." She blushed before continu-ing, "And, to be truthful, I didn't want to leave you. Now, I promised your daughter," She raised the phone, pushed speed dial, waited a few seconds and laughed into the phone, "Your Dad wants to see you!"

•————•

I heard the Converse All-Stars slapping against the lino-leum floor just before the door burst open and Max flew onto the bed and wrapped her slender arms around my neck. Tears streamed from her eyes, washing both our cheeks and she cried, "Oh Daddy, I was so worried. I tried to be brave, but I kept thinking about what would happen if I lost you too!"

Pain shot through my shoulder and arm, but I didn't care. I growled softly, "Sweetie, I'm too ornery to die and besides, I'd never leave you. You're the joy of my life. How's my baby?"

She pulled back and solemnly stated, "I'm really good now that I know you're okay, but how about our detective agency goes back to finding stray cats?"

I chuckled, "You've got a deal, sweetheart. I don't think I can stand any more excitement for a while."

As we were talking, the door opened and I heard a soft whining as Sister K and Jessie strolled in. Lobo squirmed free from their grips and then launched herself onto the bed, pushed herself between Max and me and licked both our faces.

Max giggled and the two of them slipped off the bed to make room for Sister K. She took my hand and tried to give me a stern look until a smile pushed through, "Ezekiel Jones, you gave us such a fright. I had hoped when you moved up here you wouldn't be in danger, but now you've gone and got yourself injured chasing bad guys again." She reached up and brushed my cheek with her lips, "What am I to do with you?"

I tried to look contrite, but my love for this woman who came to my rescue all those years ago burst through my expression with a big smile, "Sister K, I knew that I was protected by your prayers. I never doubted that I'd be back with you and Jessie."

I looked over her shoulder at a smiling Jessie, tears bubbling around her eyes, "Hey, Big Sis, come give me a hug." She stepped over to the other side, weaved her way around the IV and past the cast and took my face in her hands, "Little baby, you had me worried." Her voice broke and she kissed me on both cheeks and my forehead. "Sorry sister, but damn Zeke, you can't do things like that anymore. I forbid it." She kissed my cheek again and smiled, "Never mind, I know you and how you attract these situations like moths to a flame. I'm just glad to have you back, but I'm sticking around to keep an eye on you!"

I was starting to fade and my shoulder was throbbing when the door swung open and a slender man wearing a white smock and a stethoscope looped around his neck came in followed by a nurse with short-cropped silver hair and a stern look. The doctor looked around at my clan and cleared his throat, "Mister Jones, I'm Samuel Jacobson, your orthopedic surgeon and this is Karen Finley. We're glad to see that you're awake, but you need to rest and minimize the excitement." He reached down and stroked Lobo's head before continuing, "She's a sweet dog and, in most cases, we wouldn't allow her to be here, but your family insisted, and given your special status we'll permit it, but only this time." He looked around the room. "Okay folks, the nurse and I have work to do so you'll need to clear the room. You can come back in an hour."

Everyone stood and kissed me on my cheek before filing out except Max who stood tall and insisted on staying, "This is my Dad and I'm not leaving him!"

The nurse started to reply, but the doctor squatted down in front of her and interceded, "All right young lady you can stay, but you need to sit quietly while we take care of your Dad. Okay?" Max nodded and sat on a chair in the corner, sitting straight up to observe their actions.

Doctor Jacobson perused my chart while Karen checked my pulse and blood pressure. Her face broke into a wide grin and she sighed, "I heard what you did and I want to personally thank you. My sister was abducted twenty years ago, but she didn't have someone like you to help her." Her mouth turned down, "We never saw her again."

Doctor Jacobson spoke up, "Yes, Mister Jones, you're quite a celebrity and I'm extremely grateful for what you did for those children." He cleared his throat before continuing, "Now let's talk about your condition. When you arrived, you'd lost an enormous amount of blood. If that young girl hadn't applied pressure for the time it took to find you, we wouldn't be having this conversation. Fortunately, her mother taught her well and the EMTs on the helicopter were equipped with enough plasma to save you."

He pulled back my hospital gown and probed around and under the cast, causing sharp pain to shoot through my shoulder, neck and arm. Then he went on, "Your shoulder is another story, however. The bullet caused much damage to the clavicle and surrounding tissue. The good news is that my team and I were able to rebuild the bone. I expect ninety-five percent recovery, but you've got a lot of physical therapy for the next few months to get there."

He got up, squeezed my good shoulder and pronounced, "Again, Mr. Jones, please accept my gratitude for what you did. You'll be here for a few more days and I'll check in on you occasionally." He laid a business card on the bedside table, "Here's my contact information. I put my personal number on the back, and after you're released give me a call so I can buy you a cup of coffee or better yet a glass of wine." The corner of his lips curled up conspiratorially and he bent down and tittered "I'd be most grateful if you invited that striking Ms. McCormack to join us." He stood and walked out the door just as an orderly entered. *Hmmm! Lou's going to have some stiff competition.*

Nurse Finley and the orderly were gratefully gentle as they replaced my sheets and removed the feeding tube.

They both squeezed my good arm before leaving and my eyes drooped until I fell asleep within minutes.

———————•

Another intoxicating scent brought me out of my slumber this time. Cinnamon! I woke to Jessie, Terry, Fred and another man donning a windbreaker emblazoned with the FBI logo waiting patiently at my bedside. Terry had a white paper bag in her hand and was waving it under my nose and when she saw my eyes flicker open. She murmured, "Time to rise and shine sleepyhead."

I raised the hospital bed to a sitting position and growled, "Is that what I think it is? Are you just going to torture me or open the darn thing?"

Jessie rolled the mobile tray in front of me before Terry pulled out some napkins and laid them across my lap, handing me a wonderfully sticky bun, its soft dough spiraling around the ruddy spice, followed by a steaming cup of Joe. *Yummy, 'Breakfast of Champions' even if it is late afternoon.*

Jessie sat on the bed next to me, holding my hand, and the other three sat on chairs on either side. Jessie squeezed my hand and spoke first, "How about telling us about your adventure on that yacht before we fill you in on what's happened since."

Between mouthfuls of the gooey treasure and sips of coffee, I recounted my story. I finished stating, "Those girls were remarkable. We wouldn't have made it without their individual actions."

Fred smiled, "Duly noted, we'll make sure they're recognized. Sounds like you made a hell of a team."

Terry began telling their story, "The gunfight at the ranch rapidly ended after Beaumont made his escape and the remaining bad guys realized they'd been abandoned. Lou circled the island from above and after ensuring everything on the ground was secure, he boogied full throttle back to Friday Harbor to refuel. He immediately returned and began a search pattern for the yacht and you. Search planes sortied from the Coast Guard station. The local Search and Rescue squadron was called out and joined the search.

Lou was getting low on fuel when a flare burst ahead of him and he dove down to find the girls waving frantically. The sea was too choppy for him to make a water landing, so he radioed the position and circled until a Coast Guard helicopter arrived."

Then it was Jessie's turn, "Two EMTs rappelled down to the sea and began taking care of you." Her face scrunched into a frown before continuing, "They said it was a miracle they were so close because any more delay and you would have bled out. Shortly after, a cutter arrived and transferred everyone from the Zodiac to their ship before they strapped you to a gurney and lifted you into the helicopter for a quick flight to the hospital.

They paused there and Fred beamed, "Those guys are real professionals."

Terry picked up the story, "One of the search planes spotted the yacht ten miles northwest in international waters and circled before another cutter arrived and boarded to find the crew ready to surrender. The fire had done a lot of damage before the boat's fire suppression system had snuffed it out. But Beaumont and his thugs weren't there."

I sat straight up, causing pain to shoot through my neck and down my arm.

Jessie gently pulled me back before continuing, "They tried to escape in the Crew Tender, but ran out of gas and the Coast Guard found them after daybreak, dead-in-the-water five miles away. Naturally, Beaumont tried to pull rank and claim that he was an important government leader before the skipper of the cutter, who had been briefed on his activities, cold-cocked him, or I should say he slipped and fell during the arrest. Seems the captain had a relative who had been abducted." She paused before a wide grin spread across her ebony face, "And you got a little vengeance, Grazzo was among those you killed. Gibby got her justice. Great job, little baby!"

They went on to tell me about the information they had gained from the ranch, the island and Beaumont's home and office. It was enough to put him behind bars for a long time. And their digging also found enough information to take out senior members of both the Las Vegas mob as well as the Mexican cartel. With the head of the snake lopped off, they were out of business.

My shoulder relaxed, the tension drained from me and I leaned back into the pillows and grinning before the other agent started, "The media is all over this and they're pressuring the agency for an interview with the kids and you. We're protecting the young people's identity, but you're not shielded like they are. They don't know who you are, but the barracudas are circling."

Tension began to tighten my stomach and I growled, "No way! Keep me out of this! I know the FBI loves the limelight so you guys can take credit." I looked at Jessie and then Terry and asked, "If you guys want, they can let them interview you." Both ladies firmly shook their heads,

"You can tell them it's necessary to keep our identification secret to protect the individuals and their families. Just be sure to tell them about the bravery of those kids and how they saved me."

Jessie grinned at Fred and guffawed, "Told you so!"

She could tell that I was starting to fade, my eyes drooping, so she stood, brushed her lips across my cheek before softly uttering, "Time to get some rest little baby. We'll be back in the morning." She stood and headed for the door while Fred came over and squeezed my good arm and grinned, "Thanks for everything. It was an honor working with you."

Terry stepped up, brushed my hair back from my eyes, kissed my cheek and whispered, "Get well Zeke. Noah and I miss you."

The door was swinging shut behind them when Karen and a different orderly pushed it open to begin the evening rituals.

———•———

My night was restless and full of strange dreams. A pretty nurse with cocoa colored skin and big, beautiful eyes came in the middle of the night to check my vitals and calmed me after a particularly bad session. She stayed with me, softly stroking my hand and softly murmuring prayers until I finally faded and fell into a calm nothingness.

I woke with a start the next morning when Doctor Jacobson and Nurse Finley tried vainly to slip in without disturbing me. Karen busied herself by checking vitals, straightening my bed and plumping my pillow.

Doctor Jacobson smiled, "Well Mr. Jones, we're quite pleased with your progress," He studied my chart before looking into my eyes, "I think you may be heading home soon. But I must warn you that you're facing months of therapy to get that shoulder back into shape."

I grimaced as he probed my shoulder, "That sounds great. But since you want me to set you up with my sister why don't you call me Zeke?"

His brows shot up, his face beamed, and he chortled, "Sister! I'm sure there's a story behind that. Can't wait to hear it. And you can call me Samuel. I hate the nickname 'Sam'."

Nurse Finley laughed and crowed, "He gets really grumpy when someone makes that mistake. They only do it once. And Zeke, my name is Karen. The nurse moniker is so formal. But while you're matchmaking could you introduce me to that cute FBI agent?" *Cute? Who knew?*

I promised to arrange a meeting and they both headed out the door as another orderly arrived with a tray containing my breakfast, lumpy oatmeal, dry toast and watery orange juice. *Man, what I'd give for a burger!*

I picked at the food before dozing on and off for a few hours when the happy sound of Converse All Stars slapping on the hallway linoleum brought me out of my reverie. Max burst through the door and jumped onto the bed wrapping her slender arms around my neck before giving me a loud smooch on my cheek, "Hi Daddy, how are you? Did you sleep well? Can I sign your cast? The others are right behind me, but they're kinda slow. And I couldn't wait to see you!"

Before I could slip in a response, the door swung open and a procession consisting of Sister Kathleen, Jessie, Anne, Charlie and Danny paraded in. Charlie was carrying a laptop and proceeded to set it on the movable table before climbing up to the other side of the bed, wrapping her arms around me and muttering, "Hi Uncle Zeke. I'm so glad you're okay." before she choked up, tears streaming from her eyes.

I brushed away the tears and kissed her cheek, "I'm good as gold and ecstatic that you're here and safe. How are you and Danny doing?" I looked over at the boy and shot him a grin, "That was quite an adventure, wasn't it?"

Danny hesitated before overcoming his shyness, grabbed my hand and tittered, "Thank you Mr. Zeke, but I think I've had enough adventures for a while."

Everyone's laughter filled the room and my heart, "Why don't you call me Uncle Zeke? Mister seems so formal." I turned to Charlie, 'What's with the computer? You haven't given up books, have you?"

She jumped off the bed before opening the laptop and striking the keys with lightning speed, "Cillia, Maya and Judy want to say 'Hi'," She made a few more keystrokes and continued, "They are all back home so we set up a Skype call." She turned the computer to face me and slid it back a little so the kids and I could participate. Three blank panels appeared on the screen before the grinning faces of the three girls came into focus, one in each panel. They all shrieked and shouted at the same time, "Hi, Uncle Zeke. How are you?"

Cillia gushed "We miss you. Can we come see you in the summer?" Judy continued, "Please! We want to see you, and Charlie told us all about Oyster Cove." Maya started to cry before gurgling, "Oh Uncle Zeke, thank you so much. I still get bad dreams about what would have happened without you…."

My eyes started to fill with tears and I was choking up but managed to simper, "Now hush all of you. The only reason we got out of there and are all right is because of the bravery of each of you. Cillia, you saved us by taking out that guy before he put me down. Maya, you saved all of us with your marksmanship. And, Judy, they tell me that your first aid skills kept me alive until the EMTs arrived."

I turned to Charlie and continued, "And Charlie here navigated us to safety where Lou was able to locate us. Each of you was so brave I'm proud to have been part of your team. So, get up here as soon as possible. I can't wait to get together with you!"

I pulled Max to me and growled, "And we can't forget Max and her amazing skills flying drones, keeping us informed about the bad guys."

We laughed and cried for over an hour as we all shared our experiences. After we ended the session I hugged Charlie, Danny and then Anne before they left. Max snuggled up to me and we all settled into easy conversation. Max went on about the latest book she was reading, *Little Women.* Sister K informed us that her possessions were on the way to the retirement convent in Oyster Cove. It filled me with joy that this kind woman would be close again.

Jessie was uncharacteristically silent and I looked over at her. Her lips turned up before she gushed, "I'm moving up here also. I need to keep you out of trouble. I sold my share of the detective agency to the other guys. Detective work in Albuquerque is very boring compared to this place."

A few minutes later, Noah and Lou joined us, preceded by the glorious aroma of grease.

Noah slid the table in front of me and laid out a double cheeseburger (with extra onions), fries and an iced tea before me, "Figured you might be ready for some real food." Sister K tittered before smiling, "Let's bow our heads and thank God for this food and for watching over our boy." The prayer was barely over before I bit into that glorious sandwich. Between mouthfuls I grinned and muttered, "You're a lifesaver. Please don't stop with the care packages."

Two days later, Samuel approved my release and I found myself being rolled out the double doors of the hospital in a wheelchair by Jessie and Max. They whisked me into the back of a large SUV and we headed home.

SIX MONTHS LATER

I STUMBLED ASHORE AND OUT OF the cold water to the towel where Lobo sat, her brown eyes closely watching me as I approached. I danced around, hopping on one foot and then the other, as I peeled off the wetsuit and sat beside her. She licked my face before lying down and fell softly snoring into a relaxed sleep. My shoulder ached from the effort of the swim, but it was a good ache. Months of painful therapy had paid off and I felt like new.

The sun was warm on my skin and I lay down to enjoy the rays. My eyes were closed as I enjoyed the early morning solitude, my mind wandering.

Max was blossoming into a remarkable young lady before my eyes. She was growing like a weed and every time I turned around, I was amazed at how quickly she was maturing.

Sister K spent every day with Max and me, helping around the bookstore. I hadn't realized how much I missed her.

Jessie had settled into a small apartment down the street from the bookstore. After a lot of prompting from Terry she put her hat into the ring in a special election for sheriff. The news of her exploits in saving the girls had spread like wildfire throughout the county and she won with 95% of the vote. *Big Sis had her badge back.* She and Samuel had clicked as soon as they met and were inseparable.

Jessie's first action after winning the election was to promote Terry White Feather to Detective Sergeant. She was a natural and the two of them made a great team. The crime rate was dropping, and illegal drugs were waning. She and Noah became even closer. I expected wedding bells in the near future.

Cillia and Judy and their families would be visiting in June. Both had responded well to therapy and had resumed their lives. Cillia was studying hard and wanted to be an NCIS agent. Judy had received a scholarship and would be heading to nursing school in the fall. They both made me proud.

Maya was another story. Before her abduction, she had been living with her brother, but he was killed in a drive-by shooting, leaving her homeless. She was living on the street for two months before being snatched. As soon as Sister K learned of her situation, she and Jessie drove to Seattle's barrio on Capitol Hill, bundled her into their car and drove her home. She was living with Jessie and spent her time at the bookstore studying for her GED and helping Silas. Sister K's love was wonderful therapy and Maya was recovering nicely. Zeke's Clan just keeps growing. She had confided to me that she might be considering entering the convent as soon as she graduated and asked me to pray for help in making this decision. However, she still joined me at the range twice a month for target practice.

Charlie had blossomed into a beautiful young woman. She kept busy with her studies and studying college pamphlets hoping to get accepted into one of her choices the following year. She still cared for Maddie and Shi Shi, but only during daylight. Danny had moved with his parents Iowa, but they still kept in touch and thought maybe they might attend the same schools.

Anne and I were moving our relationship along nicely under the watchful gaze of Sister K and Jessie. We were comfortable around each other, and we were on the brink of moving our relationship to the next level, but we weren't in any hurry.

The warm sun and the gentle waves softly lapping the shore lulled me into a shallow sleep when the chirp of a police siren brought me out of my reverie. I sat up and squinted up the bank at Terry's lovely face. She smiled before shouting, "Sir, there's a law against loitering. I suggest you move on."

I stood and replied, "Yes ma'am. I was just leaving. I sure could use a cup of coffee. Any good places around here?"

She got a wicked look in her eyes, "Follow me, I was just heading for a cup myself."

ACKNOWLEDGEMENTS

First and foremost, I must give thanks to God for blessing me with the ability to put these words to paper. Without Him, I am nothing.

I cannot begin to thank my wife, Vickie, for the support she has provided in the writing of this book. She is the one who believed that I had the ability to create. She was my first editor and most helpful critic.

Many thanks to Rhonda and Bob Warner, beta-readers and proof-readers extraordinaire. *One Boat Service* would be a much lesser product without their help.

Finally, I must thank Streetlight Graphics for their formatting and design expertise.

OTHER TITLES BY J MILO

MENSCH

ABOUT J MILO

J Milo spent his formative years in California and Washington. After trying his hand at upper education he moved on to an all expense vacation in southeast Asia courtesy of the Marine Corps. His training there led him to the aerospace industry where he honed his writing skills by trying to convince customers that his products were better than his competitors. Sometime truth but mostly fiction. After tiring of the hustle-bustle of corporate life he escaped to the Pacific Northwest. After moping around for a while his wife kicked him out to the studio and urged him to write what he felt rather than what might sell. The result was his first book *Mensch*. *One Boat Service* is his latest book.

I hope you enjoyed reading *One Boat Service* as much as I enjoyed writing it. If you can, I would appreciate a review of *One Boat Service*. It will help me in my future writing efforts as well as giving potential buyers a feel for the book. Thank you in advance!

You can continue to stay in touch with me
by signing up to my mailing list that can be
found on my website at jmiloauthor.com.

Or you can connect with me on X @jmiloauthor

Keep Reading for a preview
of J Milo's novel *Mensch*.

MENSCH

Chapter 1

San Diego, 1969

Adversity toughens manhood, and the characteristic of the good or the great man is not that he has been exempt from the evils of life, but that he has surmounted them.

—Patrick Henry

IT FELT FUNNY, BEING OUTSIDE without my cover. It had been four years since I felt the cool breeze run through my high and tight. *This is going to take a while,* I thought as I walked across the parade grounds of Balboa Hospital to the chow hall for my last breakfast of powdered eggs, SOS, and crappy coffee. There were some things I wouldn't miss about the navy. This episode of my life was coming to a close, and the bright day whispered promises of new opportunities waiting just beyond the gate.

Bob Dylan's "Lay Lady Lay" on Armed Forces Radio seeped through the speakers as I shuffled along the chow line and headed for a seat. Johnny was sitting at one of the tables, massaging the stump that used to be his arm. His jet-black hair shone brightly under the mess hall lights. He looked up with a grin as I slid my tray onto the table.

"Hey, short-timer. How's it going?" he asked through a mouthful of lumpy Cream of Wheat. "Are you ready to enter the real world?"

I sipped my mug full of tepid java, wondering the same thing. "As ready as I'll ever be. It's going to be an adjustment, that's for sure." Looking into my cup, I saw that the oil slick on top of the coffee had an iridescent glow. "How's the arm?"

He grinned—Johnny always grinned—and gurgled, "Feels pretty good today, hardly any of that phantom pain. A few more weeks of therapy and I get my prosthesis. Then I'm outta here. Mom wrote and said that the whole town of Nowata is planning a big homecoming and they have a cashier's job lined up for me at the feed store. Then it's off to Stillwater in the fall on the GI Bill. Can you imagine this Okie redskin with all those cowboys? I can't wait to shake it up. How's that leg of yours? Can't hardly notice your limp."

I reached down and massaged the six-inch scar running diagonally across my thigh, smiling. "Getting better, but I won't be running any marathons for a while."

He reached across with his good arm and handed me a ring of keys.

My smile disappeared. "Are you sure you want to give her up? She's your pride and joy."

"You paid me top dollar, and besides, I can't quite handle a stick shift any more. There's a new GTO with automatic transmission calling my name. Besides, I owe you, Luke."

"You don't owe me shit, Marine," I growled. This was a conversation I didn't want to have.

But Johnny persisted. "Me and seven other guys sure as shit owe you, Corpsman. You dragged our asses out of that clusterfuck. You deserve a lot more than a '65 Mustang and that Silver Star. Those assholes should give you the Medal of Honor. Hell, they should give you the keys to the White House. Kick that sorry asshole out."

I cringed. "They need to give the medals to those guys who didn't make it. Better yet, get us the hell out of that Godforsaken country. It's not our fight, and our boys are just fodder for the generals' and politicians' egos."

As we were talking, a huge shadow fell over the table. Baby Huey slipped in beside Johnny and said, "Hey, Doc. Hey, Johnny. What are you two shitbirds up to?"

His real name was Howard, but due to his size—six feet, six inches tall in his stocking feet, with a girth of 225 pounds—and gentle disposition, the moniker was a natural. The burns along one side of his ebony face and neck took away from his otherwise natural good looks.

Johnny punched him in the arm. "Hey. Doc's mustering out today. We were just talking about the state of the world and our place in it." His lopsided smile returned. "Nixon announced that he's pulling out twenty-five thousand troops. That's a start!"

Huey let out his deep baritone laugh. "What about the other four hundred and fifty thousand? He's just playing politics. As long as we're over there, shit like My Lai is going to happen. And those hippy-skippy assholes sitting outside the base with those ridiculous signs can paint all of us with those atrocities. I'm not a pacifist, but that war is just wrong!"

"Well, I guess it ain't our concern anymore. It's someone else's problem now." I got up and shook Huey's huge hand. "So long, big guy. Stop by if you're ever up my way."

He pulled me into a bear hug that nearly crushed my ribs. "I still can't believe you carried me all the way to the LZ. Johnny's right, they need to give you more than a crappy piece of metal for what you did. Stay safe, Doc."

I just shook my head and retrieved my hand from his big mitt. "You would have done the same for me." I grabbed Johnny's shoulder. "Johnny, you better keep in touch, or I'll hunt you down and rip off your other arm."

"You too, Luke." Johnny wasn't grinning for a change. He hung his head, refusing to meet my eyes. "I'm gonna miss you."

After emptying my tray, I left the mess hall and walked past two buildings, then entered the admin building.

"What are you going to do, now that you're a free man?" Lieutenant Grogin asked as he handed me my discharge papers. "You know that reenlistment offer still stands. Ten big ones in your pocket and we'll fly you to 'Nam to sign the papers so it'll be tax free. The navy needs men like you. You could chart your own course if you chose to stay."

"Thanks, sir, but my baby sister's graduating with her bachelor's degree next week, and I'm gonna be there. Then, I'm off to school on the GI Bill for my own college career. Who knows after that? The navy's been pretty good to me, and I might consider reenlisting, but I want to get my degree and experience something else, maybe helping others with something other than a tourniquet and a morphine syringe."

"Well, Captain Perdue has been summoned to the Pentagon, otherwise he'd be here to see you off. I've heard him on the horn discussing you. Best of luck, Sailor."

I gave him a smile and walked out into the sunshine, heading for the barracks.

The hike down the street to the barracks took only a few minutes.

There, I picked up my seabag, then threw it into the trunk of the Mustang, climbed in and headed out. It was another cloudless San Diego day as I drove under the towering palms and eucalyptus trees and out through the gates of Balboa Naval Hospital. The glow of the sun trickled through the foliage, throwing nymphlike shadows that danced across the hood of the convertible. Near the gate a small group of long-haired protestors clustered. They yelled, waved their signs at the car, and gave halfhearted peace signs. Some of the peace signs were with one finger. They seemed so young. I wondered at the difference between their world and mine, and if the wounds that this war had created could ever be healed. With a quick wave back, I shifted into third and drove down the hill.

Tuning the car radio to K-Earth 101, I navigated the narrow streets, jumped onto El Camino Real, and headed north. I could have taken the new interstate and saved a lot of time, but I was drawn to the old two-lane by something deep inside. There was no rush; Riley's graduation wasn't for another week. In the words of my old friend, Andy, I had nothing to do and all day to do it.

As I navigated the narrow streets of San Diego, the roadside signs alternated between US 1 and 101 without any logic, but the brass mission bells that hung on shepherds' hooks led the way. I cranked up the radio as The Kingsmen sang one of my favorites, "Louie, Louie." I couldn't figure out what they were singing, but I was pretty sure it was erotic.

Two hours later, the sweet smell of caramel corn invaded the open cockpit of the Mustang as I passed through Santa Monica and spied the giant Ferris wheel suspended in the mist over the ocean. A few miles later I cruised into Malibu and my stomach was making threatening noises. I spotted a hole-in-the-wall beachside café and pulled onto the gravel among the half-dozen or so vehicles. Soft music strummed through the outside loudspeakers, and the blackboard out front advertised a blackened mahimahi sandwich special that sounded good.

After finding a table and ordering, I sipped my iced tea and watched the surfers trying to find a wave. The water was churning, not much action though. Harbor seals poked their heads above the surf and taunted the interlopers. The sandwich was every bit as good as I had hoped. Tangy tartar sauce teased my tongue, and the tension in my shoulders and neck started to ease as I stared across the blue waters. Something about large bodies of water calmed my inner being.

The afternoon sun warmed my head and shoulders on the winding course up the Pacific Coast Highway. Coming over a hill and around a curve, I was surprised by a flash of light and smoke billowing from an area along the coast. A dark projectile climbed out of the smoke, headed out to sea, and banked left, running parallel to the coast while navy cruisers tried their best to shoot it down.

Must be the boys at Point Mugu playing war games, I thought. Just then, a dartlike projectile shot from one of the ships and the target missile burst into flames. "Nice shooting, sailor!"

The Mustang's motor purred, and the car dropped into the western edge of the Oxnard Plain. The memories began to crystallize, and my mind drifted back to that summer.

And what a summer! The summer of the great adventure...